"Your fiancé?" Colette glanced around. "I did not see him with you earlier."

Shelah giggled. "Oh, he's right here." She looked up at Matthew, her eyes full of adoration. "Matthew and I are to be married after Christmas."

Matthew wanted to grab Colette and run, so he could explain. He'd asked Shelah to let him announce the news in his own time since he had not formally asked her to marry him. But Shelah only lived on Shelah's time. She *thought* they should marry, and now she'd gone and announced what she wanted people to know. His only choice was to verify the truth.

"We have to get things organized before . . . then," he said, but that sounded weak even to his ears.

Colette's smile froze into an expression he'd never forget, but the look in her eyes as she glared at him shouted despair. To her credit, she held her emotions tight. "Well, isn't this a surprise. Matthew, you failed to let us know you were *engaged*, but it seems Shelah is very excited. Congratulations."

Also by Lenora Worth

The Memory Quilt

The Forgiving Quilt

Published by Kensington Publishing Corp.

The CHRISTMAS QUILT

THE SHADOW LAKE SERIES

LENORA WORTH

ZEBRA BOOKS
Kensington Publishing Corp.
www.kensingtonbooks.com

ZEBRA BOOKS are published by

Kensington Publishing Corp.
119 West 40th Street
New York, NY 10018

All Kensington titles, imprints, and distributed lines are available at special quantity discounts for bulk purchases for sales promotion, premiums, fund-raising, and educational or institutional use.

Special book excerpts or customized printings can also be created to fit specific needs. For details, write or phone the office of the Kensington Sales Manager: Kensington Publishing Corp., 119 West 40th Street, New York, NY 10018. Attn. Sales Department. Phone: 1-800-221-2647.

Zebra and the Z logo Reg. U.S. Pat. & TM Off.
Bouquet Reg. U.S. Pat. & TM Off.

First printing: September 2023
ISBN-13: 978-1-4201-5249-4
ISBN-13: 978-1-4201-5250-0 (eBook)

10 9 8 7 6 5 4 3 2 1

Printed in the United States of America

CHAPTER ONE

ℋer sister was getting married today.

Colette King watched as Mamm helped Eliza with her pretty mint green wedding dress, her hands gentle as she tied the white apron sash and then pinned a mauve flower made from fabric scraps onto the front of the apron. Then she adjusted the organza *kapp* she'd made for Eliza a few weeks ago. This was a sweet, solemn moment, since Eliza would one day be buried in the apron and the matching white cape. But it would be a long time before that happened, *Gott*'s will.

And it might be a long time, too, before Colette wore that traditional apron and cape on her own wedding day. Her man was not here where he belonged. Maybe she wasn't the marrying kind. Maybe she'd just stay safe and sound with Mamm and Daed all her life. Find a cat to love. Or she'd be the library lady, loaning out her precious books. She had a great cookbook collection. She'd always enjoyed experimenting with food.

"There," Mamm said with a satisfied smile, her gaze moving over Eliza and ending Colette's lament over her own situation. Mamm patted Eliza's hand. "You look lovely, Eliza. I hope you and Levi will always be as happy as Daed and I have been all these years."

Eliza blinked back tears, her eyes bright. "I've never been so happy, Mamm. *Denke.*"

"I'll bring you a bite to eat," Colette offered. "You might forget about food during the celebration."

They'd turned the quilting room into the bride's room for today. Eliza stood and looked out the window at the light November snow. "Finally, a year after he proposed, Levi and I are getting married. A happy day."

Today *was* a happy day. December was coming, and with it Christmas. Colette loved Christmas. It always made her happy. Well, almost always.

Levi and Eliza had waited because his *mamm* suffered from Parkinson's, and Levi had wanted to get Connie the best help possible. That had taken priority, but Connie was doing better now. The King family owned and managed the Shadow Lake Inn, so Levi and Eliza had finally agreed that with both of them working at the inn, it was most practical for them to live on the grounds. That gave Daed and Mamm the opportunity to offer the young couple the cottage where they had lived ever since they got married. Her parents decided to build a *grossdaddi haus* just behind it. All of that had happened over the last year. So today had to be a happy day.

After hugging her sister, Colette hurried from the room and went out to get some air. Although a bit of snow had fallen last night, the temperature was mild enough for the planned outdoor wedding, especially with the sunshine warming the air. She glanced around the grounds of the Shadow Lake Inn, her gaze moving over the new pavilion they'd built earlier this year. It glowed a stark shimmering white against the dusting of last night's snow. The huge beamed structure was filled with rows and rows of folding chairs and long benches they'd brought in on bench wagons.

Eliza would marry Levi Lapp under the shelter of the pavilion, with two firepits burning on each side to keep the chilly air at bay. They'd all worked hard to string evergreens and white ribbons through some of the beams and posts. The pavilion would look festive for this wedding and for the four weeks of the holiday season, when tourists would rent out the inn for parties and get-togethers.

Today, however, the inn was closed because of the wedding. A private event with a mixed group of attendees—mostly Amish, with some *Englisch* who worked here, such as Henry Cooper, who ran the front desk and watched over the huge lobby, as well as *Englisch* vendors who provided the necessities to run such an establishment. Mamm and Daed would preside over the event, and Colette and her older sister Abigail would be in the wedding party. Levi's younger brother, James, and their sister, Laura, would also stand by him.

But would Matthew make it back in time? They'd argued the last time he'd called. And now his letters had trickled down to one or two a month. She wished she could take back her words to him. They'd planned to marry, but they couldn't announce it properly until they talked to the bishop and acquired a *Zeugnis*, which would then be delivered to a minister. Once that happened and Colette, the bride, had a talk with the minister to be sure she had no hesitation, the wedding would be announced to the church.

That should have happened by now, but Matthew had been called away before he could talk to the bishop.

Abigail shouted out to her from the inn's back entrance.

"Colette, *kumm* help me with Jon, please."

Colette pivoted, her dark burgundy dress and crisp white apron swishing against the leggings she wore underneath to keep warm. Tugging at her black cape, she called, "On my way."

She entered the bustle of the industrial kitchen, where large pans of baked chicken and savory corn bread dressing were lined up on the counter alongside macaroni and cheese, creamed spinach, and various other side dishes. They were having a huge dinner after the noon wedding. Eliza looked so happy as she and Mamm hurried back into the quilting room.

"Let me take Eliza a small plate," Colette said, hurrying to gather cut meat, some cheese and bread, and a handful of freshly made wedding mints, so her sister would have a sweet taste after eating.

She offered her sister the food and nodded her approval. "I have to tend to Jon," she said, so she could escape before she ruined her sister's joyous mood.

But her heart hammered that familiar refrain with each step: *I miss Matthew. I miss Matthew.*

Would he be home soon? And if so, would he still be mad at her for wanting him home?

Her Mattie had been gone for six long months, due to an ailing uncle who'd needed help on his Missouri farm.

"I'll be back in a few weeks," he'd told her the night before he left. "Just through the harvest, and then we can officially become engaged."

"You'll need to get back soon. Abigail has a baby now and Eliza is getting married the last week of November. We need your help more than ever."

His gaze moved over her face. Matthew had beautiful golden-brown eyes. "And do you need me, Colette?"

"You know I do. I love you."

It had taken her a long time to say those words, but she truly loved Matthew Mueller. Last Christmas, after they'd flirted and laughed and whispered sweet nothings to each other, he'd given her a quick kiss at a youth singing and told her that he'd loved her since the day she'd been born. Two years older than her twenty-one, he'd known her as a baby, a toddler, a *kind,* a teen, and, now, a woman. And loved her all that time. They'd been courting since that night.

But it had taken her too many years to finally realize she loved him, too. Wishing she could take back all the times she'd ignored him or brushed him away while they worked side by side in the inn's kitchen and café, Colette had savored their brief time together, but then he'd up and left a few months after she'd declared her love. They'd communicated through letters, but Matthew wasn't the chatty type. His letters had been practical and hadn't revealed very much other than that he missed her and couldn't wait to get home.

But three weeks ago he'd called her. Happy to hear from him, Colette asked when he'd be home.

"I don't know. A lot is going on here." He went quiet. Matthew tended to put on a good face and hold all his angst inside.

"Matthew, what's wrong?"

"I can't talk about it."

"Can't or won't?"

"I just wanted to hear your voice. I'll be home when I can get there." The gruffness in his tone pierced her heart. They'd never argued before, but he sounded so angry.

Frustrated, Colette snapped back at him. "I know

you're a big help to your *onkel*, but you should be here. Will you be able to attend Eliza and Levi's wedding?"

"Right now, Colette, I don't know."

The rest of the conversation had not gone well. The call had ended on a bad note, and she'd not heard from him since.

Had she lost her Mattie?

"Stop pouting and take Jon for his morning nap in the nursery room, please," Abigail said, handing her giggling son, Jonah Junior, over to Colette when she entered the kitchen. They called him Jon, but he looked exactly like a junior Jonah. And he was loved by the entire family. Born in the spring, he was now the apple of the family's eye, and he loved to crawl into anyone's lap.

"*Kumm*, little pumpkin," Colette said to the *bobbeli*, glad to have something to occupy her time before the wedding. "You'll have to sleep right through the best part, but don't worry, you won't miss out on the wonderful food we plan to eat."

Jon bobbed his head, his dark curls so like Jonah's, and babbled a response. At almost seven months old, he babbled a lot.

"Nap, nap," she sang, dancing him around the room. "Ruth Ann will watch over you and read you a funny story, ain't so."

Jon giggled and grabbed at the strings of her *kapp*.

Colette kissed his baby-sweet cheek. "What a joy you are."

Abigail let out a sigh. "Two more hours and then our sister will be married to the man who kissed her for the first time."

Colette danced around with Jon, making him giggle again. "*Ja*, and we well know how that turned out."

"She is marrying him after he went away and returned and they finally stopped circling and decided to be honest with each other—that is how it turned out," Mamm said as she came in with Eliza, both of them beaming. "Colette, stop worrying about Matthew. The man loves you. He will be back."

How did Mamm do that? She could take one look at any of her daughters and know exactly what they were fretting about.

Eliza's eyes held a dreamy sheen, but she tried to commiserate. "I know Matthew. He wouldn't tell you he loved you and then never return to make good on that declaration. Something is holding him up."

"It's been longer than I expected," Colette replied. "He's mad at me for wanting him home for this wedding, but really I want him home forever. What if something happened to him? The weather has been bad to the west."

Mamm and Eliza shot Abigail a speaking glance.

"What is it?" Colette demanded, her instincts on high alert. "Something has happened. Is he okay?"

Mamm took Jon into her arms and directed Colette off to the side. "Do not fret about Mattie. I have it from a *gut* source that he's on his way home. His uncle passed two weeks ago."

"Where did you hear that?"

"From your *aenti* Miriam, first thing this morning," Mamm replied. "You know my sister is like a sieve when it comes to gossip. She can't keep it in." Mamm kissed Jon. "But I made her promise not to tell you or anyone else, because I knew it would upset you to hear he was coming without letting you know."

"But who would be gossiping about Matthew?" Colette asked, thinking her mother probably knew more than she was saying.

"Just someone who has relatives in the same community. That's all Miriam told me. His uncle died and Matthew will be home by Christmas at the latest. Don't ruin Eliza's big day, *Dochder*."

"But Christmas is over a month away." Colette bit her lip. "I'm sorry. I won't mention this again now, but once the wedding is over, I aim to corner *Aenti* and find out what's going on."

"Well, I wish you the best on that," Mamm replied. "Now I have to get finished with this busywork and get your *daed* bundled up and ready for the wedding." Mamm tugged her close while Jon giggled and reached out his hands. "You look so pretty today, so get that smile of yours into shape and let's celebrate this wedding."

Colette kept one eye on the ceremony and one eye on the lane leading up to the inn. Lined with buggies of all shapes and sizes, it looked like a strip of black quilting material. But she wasn't thinking about quilt patterns. She wanted to hear the clip-clop of one more team of horses, of one more buggy pulling up alongside the others.

Matthew had to make it back before Christmas. She didn't like feeling this helpless, yet she had to show patience and grace because he'd done a *gut* deed. He's answered the call for help from an elder in his family. He could be dealing with the estate or staying to finish winterizing the farm so he could shut it down.

Then it occurred to her: What if he had to stay there

indefinitely, like forever? What if after their quarrel, he'd decided he no longer wanted to live in Shadow Lake?

Or be with her?

Colette saw her mother frown, so she went back to listening to the vows Eliza and Levi were exchanging. Vows to love and honor each other. They were short and sweet, but the minister would also provide a sermon to remind others that marriage was a sacred promise between a man and a woman.

Forever.

That thought scared her. Was that why she'd pushed Matthew away so many times? Eliza had struggled with the responsibility of becoming a wife, and now Colette saw the gravity and the finality of marriage.

Did she want that? Could she do that?

What would happen when Matthew came home?

She didn't have to wait too long for an answer.

As soon as the minister finished, they all headed to the inn to get warm and have dinner. As the crowd moved toward the inn, Colette glanced up to see Matthew walking toward her with a dour look on his handsome face. Then she noticed the young woman clinging to his arm, smiling up at him. In the same way Colette smiled at him each time they were together.

Had Matthew found someone new while he was gone?

CHAPTER TWO

Matthew Mueller felt sweat moving down his spine like tickling spiders. The look on Colette's face earlier had told him everything. Her expression had held disbelief, her eyes had shone bright with a hundred questions, and her lips had jutted in a confused pout. He'd just broken her heart into pieces, and there wasn't a thing he could do about it.

He'd hurried inside the inn to find a seat in a corner. The reception would take place here, and it couldn't be over soon enough for Matthew. He and Colette had had a fight over the phone, and now he wished he could take back his harsh words. But perhaps it was best that she thought they were done, because now he could not marry Colette. He could not be with Colette at all.

The woman clinging to his coat smiled up at him, reminding him of what lay ahead. "This inn is amazing, Matthew. I can see why you loved working here." Her dark brown eyes took in the scene with a dismissive blankness. "I'm sure you'll miss it."

"*Ja*, it's a *gut* place to work. The best." He'd be fired now, of course. But that might be for the best, because he wouldn't be able to stay in Shadow Lake now, or work here in the kitchen either. "I will miss the inn and the people I've known all my life."

But he had close to a month here, at least. To get things figured out with his family. To right a wrong. To accept his fate.

Colette walked by with her sister Abigail; then she whirled to face Matthew. He wanted to turn and leave. But the two women stood and stared at him, both with quizzical expressions. Abigail's smile held friendliness and curiosity. Colette's stare held daggers and hostility.

His companion nudged him. "Matthew, aren't you going to introduce me to the King sisters?" She smirked at them. "I've heard so much about all of you, I feel as if I know you already."

Colette's blue-green eyes brightened like a forest about to burn. Putting her hands on her hips, she said, "*Ja*, Matthew, why don't you introduce us?"

Matthew swallowed his shame and said, "Abigail and Colette, this is Shelah Frantz. A friend from Missouri."

Colette's skin blazed pink. He'd embarrassed her and humiliated her, and at her sister's wedding at that. "A friend from Missouri, now? Interesting."

Abigail held out her hand. "It's nice to meet you, Shelah. How long will you be with us?"

Shelah giggled, ignoring Abigail's kind gesture, and clutched Matthew's arm. "As long as needed for my fiancé to make the arrangements to bring his family to Missouri. We have plenty of room, since Saul Mueller's home is rather large."

"Your fiancé?" Colette glanced around. "I did not see him with you earlier."

Shelah giggled. "Oh, he's right here." She looked up

at Matthew, her eyes full of adoration. "Matthew and I are to be married after Christmas."

Matthew wanted to grab Colette and run, so he could explain. He'd asked Shelah to let him announce the news in his own time since he had not formally asked her to marry him. But Shelah only lived on Shelah's time. She *thought* they should marry, and now she'd gone and announced what she wanted people to know. His only choice was to verify the truth.

"We have to get things organized before . . . then," he said, but that sounded weak even to his ears.

Colette's smile froze into an expression he'd never forget, but the look in her eyes as she glared at him shouted despair. To her credit, she held her emotions tight. "Well, isn't this a surprise. Matthew, you failed to let us know you were *engaged*, but it seems Shelah is very excited. Congratulations."

Then she gave Shelah a burning once-over, pivoted like a top, and swished her way through the swinging doors to the kitchen.

"Is your little friend always so abrupt, Matthew?" Shelah asked in an innocent tone.

"Colette is . . . just being Colette," he replied, his gaze following the still-swinging doors.

Abigail gave him a shrewd stare. "So *gut* to meet you, Shelah. And Mattie, I'm glad you're home. We have a lot to catch up on, ain't so?"

Before he could speak, Shelah touched Abigail's arm. "Only for a while. I mean he won't be here for long. We'll be leaving again in a few weeks. We have a big wedding to plan."

* * *

Four hours later, Colette wiped her face with a brisk passing of a handkerchief across her nose. "He is engaged and never once told me. Even when he called. But I knew from the way he was acting something was wrong. And then we had that terrible fight. In all the letters back and forth, he never mentioned he had fallen for another woman. And a nasty woman at that. I am never, ever falling in love again."

Mamm and Abigail glanced at each other and back to her. Eliza, flush with happiness, had left with Levi to hop a bus to Pinecraft, Florida, where they would honeymoon in a quaint little beach cottage and soak up the warm sunshine.

While she sat here in her family home, drowning in sorrow and tears. So not like her, but this pity party was necessary. Despite her happiness for her sister, she only wanted to wallow in her sadness now and listen to the beat of her broken heart.

"This is not like Matthew," Mamm said. "He doesn't have a cruel bone in his body. Maybe he met her after you two had your fight. He could have thought he'd lost you, so he turned to someone else. Someone who made herself available?"

Colette thought about that. "Or perhaps the fight gave him an excuse to turn to her? We did say some unpleasant things to each other. I was upset and I wasn't kind. Now I've lost him forever."

Mamm patted her hand. "Colette, this might not be your fault. Matthew does not look like a happily engaged man. In fact, he looks downright dreadful. Shelah, on the other hand, is cooing like a love dove. Something is not right with those two."

Just thinking of them together upset Colette's stomach.

"I had to endure them sitting together during the whole dinner reception. I couldn't eat, couldn't enjoy the beautiful cake Edith and I created. All I could think of was pushing Shelah's face into those red roses we made for the top layer of the cake."

"We don't do such violent things and you very well know it," Mamm replied, her tone firm but calm.

Colette bobbed her head. "I do know, Mamm. But still . . ."

"But still, truth be told, I'd like to do that very thing myself," Mamm admitted in a fiery whisper.

Colette loved her *mamm* even more than ever.

"I cannot believe our Matthew would do such a thing," Abigail said, her tongue clicking. "Why?"

"Her," Colette said. "Did you hear her? See her? She's pretty and apparently very confident. She made it a point to tell us Saul had a huge home and they plan to live there. She obviously thinks she deserves that."

"She could be using Matthew to get that huge home," Abigail said while she rocked Jon to sleep. The poor toddler was as tired as the rest of them. But he had entertained all the guests with his sweet smile and his love of people.

Colette wanted to cry all over again. Now she'd never be a mother to any child. Matthew had humiliated her in front of the entire community. If only she'd held her temper and not demanded he get home quickly, they might still be together. But he'd been shuttered and untalkative, and she'd snapped. She wasn't proud of it, but they could have talked the problem through. And it was too late now.

"I'll never show my face in public again," she decided

out loud. "I need answers, however, and I intend to find them."

"I've heard from Matthew's *mamm* that Saul was a bachelor and well-off," Mamm replied as she handed Colette a cup of spearmint tea. Mamm believed tea cured anything. "Miriam asked around, and apparently Matthew has inherited Saul's entire estate and plans to live on his farm."

Colette let out another sob. "How can I compete with that?"

Abigail grabbed her hand. "There is no competition. If he is engaged to Shelah Frantz, then that is that."

"Not until I get some answers," Colette said. "He owes me that much for ruining my life."

"You should be careful there," Mamm warned. "If Matthew is truly to marry Shelah Frantz, he can't be seen with you now. That won't set well. Not at all."

Colette lifted her head to stare across the table at her mother. "We are well past being unseemly now. Matthew Mueller owes me some answers, and I will get them."

She might be humiliated, but she would rise up and find the truth—then she would declare herself an *alte maedel*. She'd need to find some cats to keep her company. Colette loved cats, but the thought of not being married to Matthew made her burst into tears all over again.

While Colette was across town lamenting her broken heart, Matthew was sitting at the supper table with his *mamm* and *daed* and Shelah, wishing he could talk to Colette. He'd planned to do that first thing, but his plan had not worked.

Shelah had taken over his life and his world.

How had he let this happen? Well, he'd had no control over the events of the past few weeks. His whole future had been turned upside down, and the worst part was he couldn't tell anyone what had truly happened.

Now he glanced between his parents, wondering how they'd managed all these years. There was a secret that involved his family, a secret that had never been told. A truth that needed to be told. But he couldn't be the one to do it.

"Your brothers need to learn to be on time," Shelah said now as they waited. "My ham and potatoes will be dried up and cold soon."

Mamm, ever the peacemaker, smiled despite the tense lines marking her expression. "The boys won't mind a cold supper, Shelah. And while I appreciate your offer to cook tonight, you did cook a little early. We're all rather full from the wedding dinner, and they are used to supper after chores."

"I understand," Shelah said. "You have to do chores yourselves. Saul always had *gut* help to keep his place running. Which means Matthew and I will be able to have early suppers and more time together in the evening." Her smile beamed on Matthew like a spotlight.

Titus Mueller glanced around the table. "My sons work hard, and it would be wrong to hire others to do the work we are capable of doing ourselves." He glanced at Matthew with the same questioning expression he'd seen on many faces today.

Why is she here?

"Saul had a lot of money to pay people," Matthew pointed out. "And as Mamm said, none of us is really hungry after that big wedding feast."

"I see." Shelah passed the potatoes. "Eat a bit and I'll wrap up the rest for later." Her nose looked out of joint, so she obviously was offended. Shelah got offended easily.

"We must try this . . . food Shelah worked so hard to cook," Mamm said in a neutral voice. But she kept casting worried glances at Matthew. He needed to talk to his *mamm* in private, and soon.

Matthew stared at the sad potatoes. The woman had boiled them to mush and then dumped them on top of what could have been a great side of ham. Now it was a dreary lump of scorched, soggy meat being smothered by sad, soggy potatoes.

"Aren't you hungry a bit?" Mamm asked, giving him a glance he recognized from his childhood. The *behave* glance. Followed by the questioning glance.

"I could eat a bite." He dipped from the mush and dropped the glob onto his plate. He rather dreaded the biscuits. They looked like lumps of stone. He feared for his teeth.

Daed's eyes widened as he received the bowl. He took a hefty spoonful of the mush and then gave Matthew another meaningful stare. *We will talk later.* Another stare Matthew knew from childhood.

His two younger brothers, Timothy and Aaron, came rushing in. "Did we miss Mamm's corn bread and ham?" Timothy asked.

"We have biscuits," Shelah said. "I baked them myself."

Aaron's face fell like a bucket hitting well water. "No corn bread and gravy?"

"We have potatoes," Daed pointed out with a display of potatoes dripping from his spoon.

The boys both turned to Matthew. "What is going on?"

Matthew wished he knew the answer to that question.

Shelah's gasp caused him to look around. "I forgot. I made a sponge cake, too."

Aaron nudged Timothy in the ribs. "We might need a sponge, ain't so?"

Shelah didn't get it. She kept passing food and encouraging everyone to eat. "And come Sunday, I'll prepare sandwiches for church with my own special bread recipe."

"*Wunderbar*," Mamm said. Then she shoved a spoonful of mush in her mouth and bobbed her head.

Matthew decided then and there he couldn't do what Saul had asked of him. He could not marry Shelah, because he didn't love her. And she surely did not love him. Shelah loved two things: herself and money. They would not make a *gut* match.

But how in the world could he convince her of that when she knew the real reason they were to marry, and she had held his promise over him like a flame about to burn him?

How could he explain to Colette that he'd made a terrible mistake? And that he still loved her?

He didn't know where to begin, because he'd learned some disturbing news in Missouri. News only the lawyer, Shelah, and Matthew knew. But now, looking at Mamm, he had to wonder if she'd figured things out, too.

CHAPTER THREE

A week later, Colette stood in the inn's industrial kitchen, staring at a big lump of rising dough. They had rooms booked well through the new year, so she had to continue helping in the kitchen. But all she could think about was Matthew and Shelah.

"That bread won't make itself turn into my famous cinnamon rolls," Edith said from behind Colette. "Especially if you keep staring at it."

Colette jumped and turned to face the ornery cook. "Aren't you thinking about retiring?"

"I am," Edith said, her *kapp* askew and her apron barely tied. "And today, I'm double thinking that, especially these days. What's your excuse?"

"I want to learn," Colette said, deciding her future. "I want to learn to cook more and better. I need you to teach me all of your recipes, all of your secrets. I need to stay busy for a long, long time."

"*Ach, vell,*" Edith said, bobbing her head. "This is about Mattie, am I right?"

"*Neh*, nothing to do with him at all." Colette struggled to validate her request. "It's just that I'll be here at the inn for the rest of my days, and I'll be running this kitchen one day. Abigail has Jonah and Jon now, so she's already delegating work to me and others. Which is the way of it, of course. And now Eliza is off on her romantic holiday near the ocean, and she'll come home to a new way of life. You know she and Levi have moved into the cottage and Mamm and Daed are getting settled into the *gross-daddi haus*—newly attached to the cottage. I'll be . . . I'll be staying on in my room. I did get an upgrade to Abby's old room, but still—"

"But still," Edith interjected, "you'll be the last sister standing, ain't so?"

Colette heard the finality of that assumption. "*Ja,* the last sister who isn't married or deeply in love. Only I am deeply in love, but I treated Matthew with disdain until I finally saw him for who he was. Then somehow, after opening my eyes to the possibility of walking out with him, I found that I liked him. That I loved him. But we argued over silly things, and he has turned to another."

Edith glanced around as if looking for an escape route. "Have you told him you still have feelings for him?"

Colette took the bread dough and began to pound it. "I haven't. What's the point? Shelah has taken over his life, and he seems to put up with her. He hasn't even bothered to explain anything to me. He . . . he doesn't love me anymore, and it's my own fault really. I talked rudely to him, and he's had enough of that. I practically demanded he return home so we could officially announce our wedding."

Edith grunted and grabbed the now flat dough away from Colette. "Cinnamon rolls demand a deft hand and a lot of sugar and cinnamon."

Colette sniffed. "Obviously."

"They also require love and understanding—when we

bite into a flaky, warm cinnamon roll with vanilla icing, we know the meaning of love and family and hope."

"We do," Colette said as she watched Edith loop and twist the bread as she'd done for years and years.

Edith kept at it. "You cannot make passable food without having a passion to make that food with love. If you don't have the love of what you're doing in your heart, the whole thing will fall flat."

Colette stopped torturing the roll she'd tried to create. "I think I understand. You are telling me that Matthew loves me like a cinnamon roll, but his fling with Shelah will fall flat because he doesn't love her with cinnamon and sugar and icing on top?"

Edith looked confused for a moment but then smiled. "That is it exactly."

Colette nodded and straightened her spine. "I'm going to fight for my man," she announced. "And I'll start with making him a *gut* batch of cinnamon rolls. Edith, you are so wise."

Edith beamed and grabbed Colette's hands. "Now let me show you how it's done. Without all the drama."

The heavy weight fell from Colette's shoulders, so she ignored Edith's comment about drama. She was only pouring out her heart, and she did want to learn to cook better. "It's always best to follow the recipe, I reckon."

Edith grinned and then she laughed out loud. "Now you are speaking my language."

While Colette was pounding out her troubles with dough, Matthew was sitting on the other side of the inn in the employee room, staring across the table at Abigail.

"Well," Colette's older sister said, tilting her head to one side, "what's going on, Matthew?"

Matthew let out a long-held grunt. "I'm not so sure myself. Saul passed and I inherited his property. A vast property that comes with much responsibility and . . . Shelah Frantz. We are to be married in the new year, and that's that."

"He left her to you in his will?" Abigail asked, her kind eyes showing suspicion. "Surely you can explain better than that."

"I want to explain to Colette, but she is avoiding me."

"Do you blame her?" Abigail asked while she folded clean white cotton napkins. "You broke her heart and embarrassed her. She's distraught and is blaming herself since you two had a major fight, over the phone of all things. She's not exactly in an understanding mood these days."

"I don't blame her," Matthew said. "I am to blame for all of this. Saul was a bachelor. He had a displeasing disposition, but he was kind to me when I went to help him."

"And he left you with this huge responsibility. It's understandable that you have all sorts of doubts right now." Abigail studied his face, then asked, "Have you met with the bishop there? Has this marriage been announced?"

"*Neh*, not yet. I had to come back here first, and I thought I'd be alone when I returned."

Abigail took that information in and would probably report it back to Colette. Nothing was official with either of his possible brides.

"But Shelah was there the whole time and things got complicated. I'm not sure—"

Before he could finish explaining, the door to the employee room swung open and there stood Colette.

She looked so shocked and so pretty, her blue-green eyes reminding him of the lake, her fiery hair caught between being golden-colored and strawberry blond. Matthew had to catch his breath. "Colette . . ."

Colette held up her hand. "I'm only passing through. I have things to check on. I've taken on a lot of tasks around here because we've been shorthanded. Excuse me."

"Wait," her sister said, getting up to block her. "You two need to have a conversation. Have it now, and I will make sure no one interrupts."

"I don't want—" Colette retorted.

"Not a *gut* idea—" Matthew said at the same time.

Abigail shook her head. "This has to be done, so we can all find some peace. Talk and get it all out there. Then we'll decide what should happen next."

Colette shot a glance to Matthew. "I think we've all figured out what will happen next. He's only here to move his family to his new farm and his new life . . . with his new fiancée."

"It's not that simple," Matthew said, his heart shattered into a million pieces.

"Then you explain why it's so complicated," Colette said.

There was no easy way to explain things to Colette. Best to let her think the worst of him. He'd be gone soon enough, and she could move on with her life.

His silent musings only fueled her fire. "See, you don't have a logical reason for all of this. If I'd known a simple disagreement between us would cause you to turn around and ask another woman to marry you, I'd have spent my time on someone who truly does like me."

Abigail let out a sigh. "Stay here and talk." Then she marched out the door. And locked it behind her.

Colette ran to the door. "Abby?"

Matthew waited until she turned around. "We're locked in, and I know for a fact that stubborn runs in your family. She won't come back until she's *gut* and ready."

"Just like you'll explain your situation when you're *gut* and ready?" Colette asked, her hands on her hips, her chin out.

He loved her so much, but he had to squelch that love.

"I've been trying to find a way," he admitted. "Can we sit down and talk, please?"

Colette glanced at the door with longing, but she sat down on the chair across the table, her spine straight. "I had planned to find you and talk anyway. But now that I'm here, my plan to win you back seems silly."

"I'm sorry," he said, knowing that sounded weak and feeble, and wishing he could grab her and hug her close because she was willing to fight for him. But right now, he couldn't fight for her. "I've wanted to have this conversation for months, and I know you lost patience waiting for me."

"You could say that, *ja*."

"Colette, I inherited this huge farm and I'm over-whelmed as to what to do. Mamm and Daed don't want to uproot themselves from Pennsylvania and move to Missouri, but I'll need to do that very thing to keep the place up. It's not a long-distance job."

"That doesn't explain *her*, Mattie. Your current fiancée." Colette shrugged. "I suppose she swept you off your feet with her beauty and then after you and I quarreled, you turned to her for comfort." Her soft musings turned to steel. "Instead of trying to make up with me."

Matthew struggled with control. This time last year, he'd finally managed to attract the attention of the girl he'd always loved from afar. And Colette, to his surprise, had developed feelings for him. They'd had a few *wunderbar* months and they'd fallen in love. But no sooner had they declared their love than he'd received word that Saul was ill and asking for Matthew. He'd had no choice. Daed had told him to go and help his *onkel*. Mamm had protested, and now he knew why. Now that was his burden to carry.

"I can't explain Shelah, except to say Saul was her guardian. He hired a woman to be her nanny. Kathleen is related to Shelah and raised her, but Saul controlled the money. He spoiled Shelah, from what I can tell."

"I never would have guessed that," Colette said, her voice full of sarcasm.

Matthew reached across the table. He hated what he had to do, but right now he didn't have many options. "Colette?"

"You will not hold my hand while you tell me you plan to marry another woman," she said, standing. Then she pivoted to stare down at him. "Why, Mattie? Why?"

Matthew wanted to tell her the whole story, but it was too personal, and a tragedy at that. "Saul asked me, Colette. On his deathbed he asked me to take care of Shelah. He wanted me to marry her."

Colette's eyes flared hot. "And you readily said yes, not even thinking of writing to me, or explaining to me, or . . . telling him no because . . . we quarreled. This is because of our fight, isn't it?" Then she held up a hand. "*Neh*, you were already involved with her when you called. You wanted a fight, didn't you? That way you wouldn't have to explain how you could leave here loving me and come home engaged to her. Am I right?"

"You speak the truth," he admitted, because he had called to tell her everything and he'd lost his courage. "It appears that way."

But inside, in his heart, he wanted to take this woman in his arms and go away with her forever.

Colette's face crushed into a tormented frown. "So you got angry with my badgering, but you were already with her?"

"I have my reasons for what I've done," he said. "I can't explain everything, but before I could figure out how to handle the situation, Shelah decided that rather than staying in Missouri to wait for me, she'd come here and spend Christmas with my family. She got on the bus with me at the last minute, saying that she and I were engaged."

"Because you love each other?"

He couldn't look at her. He didn't speak.

Colette slipped down in her chair and stared at her hands. "I see."

"I had planned to explain my new relationship to everyone, but having Shelah here has made that difficult. Shelah didn't even explain to Kathleen. Just up and left— followed me. I wanted to tell Mamm and Daed about this situation before I announced any commitment."

And he still needed to be honest with his folks. Mamm was walking around in a daze. His mother had always been jittery and nervous, but she was over-the-top anxious these days, and he thought he knew why.

Colette sat staring at him as if she didn't even know him. "You sure have a lot of explaining to do, but you'll get no more time to do it with me." She stood and brushed her hands down her apron front. "But before I break out of here, answer this one question, Mattie, and then I'll leave you alone. Do you love her more than you love me?"

He couldn't speak. He loved Colette, but his heart was twisted in a vise—duty or love? Which should he choose?

"You can't even answer me," Colette said, a hand going to her face. She wiped at tears as if fighting off bees. Colette wasn't the sobbing type. Shelah had that down pat, however.

"*Ja,* I can tell you one thing," he replied, giving in just an inch, walking around the table to tug her close. "You need to trust me, Colette." Then he placed a soft kiss on her pouting lips. "Just trust me." He wanted her and only her. Somehow, he'd get out of this forced marriage to Shelah.

Colette pulled away again. "*Neh,* I will not trust you, nor let you hold me or kiss me, not when you're with her. You should know that about me, Mattie. You should know I'd never do that even if I don't want you to marry her." She stepped away, turned from him, and stared out the window. "I'm done with you."

Colette would do the right thing. She'd stand aside and let him marry a woman he did not love, because she wouldn't cause a scandal or get both of them in trouble and possibly shunned.

He'd lose her because they'd been taught to honor *Gott* and the tenets of their faith. He ached to hold Colette and tell her the truth, but he couldn't do that.

The door opened while they stood apart. Abigail took an obvious read of the room. Then she lowered her voice. "I hate to interrupt, but Matthew, there is a woman named

Kathleen here to see you, and she's hopping mad. I mean really upset."

"Kathleen Hinson? She's the woman who helped Saul raise Shelah."

Abigail glanced back. "Well, she's asking for you. Will you speak with her?"

Matthew bobbed his head. "Maybe she's here to talk some sense into Shelah and take her back home."

"And maybe you, too," Colette said as she stared him down. "Go and find out. We're done here. You no longer have to worry about my questions. I have my answers."

"Done today," he said, giving Colette a promising stare. "But not over, Colette. Not by a long shot."

He'd find a way out of this, a way to get past the secret Saul had revealed on his death bed. A secret that could destroy Matthew's entire family, and the woman he truly loved, forever.

CHAPTER FOUR

"Matthew, this simply will not do."

Matthew sat in a corner of the inn's great room, flames glowing in the fireplace and the smell of lemon oil wafting through the air with a bit of apple pie mixed in, while Kathleen Hinson's dark eyes sparked with their own fire.

"I understand," he said, hoping not to draw attention. Tourists and locals came here for meals, so he was bound to run into someone he knew. "But you know Shelah better than anyone. She got on the bus, and she refused to leave the bus until we arrived here. Now she's staying in my home."

Kathleen, the kind of firm chaperone that made Aenti Miriam look like a slacker, shook her head so fast her black winter bonnet bounced and shifted. "Not for long," she said. "I will bring her here to the inn and convince her that she is going home to Saul's place until this matter can be settled. She is not to be alone with you until your plans to marry are announced to the community."

"I know all of that," he said, trying to convince the woman. "I have done nothing to shame Shelah, or my family either. We told them of our plans right away."

Well, Shelah had prematurely told everyone. Another

thing she was excellent at—telling everyone about her wonderful life. He hadn't even seen her shed any tears for Saul, until she found out she'd only inherited a small amount of Saul's fortune. Then she sobbed buckets and decided Matthew and she were to marry, as Saul had said. Matthew believed she'd coaxed Saul in a moment when he was far from coherent.

But Saul had spoken to Matthew and suggested the match. "She needs someone to take care of her, Matthew," Saul had said. "You are perfect for her."

He didn't feel so perfect right now.

Kathleen's stern eyes softened. "You talked about another girl—Colette King. She lives on this property, am I correct?"

"You are," he said, thinking Kathleen had a keen memory. "Colette and her family own and run this entire place." He glanced toward the kitchen. "But things between us are over now."

Kathleen didn't look convinced. "No matter. If you're seen with another woman, people will talk. And you surely shouldn't have brought Shelah here without bringing me along for the trip."

"I told you—"

"Then this is what will happen," she replied with a curt nod, ignoring his defense. "Shelah will come and stay here with me. I'll get a suite of rooms so we'll both be comfortable. You have until Christmas to make up your mind. Will you do your duty and marry Shelah? Or will fondness make you turn to this other girl? Either way, I'll be here to supervise and make sure everyone involved behaves."

So like Kathleen to put herself in charge—but she was

only in charge of Shelah, not Matthew and his family or this inn. And she was certainly not in charge of Colette.

"Kathleen, Shelah has been announcing our engagement everywhere. I'm not even sure we will marry."

Kathleen let out a huff and gave him a stern stare. Then, after checking that they were alone, she leaned close and whispered low. "That girl. I told her to bide her time, but she tends to be impulsive. She had her sights on you the day you showed up, and now, well, with Saul's blessing and his estate going to you, she can't be dissuaded. I'll set her right. She's only creating a scandal where there is no need for one. My presence here will assure that you are still a free man, and Matthew, I do mean that from my heart. If you don't truly love Shelah, she has other options. Saul was old and senile and I'm pretty sure she did some tall talking to convince him you were in love with her. But you did not hear that from me."

Matthew's heart soared. If Kathleen, who loved Shelah dearly, saw through this farce, maybe he had an opportunity to salvage things with Colette. But that would mean going against Saul's wishes, whether Shelah had manipulated him or not. And that would mean Shelah would have a small inheritance, instead of Saul's estate. Matthew's estate now. Would she settle for that?

Unless there was a way to find her another man to marry. A man of means, because that's what she wanted, and she didn't mind going against the *Ordnung* to make that happen.

"*Denke*," he said to Kathleen. "*Kumm* and I'll introduce you to Henry Cooper, our front desk person. He will give you our best suite—it has two bedrooms with a view of the lake and a nice bath between them. I'll make sure your stay is covered."

"I can pay my own way," Kathleen replied, her head high. "Saul left me a nice nest egg, probably because I dedicated my life to him and that girl."

"Okay, but I can help, too. Shelah is my responsibility for now, and she will remain so for a long time to come, especially if we are to marry."

He heard a crash and turned to find Colette standing there, shock and anger in her eyes. She'd dropped a glass pan full of cinnamon rolls and now stood, surrounded by broken glass and mushed rolls smeared with white icing, staring at him with despair. And behind the shock and anger, tears filled her eyes.

Colette couldn't move. She'd planned to send the fresh rolls home with Matthew, since she'd purposely made them for him before their talk. Even angry at him, she wanted Shelah to see her gift and know Colette had baked the rolls. Now, because she'd been devious rather than truly kind, she'd ruined everything. Even her precious rolls.

"I'll get a mop," Matthew said, going into work mode immediately.

"*Neh.*" Colette blocked him from going into the broom closet. "You don't work here anymore, remember?"

The older woman beside him, who looked as shocked as Colette felt, stepped forward. "Matthew, did you lose your job?"

"I hadn't yet," he said, his eyes still on Colette. "But I reckon I'm not wanted here anymore."

Edith and Abigail came running. Edith glanced at Colette and then at the mess on the floor. "I'll clean this up," she said, the kindness in her voice breaking Colette's frozen stance.

She turned toward her sister. "Abby?"

Abigail came and took her by the hand. "Careful, you don't want to step in glass. *Kumm*, sister. *Kumm* with me."

Colette nodded and let Abigail guide her toward the kitchen, but Matthew was right behind her.

"Colette, Kathleen has come to watch over Shelah so things won't get out of hand. If you'd let me explain—"

"Things are already out of hand," Abigail replied, her tone sharp. "I'll find Henry and ask him and Daniel to clean this up."

Matthew took one last look at Colette and nodded. "Daniel, the new guy. I understand. I'll get Kathleen checked in."

"Checked in?" Colette whirled to stare at both of them. "Why?"

The woman stepped closer, clearly not afraid of the glare burning in Colette's eyes. "I'm Shelah's chaperone. I raised that girl, and she ran off without my even knowing it. Don't hold it against Matthew. She will be out of his house today and we'll both stay here until . . . until things are crystal clear and settled."

Colette's glare deepened while her skin burned. "'Settled'? Do you think you can settle this situation?"

Kathleen drew herself up, her spine going straight. "I do, young lady. And I will, one way or another."

Abigail tugged at Colette. "Let's go."

Colette didn't argue. Now she'd have to see Shelah every day. How could this be happening? How could Matthew do this to her? And in her own home and workplace at that? Nothing made sense to her anymore. She'd been foolish to think she could so easily win him back.

She'd never make another batch of fresh cinnamon rolls for him again.

Matthew pulled his buggy up to his house, then glanced over at Kathleen. He'd gotten her the nice corner room that he'd promised, with an adjoining sitting room. Kathleen had insisted on a big bed that she and Shelah could share.

"That way, I can keep an eye on her even while I sleep," Kathleen had said with a smug nod.

Matthew could believe the woman slept with one eye open. She had always been in the know about everything at Saul's place. Well, not everything—but he wouldn't be the one to tell her what he knew.

Now she studied the small white house with winter-bare bushes all around it. "This is nice, Matthew. Very cozy."

Wondering if that was code for *small and insignificant*, Matthew prayed for grace. It would be a long afternoon. "*Denke.* It's home."

"I'm sure you're glad to be back here, even under such confusing circumstances," Kathleen replied. "We'd best get in there and get this over with."

"I am glad to be back, *ja.*"

He dreaded going inside, however. Shelah wouldn't take this new development very well. The woman had a mind of her own. Saul had let her have the run of the house, and Kathleen had stretched herself thin trying to keep up. But Shelah did listen to Kathleen. Sometimes.

Before he could get down off the buggy, Shelah and Mamm came out onto the porch. "What?" Shelah said, staring at Kathleen. Then she glared at Matthew. "Did you bring her here?"

Kathleen got down off the wagon without his assistance and marched to the porch. "I came of my own accord, young lady. You neglected to tell me you were coming here with Matthew. I had to do some investigating to even find you. This will not do."

Mamm looked embarrassed, but her lips held the hint of a smile. Maybe she didn't want Shelah in her home after all.

Shelah glanced from Kathleen to Matthew. "Make her go away, please."

Kathleen ignored her rudeness and kept going up the steps. "Hello, I'm Kathleen Hinson," she said to Mamm. "I am so sorry you have unexpected company. But we are going to remedy that right now. Shelah, go pack your clothes. We are moving to the Shadow Lake Inn."

"*Neh,*" Shelah said. "I'm staying here with my future husband."

Kathleen shook her head. "Matthew has not asked you to be his wife, nor has he declared his love for you. And until that happens, it is not proper for you to be here. You either go with me to the inn, or we'll just take the next bus back to Missouri."

"Tell her, Matthew," Shelah said with a soft stomp of her foot. "Tell her we are to be married."

Matthew stood staring up at the woman who had been like a thorn in his side ever since Saul's deathbed request. "We have a lot to discuss and decide," he replied, his heart telling him he had to stand up to Shelah or his life would be full of misery. "And until then, I agree with Kathleen. You need to stay somewhere else."

Shelah's cheeks turned a vivid red. "But I want to be here with you. To cook for you and care for you." She lowered her head, her gaze sharp. "Have you forgotten our agreement?"

"What agreement?" Mamm asked.

Kathleen snorted. "You don't cook, and you never clean up after yourself." She glanced at Mamm. "I'm guessing she's left clothes all over her room?"

Mamm nodded. "*Ja*, but—"

"But nothing," Kathleen said, taking Shelah by the arm. "You will go with me, and you will behave, understand?"

"*Neh*." Shelah pulled away. "You can't control me anymore. Saul is gone and . . . he wanted us to be married."

Matthew stared at Mamm, but he feared Shelah would blurt out more than she should to force his hand.

Mamm gave him an understanding nod. "I do believe it would be best if you stayed with your . . . chaperone . . . at the inn for a while, Shelah. It's roomy and so beautiful. And the food is *wunderbar gut*, and you won't be so lonesome there."

"I'll be forced to see that horrible woman who thinks she's going to take Matthew from me."

"You won't be bothered by Colette," Matthew said, raising his voice at her harsh description of Colette. He had to stay in control, so he held in his anger. "I need time to decide about all of this. I'm still mourning my *onkel*, and even if we do marry, it will be a while from now. So do as Kathleen is asking. Give me some time. Just a few weeks with my family. You'll be much more comfortable at the inn."

"Weeks? I don't have weeks," Shelah replied. Then she put a hand to her mouth. "I mean, I don't want to wait for weeks."

"It is decided," Kathleen said. "And if you run away

again, you'll be on your own without money or family. Think of that before you do something impulsive."

Shelah pouted and looked off into the distance. Matthew had made one decision. He had to get her out of his house. Mamm and Daed didn't need to deal with her. They hadn't even been able to go to Saul's funeral, so they sure didn't need a reminder of their loss every waking hour. Especially Mamm. He wished he could talk to her and confide in her, but it would only bring her pain.

Daed and his brother Saul had never been close. And now Matthew knew the reason why. But he couldn't tell anyone that reason.

And he hoped and prayed Shelah wouldn't reveal it in frustration either. She'd certainly hinted that she might blurt out the truth, and it had become a way to threaten Matthew. But he wanted to be the one to tell this story. It wasn't Shelah's to tell, after all. She'd told him she'd keep quiet about it, but he knew she could change her mind on a whim.

"I'll go," Shelah finally said. "But Matthew, I expect to see you each day. We have much to discuss, remember?"

And there it was. The secret she was holding over his head. The one thing about him she knew to be true. And it was the one thing that could tear his family apart and put Colette out of his reach forever.

CHAPTER FIVE

Colette sat in her room later that week, still fuming over her brief talk with Matthew. He couldn't even tell her he loved her still, though he hadn't told her he loved Shelah either. But after what she'd heard him say to Kathleen, it seemed that baking cinnamon rolls wouldn't win him back.

It felt as if she'd known Matthew forever. He'd always been very shy, but Colette could draw him out. So she'd flirted with him, just to see where it would go. Not to hurt him or deceive him. She really did like Mattie. But they were always so busy, coming and going as they worked together, the inn always needing their attention. She'd taken him for granted, as a friend and a coworker. Until last year when Eliza had been caught up in loving Eli, and Abby had been preparing to have her first child. That left Colette on her own a lot.

Then she and Matthew had kissed after the Christmas singing. Kissed and held each other. She'd never felt so at peace. She'd fallen in love, maybe because her sisters had both found love and she'd longed for the same. And Matthew was there. He'd always been there right in front of her eyes.

But that night, she'd looked up and really seen him. Then she'd poured out her heart to him and he'd kissed her and held her.

Maybe she'd opened up because Matthew had been talking to her more, really talking to her. Matthew had been there to calm her, to listen to her.

"You know something, Colette," he said that night, his lionlike eyes as always so strong and sure, "you are not alone. Your sisters will always be your sisters. And you'll have nieces and nephews and all those in-laws, too. And you have me. The one who's known you since you were born."

"And what do you know about me, Mattie?" she asked, so naive and yet so flirtatious. She enjoyed his attention. But his next words caught her heart and opened it wide so that she saw what was there right before her eyes.

"I know that you secretly love to cook, but Edith won't let you experiment with your new ideas. I know that you like to read, same as Eliza, but you really take books more seriously than your sisters. You sneak off to that small library in the inn and read. You twist your lips or sigh when you're reading, and you hate finishing a book. You look sad until you find another one. Like the ones I've left here and there in the inn for you."

Colette let out a gasp. All this time and she'd never figured out who'd left her those special books. She should have known. She should have.

"That was you? I thought it was Eliza, and she kept telling me she didn't know anything about the books, but then her thoughts were always lost in her horses."

"I didn't want you to scold me, or think I was strange."

"Well, you are strange, but it's a lovable strange."

"Why do you say that?"

"I've seen you rescuing baby birds and petting the lambs and playing with the children who pass through here." She grinned at him. "I know you take Samson treats."

"I like animals and I like children."

"And you work hard. You're the first person we call when something goes wrong in the kitchen or the washroom."

"My family has to eat. I love my job here. It's nice to meet new people who pass through or visit with the ones who return. And it's nice to work with someone like you."

His gaze spoke so many things, his dark eyes bright with hope.

"Mattie, why do you put up with me?" she asked, realizing for the first time just how much she did depend on him. And care about him. Colette's heart changed that night. It lifted and opened and beat a new rhythm. She felt a rush of love.

He smiled at her, and even though she'd seen that smile a thousand times, this time she saw Mattie. Her Mattie.

"Do you have to ask? I've known you since we were born. I've watched you grow up while I grew up. I've watched you chase butterflies and learn to make pies. I've watched you turn down boy after boy, and now I am the last man standing."

"Here with me," she said. "I like that, Mattie."

"Then maybe you'll finally see me as fully grown, hardworking, and here. Always right here."

She had seen him that night. After he'd kissed her, Colette had thought her heart would burst out of her chest. No more wondering who she might fall in love with. She was already in love with the boy who had followed her around forever, antagonizing her at times and annoying her at others, but always right there if she needed him. And . . . she'd always needed him.

"I took you—us—for granted," she said to herself now.

Then her door burst open and Eliza, fresh from her honeymoon and glowing, grabbed her up and hugged her tight. Abby followed close behind, her smile soft and quiet.

"We wanted to check on you," Eliza said. "I brought you something from Pinecraft."

She pulled out a pretty pink pair of flip-flops. "For summer."

Colette studied the strange shoes. "I'll fall right out of these."

"You get used to them," Eliza said, her cheeks pink with love. Maybe even pinker than the shoes.

"Just don't wear them in the chicken coop." Abigail snorted, and they all laughed.

Well, Colette tried to laugh, but tears seemed to blur her eyes. "I don't know what to do with myself. That girl is in the inn right now, plotting ways to keep Mattie and me apart. I don't think he wants me to try to win him back. He implies he must marry her. My only hope is that he does not seem to be in love with Shelah."

"She's a bit obvious," Eliza said. "She wants status and money, so clearly she never paid attention to the reading of the *Ordnung*."

"Clearly," Abigail echoed. "So far, she's managed to make everyone from Henry to Edith angry. She demands fresh linens and towels when we've just changed the beds. She sends waiters up and down the stairs with silly requests. And that poor nanny woman chases her, fussing at her." She shrugged and rubbed her forehead. "I have a headache."

Eliza made a face. "I'm so glad I won't have to deal with her, but Sister, if she messes with you, I might not be kind."

"*Denke*," Colette said. "Maybe I'll just stay here in my room for a long time."

Abigail shook her head. "*Neh*, that's what she wants. You need to remember who you are, Colette. Our parents didn't raise us to be brash or proud, but they did raise us to be strong. You keep at what you do best. Help Edith run the kitchen. From there you can keep an eye on Shelah."

"But I'll see Matthew. Jonah told me he hasn't been fired."

"Not fired?" Eliza said. "Why not?"

Abigail dropped her hand away from her forehead. "We need the help, and I decided Mattie needs to be here around us for the next month. He's carrying a heavy load and he has to make a decision by Christmas. Saul's place can't be vacant for long. It's a big operation."

"*Ja*, a big operation that one smooth operator apparently wants for herself," Colette said.

"And marrying Matthew is the only way she can get it," Eliza finished. "You know what you need to do, Colette?"

"Run away?"

"*Neh*, you will do no such thing," Eliza said. "You should make a quilt. A Christmas quilt, since this time of year is when you truly fell in love with Mattie. You can show past Christmases, including the night he kissed you by the tree. That special night."

"We had a lot of special nights before he had to leave for

Missouri," Colette said. "I thought my life was complete. Now I have no hope."

"There is always hope," Abigail said. "Make a quilt. It worked for both of us." She patted Colette's hand. "The truth will be in your quilt, and Matthew will see that, just as Jonah and Levi saw our stories."

Colette sat up straight, her heart beating faster. "And maybe Shelah will see the truth, too, and get on a bus out of here."

"There's the Christmas spirit," Abigail said, laughing. "We have other ways to distract Shelah. *Gut* ways."

Colette could only think of bad ways. "How so?"

Abby pressed her lips together in a prim smile and then said, "We can hold youth frolics and invite all the eligible boys and men we know."

"The ones with money," Eliza replied. "She seems to have that at the top of her list."

Colette nodded. "You are both so *wunderbar gut* to help me."

"It is a big task but we can do it," Abby said as she stood. "I must go. My husband is waiting downstairs. And, Eliza, you and Levi are in charge of this home now that you've returned. The men are finally finished moving Mamm and Daed into the *grossdaddi haus*."

Eliza's smile said it all. "It was *gut* of Levi's *mamm* to insist we move in here after the add-on, because we both work here. Levi has found an overseer for their farm, so once the crops are in, there will be some extra money for his *mamm*'s care. But Connie knows Jamie, Laura, and she are always *welkom* to live here with us . . . when things get bad with her Parkinson's disease."

"Always *welkom*," Abby said. "And now that Connie's home has been renovated and Aenti Miriam is there to nurse her as needed, things are looking up for everyone around here."

Colette groaned. "Everyone but me." Her world was changing so fast, she felt like a spinning top. "I'll be the woman who lives upstairs forever."

"*Neh*, we have a plan," Eliza reminded her. "You can stay here as long as you like, but I don't think it will be for very long at all."

"*Gott*'s will," Colette replied. "I want to believe Matthew and I belong together, but it might take a while for that to happen."

"Just like Levi and I did," Eliza said with a warm, happy smile. "It took us years, but once it happens, well, it's worth the hard time of waiting."

"You both know I'm not good at waiting," Colette said.

"We do. But *Gott* knows better than we do, Sister." Abby kissed Colette's cheek. "Get your rest. You will be busy soon enough."

Colette waved to them and then lay in her bed, dreaming of Matthew coming to her and declaring his love. Dreaming also of Matthew putting Shelah on a bus to anywhere but here.

But what if he didn't do that?

"I need to talk to Shelah," Matthew told Jonah the next morning while they mended some boards on the inn's front porch.

"I'm sure you do," Jonah answered in his quiet way.

He'd become the go-to person at the inn now that the girls' father had heart trouble. Jonah was smart, and he'd been out in the world. He knew how things worked. But like all of them, he'd struggled to figure out the three King sisters.

"Should I, though? Colette already hates me."

"She doesn't hate you," Jonah said as he measured a two-by-four and placed it to the side while he searched for nails. "Quite the opposite. She thought you two were to be married next year."

"We were. That was the plan," Matthew said. "Then Saul died, and my life got messy."

"Two women vying for you is a hot mess," Jonah replied.

Frowning, Matthew figured "a hot mess" must be an *Englisch* term. "If that means double trouble, then you are correct."

Jonah chuckled. "Why did you agree to bring Shelah here, Matthew?"

"I didn't, really," Matthew replied. "Saul asked me to marry her, but he was very ill and hardly recognized any of us. Shelah sat with him a lot and I think she implied things."

Jonah stopped measuring and stared at him. "Things such as you and her getting married?"

Matthew nodded. "I was as surprised as anyone when he told me he wanted that."

"Shelah thought you'd stay in Missouri and make it right?"

"She did, but I tried to explain I was . . . taken. I told her about Colette. How much I love Colette. I stressed that I was to marry another, not Shelah."

Jonah handed him two nails and a hammer. "And yet, she came here with you."

"*Ja*, like glue stuck to my arm. I shouldn't have told

her I had not spoken to the bishop about my intentions with Colette. She zoomed in on that one little misstep."

Jonah measured another board. "Is there some special reason she thinks you'll marry her?"

Confused at first, Matthew shook his head when he realized what Jonah was asking. "I've barely kissed the girl. It's not that kind of forced marriage."

"So no *bobbeli* on the way," Jonah said, his stern gaze on Matthew. "But you have kissed Shelah?"

"Shelah has kissed me," Matthew admitted. "I was caught completely off guard."

Jonah lined up the new board to match the still-solid old ones so they could nail it and then paint it. "Hammer that nail, Matthew. You need to work off some steam."

"A lot of steam," Matthew said. But he took Jonah's advice and hammered away, wishing he could nail all his worrying into this floor.

Remember Gott *and His son who suffered for your sins*.

Matthew said a silent prayer, and then he went back to hammering. Until he looked up and saw Shelah coming from one direction and Colette headed toward him from another.

"Jonah, I need to—"

"Hide?" Jonah shook his head. "Matthew, you're not a coward. Why don't you send Shelah packing and tell Colette you still love her?"

"It's complicated." He glanced at the determination in Shelah's eyes as she came up the path from the lake, her black wool cloak blowing in the wind.

Colette had spotted him and Jonah and now marched down the hill toward the big inn, her black bonnet covering most of her face. But she lifted her head and gave him a quick glance before she saw Shelah.

"They're going to meet right here," he said, thinking he should have found other work today.

"And you will stay right here and handle this."

Jonah never had to ask twice. His voice held a certain command. And Matthew had never run away from anything or anybody. Sure, he was younger than Jonah or Levi, and they treated him like a little brother. But he was also strong and healthy and ready to marry and have a family. He'd never been scared of much in life, but losing Colette scared him. Deeply scared him. His whole life had revolved around this inn and Colette King. How could he just walk away from her and marry a woman he barely knew and to whom he wasn't attracted?

He wanted to be with Colette. Always Colette.

Now Shelah approached him, that look of disappointment in her brown eyes. "There you are. I thought we were supposed to take a stroll down to the big lake today. I had to go by myself when I couldn't find you."

Matthew pushed at his shaggy hair and said a silent prayer for grace and guidance. "I'm certain sure I told you I'd be working, all day."

"Don't you get breaks?" Shelah asked, her tone full of doubt. "I can't understand why you feel the need to work. You are a landowner now."

"*Neh*, not many breaks," he said, ignoring her jab. "Always something to do around here."

Shelah adjusted her cloak, shot Jonah a curious stare, then fixed her gaze on Matthew. "Well, when we get home you'll have people to take care of petty stuff like this."

"This is not petty," called out a feminine voice on the other side of the porch. Colette came up the side steps and stood with her hands together in a prim way, while her rosy cheeks burned with indignation underneath her bonnet. "This place has been here since the early eighteen hundreds. Presidents have stayed here. Movie stars have stayed here, as well as hundreds of *Englisch*, along with Amish. We don't get all starry-eyed about our important guests, but we are happy to serve anyone because we love this inn, and it is our livelihood. We consider any guest important, because this place provides a *gut* livelihood and one we do not take for granted. Even when a rude guest appears."

Shelah gasped and glared at Colette. "I wasn't rude. I was merely stating a fact. Matthew doesn't need to be doing demeaning work. He has inherited a farm twice the size of this old place."

Matthew looked at Jonah. Jonah's face remained blank, but he had a brightness in his eyes that showed pride.

Matthew turned to face Colette. "You are for certain sure right about everything. This place is special and historical, and everyone loves it here." Then he glanced at Shelah. "Well, almost everyone."

Colette remained quiet, but her eyes locked onto him, the hurt in her gaze breaking him. He wanted to go to her, but before he could make a move, she turned and headed around to the kitchen porch on the other side of the inn.

"She's an odd one, isn't she?" Shelah asked, clueless about anything but herself.

"She's a unique individual," Matthew said. "And, Shelah, you need to understand I was once engaged to her. At least be kind to Colette."

Shelah gave him a look that twisted her pretty face, her chin jutting out, her eyes flaming with anger. "But you are not engaged to her anymore, Matthew. Remember what you promised me?"

Then she turned and whirled away in a huff.

Matthew let out a sigh and grabbed more nails.

"What exactly did you promise her?" Jonah asked, glancing toward Shelah's departing back. "What is she holding over you, Matthew?"

CHAPTER SIX

"We are less than four weeks away from Christmas," Abigail said the next Monday. "We have a lot left to do."

Colette glanced around the table where all the inn's employees were gathered for their weekly meeting. They never overdecorated; that was not the Amish way. But they did put up trees with simple handmade ornaments, and they put battery-operated candles in all the windows—and there were a lot of windows. That took a whole day and most of the staff. They put natural wreaths made from holly leaves and twigs and tied with bright red ribbons on the main doors and windows. The whole place looked festive but old-fashioned and not at all over-the-top.

"As we know, most of our guests come back year after year," Abigail said. "They like the charm and the simple decorations."

Colette took a quick glance toward the man sitting near the door. Then she thought about Shelah's mean words to Matthew the previous week. Did he think his work here was beneath him now that he owned a vast property and had a big bank account? He had defended the inn and his work. But Shelah's words might have changed his feelings about everything, including the inn.

Neh, not her Mattie. He'd worked here since he was fifteen, almost ten years. But Shelah's arrogance could had worn off on him and given him high-flying ideas. Who could turn down the kind of place she'd mentioned? And a wife ready to come with it at that. A pretty wife with an ugly attitude.

"And, Colette, I hear you're helping Edith with the baking. We'll need snickerdoodles and our favorite almond cookies out on the buffet each day."

The room went silent while Abigail waited for her answer. Colette looked up and saw everyone staring at her. Even Matthew, who'd sat as far away from her as he could.

"*Ja*, lots of cookies. It's covered. All kinds of cookies."

Where was Edith when a person needed her? She left early every day because she arrived before everyone else to bake. Lately, because she couldn't sleep, Colette had been helping during those morning shifts. Now she'd be knee-deep in cookie dough for the next few weeks.

"You sound very enthusiastic," Eliza said from her corner. She was waiting to escape to the stables.

Colette slid her gaze over the room. "I am enthusiastic. You know I love Christmas, for so many reasons." Her gaze stopped on Matthew and she went silent.

"Okay, time for work," Abigail said, standing; she obviously wanted to avoid a nasty conversation. "You all know what needs to be done. Remember the buggy rides and hot chocolate, twenty-four seven. Now that we have the new pavilion with the firepits nearby, we should have a steady supply of ingredients to make s'mores, too. I could go for one of those right now."

Jonah laughed and took her hand. "We'll do that soon—share some s'mores together."

Colette wanted to scream. Those two were so in love, and now Eliza and Levi were giggling to each other. While she sat here seething with an ugly kind of envy that wouldn't go away until that annoying woman was out of Mattie's life.

After everyone had left, her sisters stood watching her. "What?"

"You're not yourself," Eliza replied. "You're lost."

"I am that." Colette plopped down on her chair, out of breath from fretting so much. "I can't stop thinking of this horrible situation." Then she perked up. "But Mattie did take my side the other morning when she-who-won't-be-named said the work he does here is beneath him, petty, and demeaning."

Eliza's eyes flared hot. "Does she realize what this place means to all of us?"

"Oh, I told her what it means, and she heard me, all right. But she was defensive and reminded me that Matthew Mueller is now a landowner, and he doesn't need to do menial work anymore, as if his job here was somehow insulting."

"She is the one who is insulting," Abby said. "How ungrateful."

"She wants what she wants," Colette replied. "And that is Matthew."

Abigail started to speak, then stopped.

"What?" Colette knew that look. Jonah had told her something she wasn't supposed to repeat. "Tell me or I'll just hound Jonah until I get it out of him."

"Oh, all right," Abigail said. "He thinks Shelah is holding something over Matthew's head, forcing him to give in to her." She lowered her voice. "Matthew wouldn't tell him what's going on, but my husband is *gut* at reading people. I think he's right."

Colette's heart bumped too hard. "That would be cruel. But what could she use against Matthew?"

"I don't know," Abby said. "And neither does Jonah. He asked Mattie to tell him so we could help. But Mattie just shook his head and went back to work."

Colette felt hope for the first time in days. "That would explain why he keeps saying they are to wed. Not 'We want to get married soon' or 'I'm sorry, but we are so in love.' I find it strange that he does not seem to be in love with Shelah, and that he is so sad. I wanted to believe that was because of me, yet he has not shown any indication that he'll change his mind. He never did answer me when I asked if he loves her more than he loves me." She held her hands together, thinking. "So maybe if we try something different with Shelah, we can find out the truth. Or maybe he's in love with both of us."

"I don't think that's it," Abigail said. "He does not look at her the way he looks at you—has always looked at you."

That made Colette's heart warm, but still . . .

"What would that something different be?" Eliza asked. "We can't nab her and put her back on the bus." Her eyes widened. "We could grab her and bring her here and take her up to Colette's room and question her."

"You've been around my husband too long," Abigail replied. "And you know we can't do that."

Colette didn't see why not, but she would refrain from going to such drastic measures. Mamm wouldn't approve. She grinned, then turned serious. "We should befriend her."

Eliza grabbed her arm. "You've lost your mind. Why would we do that?"

"To catch more flies, as Mamm would tell us," Colette replied. "We hold a holiday youth singing as we planned, and invite lots of eligible men, and we treat her nice and tell her we want her to feel welcome. I'll pretend that Mattie and I are done forever. And then I'll question her. She's so vain, she'll talk about all of it, I imagine."

"What if Mattie believes her, about you and he being finished?" Eliza asked.

"I don't care. He's made no effort to say that we're not. I'd like to believe he'll fret about it, but so far he has not." She gave both her sisters a piercing stare. "And you two are not to let on. As far as the world is concerned, Matthew Mueller and I are finished, broken up, not getting married. It's over. And really it has to be over, regardless of our feelings for each other. I've already told him that."

"We need to make this believable." Eliza looked worried, but her eyes held a hint of anticipation. None of them wanted Matthew to leave with Shelah. Not if he didn't really love her.

"It's a bold idea, and risky," Abby said, glancing around. "I gave up sneaking around when I married Jonah."

"Not sneaking. Just showing grace to a woman who doesn't deserve it," Colette said. "I have a feeling she'll be only too happy to let me know what's what."

Mamm came into the room. "What are you three cooking up now?"

"Nothing." Colette stood and glanced around. "I'd better check on the biscuits for breakfast tomorrow."

"Right." Mamm looked at Abby and Eliza. "I don't suppose you'd like to clue me in?"

"We're just wondering what Matthew might decide about . . . things," Abigail replied. "We're all still a bit shocked."

"Tell me something I don't know," Mamm said. "I got a complaint that the hot water ran out in the West Suite."

Shelah's suite.

"Oh, that suite. I see," Abigail said. "I'll have Jonah check on it."

"But the hot water never runs out around here," Eliza said.

Mamm smiled. "Truer words have never been said. Maybe that's why you three land in hot water so often. And I'm hoping what I walked in on isn't one of those times."

She waited a beat, then shook her head and left, but Colette knew her *mamm*. Mamm would find out the truth.

So their plan might be called off before they even got started.

Colette listened as Edith explained seasonings.

"You don't want too much. A palate doesn't need too many spices. Mild seasoning is best because we have a variety of visitors who eat here. Savory and sweet. A little pep, but not too hot. The digestive system prefers a smooth taste."

Colette nodded while Edith threw a dash of this and a pinch of that into the potato casserole they were making for today's menu. Savory and sweet—she should try that with Matthew and maybe he'd open up to her. She'd failed with the cinnamon rolls, and ruined a perfect baking pan at that. If she decided to make a quilt as her sisters had done, she'd add a cinnamon roll to it to show she'd tried. Meantime, she planned to seek out Shelah, though she'd have to try hard not to grimace with pain as she befriended the woman.

"Are you understanding me?" Edith asked, bringing her thoughts back to the present.

Colette nodded. "Don't overdo anything, but give it a boost so the taste will be pleasant and enjoyable."

She'd try that with Shelah.

"That's correct." Edith studied her, obviously beginning to see where Colette's thoughts were wandering. "We're not talking about potato casserole, are we?"

Colette began mashing the potatoes they'd peeled and boiled earlier. "I'm just so interested in getting it right, Edith."

"I understand."

"I think I've been seasoning things the wrong way with Mattie, and now we are officially broken up," Colette continued. "I'm going to try savory and sweet by accepting his upcoming marriage and life with Shelah. I don't want to pain him. I want them to be happy, with my blessings. I can't control their actions, so I'll just season the whole thing with grace."

"Uh-huh." Edith sighed and went back to her potato casserole tutoring. "Not too mushy, mind you. That never works." Then the buxom cook leaned in. "And you might want to lay off the sweetness, dear. Faking it is not becoming on one whose face shouts honesty. You look like you've swallowed a frog when you speak of that woman."

"*Neh*, I'm fine with her. I won't even cry one tear. I'm not a fading violet, after all."

Edith gave her the side-eye. "I believe that's a shrinking violet, and you certainly are not that. Not at all."

"*Denke*." Colette used the handheld potato masher to let out her frustrations. "I refuse to cry. I'm taking the high road." She mashed the potatoes flat.

"You know what they say—no tears in the taters."

"Do they really say that?" Colette asked, coming back to reality.

Edith shook her head. "I think when it comes to Matthew and Shelah, you should start with cookies. And a pan that won't break if you drop it."

"You are so wise, Edith. Cookies it is. I happen to know he loves sugar cookies. But would that be too sugary?" Then she dropped the potato masher and gasped. "I mean, would that be too sugary for Shelah? I'm done with making food for Matthew. I'll make cookies for Shelah."

"*Ja*, that's a fabulous idea." Edith scratched her head and frowned. "Can we finish the potatoes since they're on the menu today? And then this afternoon I'll tell you all the secrets to baking cookies . . . for Shelah, *ja*?"

"A *gut* plan," Colette replied, even though she'd helped bake cookies since she was twelve, and even though she hated the thought of giving Shelah anything. "How long do we bake this casserole?"

"About an hour or until the cheese is nice and bubbly."

"Bubbly! I'll be bubbly, too. *Denke*, Edith. You always help me figure things out."

Edith nodded, then laughed, then looked concerned. "You're *welkom*. I think."

* * *

A day later, Abigail asked Matthew to help with winterizing the inn. He checked all the outdoor faucets and pipes and made sure they were covered. A big snowstorm was predicted for the rest of the week. The inn was booked up through the new year, so they couldn't afford a frozen or broken pipe. The inn had to have running water and electricity, not to mention propane for the many ovens and stovetops they used in the industrial kitchen. For years now, Edith and Abigail had relied on him to manage anything connected with the kitchen, from the stoves to the plumbing. He'd even taken courses to learn more about maintenance. He'd just gotten a nice raise before he'd been called to help Onkel Saul.

Saul Mueller had been a paradox to Matthew. Even now, he couldn't believe what he'd found out. It was hard to think of Saul, to call him *onkel*, because no one had really known the man. Saul was a loner and someone who didn't always follow the rules. Conflicted, that one.

Especially with Matthew's family. From what Matthew had learned through conversations over the years and before he'd discovered the truth, Saul and Daed had had a falling-out long ago. But no one ever talked about it. They never visited each other, which Matthew had always thought strange. Relatives always visited back and forth unless someone was shunned.

But now, Matthew had figured out so many things. Things he couldn't share with anyone. How he longed to talk to Colette. Just sit and talk the way they had before he'd left. Their love had been so fresh, so new, after years of dancing around each other and teasing each other. After years of him waiting for Colette to really see him as someone other than a friend and a coworker.

I had it all. My life was full. Colette loved me.

But by inheriting a huge estate he'd never asked for or wanted, he'd lost the most precious thing in his life—Colette.

How could she understand or forgive him when he'd walked into her sister's wedding with another woman? He'd planned to show up alone and explain everything, but Shelah, who'd had to stay at his house since she had nowhere else to go, had hopped into the family buggy at the last minute. Then, after he'd parked the buggy, she'd latched onto him. He couldn't make a scene at the wedding, so he'd tried to ignore her. But Colette had seen them before he'd even gotten himself together, and that was that. Now Colette had made it clear they were finished.

Caught between the truth that would ruin his family and hurt the woman he'd always planned to marry, Matthew went about his business with his head down. The King family had been kind to him, considering all he'd brought home to them.

At least Shelah was under the watchful eye of Kathleen now. That woman wouldn't let Shelah do anything to compromise herself or Matthew. Kathleen might even get her to give up this marriage notion and leave before Christmas. He planned to stay the whole month. One last Christmas with his family and friends before his life took a different turn.

He prayed Kathleen could convince Shelah to leave. He needed time alone to salvage things with Colette. If they could not be together, he at least wanted her to know he would always care about her. Of course, that would sound like an insult and a brush-off.

He rounded the back corner of the inn and saw Colette coming toward him with a small basket. He wanted to talk to her but hadn't found a time or place where they could be alone. And he was afraid she'd only tell him how angry she was. Angry and hurt and disappointed.

Then she called out to him. "Mattie?"

He pivoted, his toolbox in his hand, surprised that she'd called him Mattie instead of Matthew. "*Ja?*"

She walked up, a tentative light in her eyes. "I made some sugar cookies for you to take up to Shelah later."

Not sure if she was being kind or giving him poison cookies, he forced a smile that might have been a frown. "Why?"

"Why not? We always give our guests cookies, but since she rarely comes downstairs, and you visit her up in her suite, I thought we could still show her the same courtesy. She is a guest here, after all. A long-term guest, as it turns out."

Because he was so surprised and because he knew Colette too well to believe her sweet explanation, he stared at the basket; the smell of freshly baked cookies tantalized him. "I'll see that she receives the basket."

Colette smiled big. "*Gut.*" Then she gave him a solemn glance, making him think the real Colette was about to be unleashed on him. But instead, she shocked him yet again. "You can have some now if you'd like."

Okay, Colette being nice to him was almost as concerning as Colette being angry at him. What had she and her sisters cooked up? "I'd like that," he said. "Want to go over by the fire Jonah built?"

She lifted her head. "I would normally love that, but you know I can't be seen with you. What if Shelah glanced out the window? After all, these cookies are technically for her."

"Oh, so you don't want to talk privately?" He squinted at the cloudy sun. "You're still mad at me, ain't so?"

Colette sank down into one of the heavy wooden Adirondack chairs her *daed* and Jonah had built and handed him the small basket. It felt warm from the fresh-baked cookies.

"It's chilly," she said. "I hear a big storm is coming. So I'd rather be inside where it's warm. I'd be glad to take Shelah the cookies myself."

"That won't be necessary," he said, grabbing the basket, his appetite gone. Such a visit could turn into a disaster.

She stood and shivered. "I'm going home—to the cottage—where I still have a room. Being single does have its perks." Then she motioned toward the firepit. "You should go get warm. Seems Abigail is keeping you busy these days."

Colette was tormenting him, that she was. He got it now.

"*Ja.* I've been checking everything, wrapping plants, making sure the pipes and faucets are secure, same as I always do."

"In case you leave again?"

And there it was. She was ready to let him have it.

He looked at the basket in his hand. "I plan to stay here through Christmas. My folks need help with some things, repairing fences and making sure the barn is in working order."

"Mattie, you stay as long as you and Shelah need to. You've chosen her, so that's the way of it. I'm okay now and I'm sorry about how I've behaved."

But she didn't look okay. Colette's eyes held a sad darkness that made his heart flame with regret. Her words indicated she'd get on without him though. She was just that stubborn. She'd make herself give up on them.

But that was how it had to be. Or was it?

"Is that your way of saying things are truly over between us?" he asked.

Colette looked into his eyes with a gaze that hid nothing, a gaze that filled his hurting heart with a cutting regret. "I'm accepting what I've seen with my own eyes," she finally said. "You blindsided me in front of most of the community. I dread even going anywhere. People are whispering and gossiping, but I can deal with that. I have to go on with my life—and with very little explanation from you."

"I've tried to explain several times."

"So try one more time," she said. "Even though we're done, I can't help but be curious. I need to understand. I need this to make some sense."

Matthew took a deep breath. Now was his opportunity to be open with Colette. But if he told her the whole truth, he'd bring shame to the ones he loved. He couldn't do that to his family. He'd tell her only what she needed to know.

Letting out a sigh, he began. He could tell her the public facts, at least.

"Colette, inheriting Saul's farm has thrown a wrench into my plans. It's a big place, a thriving business with silos and barns and more livestock than I've ever seen, and two dozen people employed to do everything. It has its own produce market and a tree farm that brings in loggers and makes money. Saul hired Amish loggers who use horses and trailers to do the logging, so the whole community looked up to him. It's amazing."

Especially amazing considering what Matthew had learned about the real Saul.

She gave him an earnest gaze. "So you'd like to take all of that on? Is that the reason you're acting so strange? And of course, it's clear you and Shelah found feelings for each other. It does make sense if she comes with the package, right? She's pretty and she knows her way around Saul's home. She's the right age and available and equipped to be your helpmate. Maybe she's right about your work here being demeaning. You'd be set for life, and you could do *gut* things in that community."

He longed to tell her his heart belonged here with her. Best now though to let her believe the worst. "I have been given a blessing, a place that will take care of my family's needs for a long time to come. I can't turn my back on that without a lot of consideration."

"But you can turn your back on us, Mattie? On this place where we grew up together and worked together?"

Matthew held back the slow rage building inside him. If not for Shelah's presence, he could have Colette and keep Saul's place too. "I don't have much of a choice, and I don't have a lot of time to contemplate my next step."

Colette's eyes misted with tears he knew she wouldn't shed. "Well, now that you've explained things so clearly, don't let me hold you back. I've decided I can't avoid you or Shelah, so I'll accept what is, and I'll get over what might have been."

She leaned toward him. "But one day, Matthew Mueller, I want the truth. All of it. You owe me that much at least. And you'd better come up with a good reason why you're leaving me for her." Then she motioned to the basket.

"Now, take some time to give those cookies to Shelah. You two can enjoy them together."

She held her head up and started to turn away. She might as well have added what he could see in her gaze. *And I hope you both choke on them.*

CHAPTER SEVEN

Matthew tugged at Colette's arm and put a finger to her lips. That stopped her cold.

Only her lips were warm and soft, and before he knew what he was doing, he pulled her close to kiss her.

Colette's lips were an inch from his, a sigh leaving her body, when she pulled back and stared at him. "What are you doing?"

"What I've wanted to do since I got home. Kiss you."

She stood and tugged at her cape. "*Neh*, that will not be happening when you're engaged to another. I won't allow you to play with my heart that way, Matthew. Nor do I want to be found in your arms and be forced to do something I might regret, like marry you to avoid a scandal. Since you belong to another now."

Anger took over Matthew's mind. He put the basket down so hard, the cookies bounced. One landed in the dirt at his feet, but he didn't care. Right now, he didn't care about anything but this moment and the truth. "I do not belong to her, Colette. My heart is still with you."

Shock widened Colette's vivid eyes. "But you want *her*, don't you? You just explained all of it. Why else would she get such a notion in her head if you hadn't encouraged her? Is she trying to compromise you, to force you to marry her? Or does she know something I don't know? Just tell me."

"I can't," he finally said. "I can't tell anyone the things I found out, the things I know now. I won't."

Colette looked up at him, tears in her eyes. "You won't tell me? Me, Mattie? We've never kept secrets from each other." She lowered her head, wiped at her eyes. "If you do love her and want to be with her, I told you I'll be all right. I'll be hurt and . . . I won't forget it, but I don't want to be married to someone who might be in love with another person."

He stood there, torn between protecting his family and confessing all to the woman he loved so much.

Colette's deflated expression showed she took his silence to mean he didn't love her, though.

"I'm asking this only once, Matthew. Just say it—and be honest, please. Do you love me, or do you love her?"

Matthew knew the answer. "I love—"

"There you are," came the shrill voice that now tormented his nightmares. Shelah stood frowning a few feet away, glaring at them. "Matthew, you're supposed to take Kathleen to visit your family and get to know them so she will feel comfortable with us being alone together at your house."

"I'll be there soon," he said, his gaze still on Colette.

Colette backed away, her eyes full of pain and regret.

Shelah advanced, her hands held primly together, her smile bordering on a smirk. "You know Kathleen wouldn't approve of this, that's for certain sure."

Colette turned her gaze to Shelah. "You're right. I was just explaining to Matthew that this isn't proper. And I need to go help with supper."

She whirled, leaving Matthew in a cold sweat. He called out, "Colette?"

But Colette wasn't listening. She practically ran all the way to the cottage.

Shelah grabbed his arm. "Let's go. It's getting late."

"Why can't you let me have some time with her?" he asked, his anger still simmering. "To explain."

"But will you explain everything?"

Tugging his arm away, Matthew said, "Shelah, if you think holding this over my head will lead to our getting married, then you need to rethink things. I won't be forced into any marriage. The sooner you understand that, the better off we'll be."

"Better for you and her, you mean?"

"There is no me and her anymore," he said, the words like nails hitting tin. "I wanted to marry her, but that has changed. You need to understand that. You don't love me. You only love what comes with me. So think very carefully on your threats and demands. A loveless marriage is not a pleasant one."

"I care for you," she said, her tone petulant. "We can come to love each other, and Saul wanted us to marry." She smiled up at him. "Just think about it, Matthew. You and I can be pillars of the community, just as Saul was."

"Do not remind me of Saul," he replied. "Go and find Kathleen. I'll take the two of you to visit my family, but this doesn't mean I'll invite you back to my home. I want to make that clear, because it's not proper, and you know that."

"Perfectly clear," she replied. "Just as being found with the woman you broke up with is not proper." Then she glanced at the basket at his feet. "Do you want to take those cookies with us?"

Matthew had forgotten all about the cookies. He picked up the basket, noticing most of them had been broken when he'd put the basket down. Broken, same as him.

Not answering, he held on to the basket. He'd take the cookies home for his siblings. But he didn't think he would ever eat sugar cookies again.

Colette hurried up the porch steps so fast she almost slipped. The raw wind chilled her to the bone and made her wish she could curl up in her bed and hide.

But she wouldn't hide. This was her home. Shelah might be a nuisance and Matthew might be keeping secrets, but she would hold her head high and do her work. She'd take care of things the way she always had, working alongside her sisters and Mamm and Daed, and now Jonah and Levi, and even Aenti Miriam and Edith. Her family. Her only family.

Matthew could no longer be a part of her family. He had to make a choice, and obviously he couldn't. So she'd make it for him.

Holding her spine straight, she entered the cottage where she and her sisters had grown up, taking in the fresh pine wreath and the handmade Christmas cards her *mamm* always brought out—some of them made by Colette and her sisters when they were *kinder*, and some of them from family and friends.

Colette touched a finger to a card she'd made long ago. A red bird perched on a snow-covered tree branch. It was an awkward child's drawing made on heavy beige paper her teacher had helped her cut and paste, but it tugged at her heart. She and Matthew had been close since birth. Now they were far apart. So near, but so far apart. She'd add that image to the quilt she had started the night before.

"What am I to do?" she whispered, tears dampening her skin.

"Colette?"

She turned to find Daed standing near the washroom at the back of the house, staring at her with concern, the wrinkle between his eyes prominent.

He opened his arms, and she ran to him. "What am I to do?" she repeated, the strength of her father's arms comforting her.

Abe tugged away and held her hands. "Let's sit by the stove and warm ourselves."

Colette let him guide her to his big chair. He pulled up a smaller slipper chair for her. "Hard day?"

"The worst," she said, wiping her eyes. "Matthew has something going on."

"*Ja*, we've all seen that something, but you and I have not talked about it."

"It's not just Shelah, Daed. He has some secret that he won't talk about. Not even with me. And I think Shelah knows that secret and she's holding it over him to make him marry her."

Daed studied her for a moment. "You mean, blackmail?"

"Something like that," Colette said. "Something that he's ashamed of or can't speak about."

"That could be many things—personal things. Do you believe he's been close to this woman?"

Colette frowned, another worry making her heart hurt. "I don't know. Could that be it? If so, he'd have no choice but to marry her. Not me, but her."

"I will talk to young Matthew," Daed said. "But he

might need to go to the bishop and be truthful—good or bad, you understand."

Colette sniffed. "I understand more than anyone the ramifications of what we're thinking. But Mattie is not that kind of man, Daed. He's *gut* and solid and so shy, it took him forever to kiss me."

She stopped, put a hand to her mouth. "I mean, he was a gentleman with me at all times."

Daed gave her the *daed* glance, then smiled. "I have no doubt, but this situation is troubling. I'll talk to him."

"Don't tell him what I've said," she replied. "He's already got enough to deal with."

"You still care for him."

Colette looked into her father's eyes and nodded, thinking Daed rarely got involved in the sisters' drama. But he was exactly the right person to talk to her now. She loved him so much for taking this time with her.

"I will always love Mattie," she admitted. "But if we are correct in our assumptions, I cannot marry him. Ever."

"I agree," Daed replied. "Let's hope we're wrong."

"Wrong about what?" Mamm asked as she entered the front door, tiny snowflakes on her cape.

Daed stood and greeted his wife. "We're discussing our concerns regarding Matthew and Shelah. Maybe a forced marriage."

Mamm glanced from him to Colette. "I think the girl is wanting that. Have you learned something new?"

"*Neh*, but now we're wondering if Matthew and she have been . . . compromised," Colette said for want of a better word. "It seems she's demanding he marry her. Which he should if that happened."

"Or perhaps even if it didn't happen," Daed said. "People will talk. Matthew could be shunned."

"People are already talking," Colette said. "I can see the pity for me in their eyes, so I'm sure the gossip is flowing."

Mamm looked at Colette again, her all-knowing eyes seeing her daughter's tears. "You had words with Matthew."

"We tried to talk, and he was so close to telling me what's really going on, but Shelah came up and insisted he take Kathleen to visit his family, which means she'll go along for the ride. I came home."

She glanced out the window. The sky was dark and ominous. The first heavy snow of the season would hit tonight.

"I hope they haven't left yet," Mamm said. "It's getting bad out there. Matthew usually sleeps here at the inn when it's snowing this hard. And I heard it will only get worse, so I hurried home from my visit with the Monroes. Their baby isn't due yet, thankfully."

Colette got up to take a closer look out the window. "It wasn't even snowing when I got home a while ago." Now she could see the big flakes falling softly to the ground. This could become a real white-out. And Matthew could be caught in it.

"Well, the storm is here," Mamm said. "I'm glad to be home. And I hope no one is out on these roads right now."

Colette hoped the same. As hurt as she was, she worried about Matthew. Where was he right now?

Matthew moaned and shivered, the cold, damp snow waking him from what felt like a nightmare. Despite his worries about the weather, Shelah had loaded herself and a begrudging Kathleen into the buggy so they could go visit his family.

Nothing he could say would change her mind, and now it all came back to him in a flood of images as he sat up straight and glanced around.

The road, icy and slick, black ice forming, snow coming in. He'd had to hold tight to his horse, Sawdust, to keep the animal on the road. Shelah and Kathleen had argued about turning around.

"We can do this another day," Kathleen had said, her words coming out in a shiver. "This is not the best weather to be in and I told you so."

"That is, on a clear day it only takes twenty minutes," Shelah had retorted. "We can't let a little snow deter us. That would be rude."

"That is on a clear day it takes twenty minutes," Matthew had pointed out. "This trip could take an hour or so, probably longer."

He could barely see the road, and soon it would be covered in fresh, wet snow.

He'd finally had enough when Sawdust pulled toward the ditch. "I'm turning us around. This is only going to get worse, and it's miles to my house. Too many miles to get caught in a white-out."

Shelah groaned. "What is wrong with you two? If we're only miles away, why turn around now?"

"Because Matthew knows this area better than we do," Kathleen replied. "Now behave so he can focus on getting us safely out of this storm."

He'd maneuvered the buggy onto the road back toward the inn and was headed that way when he glanced back to agree with Kathleen. He remembered a scream and tires screeching.

He shot up off the ground now, cold and confused as memories vied with the pounding inside his head. A vehicle had tried to pass them, but it swerved toward the buggy. Sawdust balked and lifted his front legs. The buggy had jerked and pivoted, and then it had slipped off the road.

They'd all been thrown out.

"Shelah? Kathleen?"

"Over here," Kathleen called, her voice weak. "Here, Matthew."

He followed her voice toward the deep ditch near where he'd landed, then saw her and Shelah. Kathleen sat up, her clothes wet and muddy, but Shelah lay still, the snow covering her black cape.

"Are you okay?" he asked, glancing around for help. The car that had shot out in front of them was now gone. Had the driver just left them here?

Ignoring his own throbbing cuts and bruises, Matthew rushed down the hill, slipping in the wet grass and slushy mud. Shelah lay so still. He silently prayed she wasn't dead.

"Shelah?" he called, trying to remember what had happened. Then it struck him. They'd been arguing. She was angry that Kathleen had suggested taking her for supper another night when the weather wasn't so bad. Matthew had turned the buggy around to go back to the inn.

"Surely, you know how to drive a buggy through the snow. We'll be fine, and if it's too bad, Kathleen and I can stay the night."

That had angered him because Shelah was so obvious in her manipulations and suggestions. He'd looked back at her and Kathleen just as the car had taken a chance on making it around the slow buggy. Only the road was icy and slippery, and the car had fishtailed toward the buggy, bumping it with a pounding shove.

The horse he'd brought to work every morning for years was nowhere to be found. Sawdust had been frightened and swerved too abruptly, causing the buggy to turn over. The harness and other belts had broken loose from the shaft, and the old wooden axle was probably dragging behind the horse now. The small buggy lay on its side, crushed and splintered.

Matthew couldn't do anything about that right now. He leaned over Shelah and checked her breathing. She had a pulse, thankfully. He checked her head and found no blood, but one of her shoes was missing. Taking off his coat, Matthew covered her.

"Kathleen, I have to go for help."

"I know. I'll stay right here."

"But are you okay?"

"I'm fine," the older woman said, her breath coming in huffs, her hair springing from her snow-covered bonnet. "I flew out of the buggy and landed hard, but Shelah went up in the air. She screamed, then passed out when she landed. I'm not sure how badly she's injured."

"There's a phone booth back toward the inn," he said. "Stay here and keep her warm. Get as close to her as you can, but don't move her. I'll get the blankets we keep in the buggy."

Kathleen nodded and shivered as she scooted toward Shelah. "Hurry."

Matthew limped up the hillside and found the blankets still in the buggy, then took them back to Kathleen. Next, he rushed back to the road, watching for vehicles. The snow was falling heavily now. He was halfway to the phone booth when he saw a horse and buggy coming toward him. Waving his hands, he stood on the road.

"Matthew?"

Jonah and Levi were in the utility buggy, which had heavy wheels, and big Samson snorted and tossed his mane. Matthew gave thanks that they'd come along.

"How did you know?"

"We didn't," Jonah replied as they hopped down. "Everyone was worried that you'd left in this weather. So we came looking."

Matthew bent over and propped his hands on his knees. "I was headed to the phone booth to call for help. A vehicle tried to pass us, but it fishtailed and hit the buggy."

Jonah hopped down and glanced behind Matthew. "Are you hurt?"

"*Neh*, just a few bruises and cuts. Kathleen is around the curve with Shelah. We were all thrown clear, but Shelah is unconscious. The driver left the scene."

Jonah pulled out a cell phone. "Abby made me bring this just in case. She rarely makes exceptions, but I'm glad she did tonight."

While Jonah called 911, they hurried Samson toward the wreckage. Jonah quickly hopped down to check on the women because he knew CPR.

Levi checked Matthew over. "You have some cuts that need to be cleaned. You'll come back to the inn with us for the night."

"I can't leave them."

"*Neh*, you won't. We'll wait for the first responders. They'll have questions, and they can check all of you."

Matthew bobbed his head. "I think the car was light

blue, but it happened so fast I doubt we'll ever find the driver."

He wouldn't tell them about the argument right now. He ran down to Shelah. "How is she?" he asked Kathleen.

"She moaned and told me her foot hurts," Kathleen said, her eyes wide as Jonah took over. "I hope she'll be okay."

"It's not broken," he said as he carefully checked Shelah's left foot. "But I'm pretty sure from the swelling that she sprained it badly when she fell. I don't find any other obvious contusions or lacerations, but she needs medical attention. She might be going into shock from the cold and the accident, but the paramedics are on their way."

Kathleen nodded. "I'm thankful you two happened along."

"You can thank Colette," Jonah said, shooting Matthew a glance. "She insisted we needed to look for Matthew."

CHAPTER EIGHT

Colette watched out the window for Jonah and Levi to return. Jonah had called her phone to let her know what had happened. Shelah had been taken to the closest hospital and Kathleen had insisted on riding in the ambulance with her. Matthew had given a statement to the local authorities, but it might be difficult to find the hit-and-run driver.

Matthew would be coming back here with Jonah and Levi. His parents were used to his staying over at the inn during bad weather, because his home was quite a distance away.

Would he be okay? Or would he worry about Shelah?

Would he be angry that she'd insisted on sending people after him? None of that mattered. They were all alive, thanks to her badgering her brothers-in-law, and thanks to their deciding she might be right to worry. She had the best family in the world. But her heart ached for Matthew.

When she saw a lantern moving through the night, she let out a sigh. "They're back," she called to Eliza and Abby.

Mamm and Daed had gone to bed but were probably

not asleep yet. Jon was asleep in the crib beside their bedroom in the attached smaller house.

"They're headed toward the stables." Samson would need a warm blanket and a treat, for certain sure.

All of the sisters stood at the window, waiting for their men. Only Colette had to remind herself Matthew wasn't truly hers anymore. Now Shelah would be his first concern.

When they heard the men on the porch, Abby opened the door to let them in, snow swirling and swishing all around them. Only Samson could have had the strength and power to get them home in this storm.

Abby squeezed her hand. "Let him do the talking. Too many questions cause a man to shut down. I know this from experience."

"I'm just glad they are all okay," Colette said, meaning it. She might resent Shelah, but she did not want any harm to come to her.

The men entered quietly. Jonah hugged Abigail and Levi kissed Eliza's cheek. Matthew stood there staring at nothing until he finally looked at Colette.

Her sisters quickly got their husbands out of the way by taking them to the kitchen for some hot chocolate. That left her and Matthew standing in the living room by the window.

"I'm so sorry," she said, not knowing what else to say. "I hope that Shelah and Kathleen will be okay."

Matthew finally sank down onto a chair. Eliza brought him some cocoa and a sandwich cut into four pieces. "You need to eat."

He nodded absently, then stared at the food. Colette wanted to grab him up in her arms and tell him it would all work out, but how could she promise him that? After her harsh words to him earlier, she could only pray he'd be all right.

"I tried to talk them out of visiting tonight," he finally said, his shaggy hair falling across his eyes. "I knew it would be tough getting home, but I've made the trip before in bad weather." He shrugged and took a sip of the hot chocolate. "But this storm is a monster, and it came on faster than I'd expected. They should have stayed here, where they'd be safe and asleep in the inn right now."

Seeing him in such distress only added to Colette's resentment of Shelah, but she held her feelings in check. Talking about something she couldn't change would only upset Matthew more. And right now, he seemed genuinely worried about the other woman in his life.

"Mattie, this is not your fault. You did your best."

"Did I, Colette? Have I really done my best? I left you all those months ago, thinking I'd be home soon and we'd plan out our lives. Now I can't even begin to tell you what a mess I'm in. But I do know this. After tonight, I can't do this anymore."

"What?" she asked, her voice quiet, her worst fears hovering. "What are you talking about?"

"I have to tell Shelah I don't love her. I have to make her see this isn't right."

Colette couldn't believe what she was hearing. And she wouldn't believe it until she knew it to be the truth. He was upset and in shock; perhaps he wasn't making any sense.

"Mattie." Colette took his hand. "Shelah will be fine, I'm sure. You don't have to pretend with me. You care for her, and I need to accept that. If something horrible had happened out there, I would not have been able to forgive myself."

He seemed to gather his thoughts. "I don't know if she'll be okay. Physically, she has a badly sprained ankle and some cuts and bruises. But emotionally, she is confused, and she thinks she wants me for her husband. But she only wants the life she had before Saul passed."

Realizing Mattie was finally talking to her, really talking and telling some of the truth, Colette listened. What else could she do right now?

"And she can get the life she wants by becoming your wife. We all see that, but does she love you, or just the land and status that come with your inheritance?"

"She thinks she loves me, *ja*." He looked around and then back to Colette. "And she convinced Saul of that. The poor man barely knew what he was agreeing to, but he asked me to take care of her."

Colette swallowed her pain and resentment. She could see the torment in Mattie's eyes. He was trying to be noble and do the right thing, even if it meant denying his heart. She loved him even more for that.

But she had to ask, "Are you sure about your feelings for her? As I've said, if you care about her—"

"I care about her, but I don't love her." He looked into Colette's eyes but said nothing more.

He didn't need to speak. Colette saw his love for her, but neither of them could voice that now.

She leaned close. "I will be here, Mattie. I will be here waiting for you. But I have to resist you for now—we're done. And I mean that." Then she added, "We must make it clear we are not together in any way, do you understand me?"

He nodded and lowered his head. Then he gazed up at her. "I need you to trust me, you hear? No matter what? I need you to remember that." He whispered, "I can go along with Shelah's plans for now, but then find a way to trip her up or change her mind. But not if you aren't waiting for me when this is over. Just trust me, please?"

Colette wanted to trust him, but how could she with Shelah standing between them? "I will do my best," she said. "This is hard, so hard. But you must do what you need to do. I'll be here, no matter what."

He finished nibbling at his food. "I should go. I'm staying in the carriage *haus* tonight."

He'd be close by. Colette would sleep better knowing that.

They walked into the kitchen. Abby went to get Jon. Colette asked Jonah, "Are we sure they are both going to recover?"

"They will. Getting thrown into the ditch might have saved them. We don't know where Sawdust is, and it's too treacherous to try to find him or recover what's left of the buggy tonight. We convinced Mattie to come back here instead of trying to walk home."

Levi and Eliza said their good nights and went to their room. Abigail whispered the update to their parents, then gathered up Jon and covered him in a warm blanket so she and Jonah could follow the path to their home just up the hill.

That left Matthew and Colette alone in the front of the cottage.

She walked him to the door, noticing his coat was muddy and torn. "I'll clean this and fix that tear tomorrow," she said. "I see you have a bandage on your head. Mamm had planned to check you, but Jonah said you were not seriously hurt. Do you hurt anywhere else, Mattie?"

He stood there, his eyes burning dark as he stared into

Colette's eyes. Then he took her hand and put it over his heart. "I hurt here the most. For all the pain I've caused, for all that has changed in my life, and mostly because I might lose you."

Colette couldn't speak. She could only nod and see the despair of his secrets. "Tell me? Let me help, please?"

He tugged her close and pulled her into his arms, his face against her hair. "I will one day. I will."

Then he drew back and kissed her, his lips warm on hers. This time, Colette didn't pull away. She couldn't. She wouldn't. Being in his arms, holding him like this was all she'd ever wanted and more—she needed this kiss for assurance, for trust, for hope. For a memory she could keep secretly inside her heart.

He backed away too quickly. "I must go."

She found a flashlight. "Take this and be careful. Henry is spending the night at the inn to help the night clerk, if you need anything else."

He gave her a look that showed he only needed her, but they both knew a lot had to happen before they could be together again.

Still, Colette went to bed with hope in her heart. This accident might be a turning point for them. Shelah might give up and go back to Missouri.

Or she might make things even more difficult for Matthew. Colette prayed and knew she had no control over the matter. *Gott*'s will. It would be hard to accept, but that was the way of things.

The next morning, Matthew woke early and saw the snowdrifts piled against the tree trunks and rocks. Snowed in.

He'd need to get word to his family in case Sawdust showed up there if the poor animal could find his way home. Sawdust knew the way, knew the road and the house. Maybe, just maybe, he'd made it to the small stable they had out back.

Matthew didn't want to think the worst, but he'd not slept well. Reliving the argument he'd had with Shelah, he felt ashamed he'd even let Shelah talk him into taking her and Kathleen home with him. Had she hoped they'd get snowed in together at his house? He had a bad feeling that had been her plan. When would she learn that her demands and manipulations were too obvious and she needed to stop?

He had never backed down from a confrontation, and he wasn't accustomed to letting people push him around. But hearing Saul ask him to marry Shelah had shaken Matthew to the core. He needed to talk to someone.

And he knew exactly who that someone had to be. He needed to talk to Colette's father, Abe. Then he'd consult Jonah and Levi. They were both worldly and wise.

A knock at the door brought his head around.

He opened it to find Henry standing there. "Hey, Matthew. I managed to get a message to your parents through Edith. She called to say she's snowed in. Can you work in the kitchen today?"

Matthew needed a strong cup of coffee. The last place he wanted to be was near Colette, for so many reasons. But he had to do what needed to be done, so he agreed. "Mamm and Daed know I'm okay?"

Henry nodded and stomped the snow off his boots. "Edith said she'd pass the news on to her neighbor who came to look in on her. He's going around to check on people near his place. He'll explain what happened, and he's going to watch for Sawdust, too."

"How did Edith know all this?"

"Colette," Henry explained. "She's working the kitchen today since Edith can't get here. They had a phone call early this morning." Henry shifted and adjusted the fleece-lined earflaps of his winter cap. "You're all caught up, and I've got a cup of coffee waiting for me."

"*Denke,*" Matthew said. "I'll be there soon." He freshened up and shook out his old coat. He'd knocked most of the mud off it last night, but the big tear was still there.

Just like the tear in his heart. His coat could be mended, but he wasn't so sure about his heart.

Colette. He'd thought about her all night. He should have been worried about Shelah, and he was, but Kathleen would take care of the misguided woman. And as soon as they could talk, he'd tell her he couldn't marry her.

She'd probably go to his parents and spill the secret he was trying so hard to keep. But what other choice did he have?

He didn't like being caught between two worlds and two women.

He had wanted one woman all his life. Somehow, he'd win Colette back. *Trust.* He'd have to gain her trust by telling the truth.

Right now, he would be spending the day with her in the kitchen and restaurant. Not that they'd have many visitors. A few registered guests and maybe some brave locals. His walk to the inn was cold thanks to the biting windchill from the near-frozen lake. Snow covered the entire area in a white blanket of pristine beauty. It was hard to imagine his turmoil in such a peaceful place, but it was there, blowing over him like this brutal wind.

He'd call the hospital where Kathleen and Shelah would be stuck for the day. Everything was shut down. A *gut* day to stay inside and do busywork. A day away from his troubles.

He silently thanked *Gott* that no one had been hurt worse. He might not love Shelah, but he wanted the best for her and Kathleen.

This day might give him some more time to talk to Colette. Really talk to her. Normally, he'd tell her everything. But nothing about his situation was normal.

Being able to see her again should bring him joy, but he felt only shame and trepidation. How would she feel when she found out the truth?

Colette started making the cinnamon rolls. She knew how to do that, and they could rise while she and the couple of staff members who'd been able to walk to work got the rest of the breakfast buffet started. They had about a half dozen guests who were snowed in, and she wanted to make their extended stays cozy. She planned to give them three meals while they waited out the storm. For supper tonight, she'd make a savory beef and vegetable soup with corn bread. And for dessert, a peach cobbler, warm from the oven. She and Edith had made a fresh batch of oatmeal cookies and some snickerdoodles yesterday.

She could keep their guests happy with food, and they had a small library in the lobby for reading, and some board games for bored children. Walks in the snow were always fun but could be treacherous if someone didn't show guests the way.

All that would take many hands. Abigail would be

here soon, and Eliza could help, since Jonah and Levi had everything in the stables under control.

And Matthew would be back.

Just for a day or two, they could go back to the old routine where they flirted and teased, only now Colette wouldn't ignore him or make smart remarks. She'd treasure this forced time together with Mattie, because after last night, she knew he still loved her. She'd stayed awake most of the night, praying for him to tell her the truth, asking *Gott* to guide them.

Shelah would be back soon enough, she knew. And then they'd have to be mindful. She hoped Mattie had meant it when he said he would find a way back to her. And that he'd have the courage to tell her the truth, so she could make her own decisions about the future. He couldn't keep her and Shelah in limbo. Whatever secrets Shelah knew, Colette needed to know, too.

She almost let the rolls rise too much, just thinking about Matthew. But soon she had them in the oven and the usual kitchen chores underway. Abby showed up after leaving Jon with Mamm and Daed. They'd all three stay warm and cozy in their new little home behind the cottage.

Eliza came in and went to work on getting the tables set and the coffee and other beverages ready.

"A small crowd today, but remember our guests here. They need to eat three meals and have snacks, and we might have to offer suggestions on activities so they don't get bored," Colette explained.

"Bored?" Matthew said from the door. "They won't be bored. We have sleds so the *kinder* can ride down the hillside, and Samson loves the snow. We can give the youngies a ride on him. Or Peaches, of course."

Colette stopped stirring scrambled eggs and smiled at him. "I see you have everything planned out."

He nodded, but the smile died. "Not everything. But I'm getting there. I am going to take Samson out later to look for Sawdust. Levi said he'd ride Rudolph out with me once some of the snow has softened and melted."

"I'll go, too," she said without overthinking it. "I mean if you don't mind me riding out with you on Samson."

"He's not my horse," Matthew said, glancing at her sister, who considered herself Samson's caretaker. "But if you insist."

"I do."

Abby and Eliza exchanged speaking looks and went back to their busywork. Colette appreciated that they didn't scold or fuss.

"Are you sure that's wise?" Matthew asked. "After yesterday's discussion?"

"So you don't want me to help you find Sawdust?"

"I didn't say that, did I?"

A standoff began. They eyed each other for a moment.

Abigail came by. "Make up your minds. We have work to do. I'd say you still have some unfinished business, and today is the best day to take care of it."

Abigail's eyes spoke volumes. Shelah and Kathleen were not here today. They were safe at the hospital and mending just fine, from what Colette had heard.

Colette waffled, her conscience clashing with her impulsiveness. Then she remembered that kiss last night, and impulsiveness won.

She and Matthew had always been close, but now their relationship was a mess. Levi would go with them to look for Sawdust. Could an afternoon of riding through the snow on Samson really do any harm?

CHAPTER NINE

Colette bundled up for their ride. She should stay here and watch over the restaurant, but the noon dinner was over, and she had a few hours before the supper buffet. The guests had complimented the food after breakfast and had all returned at noon for sandwiches and soup.

"I'll be sure to recommend the Shadow Lake Inn to all my friends," Mrs. Brewster had told her earlier. "Jeffrey and I have always loved it here, and being snowed in is so romantic."

"*Denke,*" Colette had replied. "It is a special place."

Now she was experiencing that feeling of romance Mrs. Brewster had mentioned. Jonah and Levi had cleared walking paths, so she followed the one to the stables, all snug in her boots and long coat with a dark wool bonnet covering her head and gloves keeping her hands warm.

When she entered the stables, Matthew was waiting with Samson. "Hello," he said, his tone tentative.

They'd worked so hard all day, they hadn't had a minute to actually talk, but she'd enjoyed knowing he was there where he was needed, and now and then, she'd glanced up into his eyes. There was a thread of connection between them that could not be broken.

"Are you sure about this?" he asked her. "Levi and Jonah had to go help with a buggy that got stuck up on the lane out of here, so it will be just us."

"Oh, maybe I should stay behind," she said, scanning the area. No one was about. Then she shook her head. "*Neh*, you shouldn't be out there alone. We'll find Sawdust and maybe stop by your house to check on your parents, too."

"What if you're late for supper?"

"I have made provisions. My sisters will fill in."

"You just want to take a ride in the snow, ain't so?"

"You know me well. *Ja*. Of course. It's a rare treat to get this much snow, even if it has shut everything down."

"Sometimes, things need to be shut down. *Gott* wants us to be still and . . . accept His word."

"I believe that. We have a big problem to overcome, but this is our time, Mattie. Time to be still and . . . figure this out. And enjoy the beauty of a snowfall, of course." Then she looked into his eyes. "If nothing else, we will make one last memory."

He nodded, the tenderness in his eyes so sweet. "Then let's go. We have about three hours of sunlight. The snow isn't melting, however. So we need to be mindful."

"It wouldn't do for us to get lost out there," she said. "Then we'd be in real trouble."

And now she had to wonder why she was willing to break her own rule that she would avoid being alone with him.

She stopped and stared at Samson. "Maybe I should just stay here. I do have a lot to do, and . . ."

"And you're afraid?"

"Not of you, not of Samson. Of my own feelings, Mattie. I've been confused ever since you came home. I want to do the right thing, to be noble and let you do what you need to do. And here I am, going out into the woods alone with you."

She turned to leave, but Matthew caught her arm. Then he pointed to his coat. "You did this, right?"

Colette swallowed and nodded. "I found it in the employee room and cleaned it and did a quick mend."

"You are doing the right thing, Colette. You're speaking to me, and that's a start. And I want you to go on a horseback ride in the snow with me. We could take a buggy, but then we would get stuck. Not that I'd mind, but—"

"But we both know that wouldn't do."

"Let's just go for a ride and see if we can find Sawdust. If anyone makes a fuss, I will take the blame. I have not committed to Shelah. I'm committed to you, but I can't shout that out just yet."

"*Neh*, we'll both take the blame." She touched a gloved hand to his cheek. "I'm committed to you, too. And that has to stay between us, no matter what."

They prepared Samson, then Matthew looked over at her.

"Have you heard from Shelah?" she asked, concern overriding her dislike of the woman.

"Shelah is going to be fine, according to what Kathleen told me this morning after I finally got through. Kathleen is bruised and has some cuts, but she assured me they are both better and will be home tomorrow. I have not talked to Shelah. She was asleep when I finally heard from Kathleen. I did leave messages for her with Kathleen and the nurses."

"Soon she'll be here and back at it, right? Which is why I'm concerned about risking this. I should have thought it through better." But she wouldn't deny her feelings. "Honestly, I wanted to ride out with you. I felt restless today, and a bit reckless. So whatever the consequences, let's just go."

"Okay, we'll cross that bridge when we come to it."

Samson snorted, obviously bored with their banter.

Matthew got up on the Percheron and then offered her his hand. Colette held on to it like a lifeline and scrambled up bchind him, her hands automatically going around his waist.

This felt right, the warmth of him, the scent of the woods around him, the familiar way he glanced back and smiled at her.

It felt right, but was it wrong? Shelah was in a hospital, and they didn't really know the extent of her injuries. As Samson trotted tentatively over the snow, Matthew told her he'd tried several times to find out more, but with the storm being so fierce, lines were down and even the cell phone towers were slow.

Henry had called a friend at the hospital and found out Shelah was stable, and the friend had found Kathleen. She'd only spoken to Matthew for a couple of minutes, assuring him that Shelah would be well soon. That could mean a lot of things, but until the storm lifted and some of the snow melted, there wasn't much to be done.

"Should we go to the hospital?" she asked as he trotted Samson toward the road.

"That's ten miles from here," he said over his shoulder. "And they won't let anyone besides family see her. I know you're concerned, and I am too. But she can't leave there, and I need to find Sawdust. It will take my mind off all I have to decide. And I want to be with you, like the old days. Just for a few hours."

Colette snuggled close and laid her head on his broad back. "I want the same, Mattie."

They rode down the snow-covered lane in silence, occasionally dusted by flakes falling from the branches. Colette felt cocooned in a quiet world that had no troubles. She imagined they were in a book, and he was the prince come to rescue the princess. She knew such notions were frowned on in her world, but right now she felt like a princess in the forest with her prince.

Safe and warm.

Loved and happy.

She'd hold on to this feeling until they had to return to reality.

Which wouldn't take long. But maybe in this short time, Mattie would open up to her and they could find a way out of this tangle of obligations. Together.

They followed the route Matthew had taken last night. He brought Samson to a halt where the damaged buggy still lay turned on its side.

After he stopped Samson, Matthew got down, then helped Colette dismount, his hands on her waist. Even all bundled up, she still felt light in his arms. He stood staring at her for a moment.

"I got distracted," he told Colette to take his mind off being near her. "I didn't see the vehicle about to pass us."

"Was it moving fast?" Colette asked. She stood staring, her eyes wide. Buggy wrecks happened often, but never before to someone she knew.

Matthew nodded. They both knew there was a rule that

vehicles were to slow down when approaching or passing a buggy. And they both knew the buggy driver was to be aware at all times. The Mueller buggy had two benches. He'd been up front driving, with Shelah and Kathleen in the back underneath a partial black cover.

"In a hurry and trying to get around a curve in the ice and snow, the driver took me by surprise and Sawdust immediately became agitated. He was already skittish to begin with, and this set him off. Then the vehicle bumped us, and Sawdust reared up and started kicking."

"What happened, Mattie? What happened to distract you?"

"We were arguing about turning back. I wanted to do so, but Shelah didn't. Kathleen was fussing at her, and I glanced around to convince her we needed to get back to the inn. In the time I turned to glance at Shelah, the car tried to pass, and then the driver hit the buggy. Sawdust went one way, and the buggy went the other."

She glanced around and then back to him. "It's amazing you're all alive."

"We all got thrown, but the snow and grass saved us. If it had been a mile farther, we'd have landed near the rocks and the waterfall."

"So Kathleen and Shelah bounced out through the open front," Colette said. "They must have been pushed forward and up."

Matthew shut his eyes, remembering the feeling of moving through the air. "*Ja*, they went right past me. Thankfully, the buggy tipped completely, tossing me out after they'd been thrown. I kind of passed out for a minute and then I woke and rushed over to them. I feared they'd both be dead."

"Do you remember anything about the vehicle that hit you?"

"A small, light blue car. I saw the blue in the fading light. That's all I remember. Blue and small, like a sports car. It had to have been damaged, too."

"That might be enough to find this person." She glanced around the scene. "Jonah still knows people in authority. Maybe he can help."

"I'm not so worried about that as I am Sawdust. He took off so fast, he broke the old wooden shafts I've been meaning to have Levi replace. Once I'd let go of the reins, he was free to run with most of the ropes and ties still in place. I hope he's not hurt. Or worse."

"We'll find him," Colette said.

"I'm worried about Shelah and Kathleen, too," he admitted. "I don't know how Shelah will react when I talk to her. She was determined to see my family . . . and I think she wanted to get snowed in at my house."

"That makes sense. Why else would she insist you all go there during one of the worst storms we've had in years? She might have wanted to stay a long time."

"Shelah wants what she wants. She had a hard childhood. I know she is related to Kathleen somehow and doesn't remember her parents at all. I think she was passed from family to family until Saul took her in, and he hired Kathleen to keep house and raise Shelah. Saul spoiled her and now she is afraid of what's next."

"You," Colette said. "You'd be the answer to her prayers. I want to feel sympathy for her, but how can she want to marry you when she knows about us?"

"I never tried to hide it from her," he said. "I told her and Saul right off that I had to get back to you."

"*Ach vell*, she did not listen."

"She talked to Saul and then he told me he wanted me to marry her. I never said yes, but I feel an obligation."

Especially after the reading of the will. Matthew was still in shock from the revelations he'd discovered since then.

"She was trying to force you again last night. This accident is her fault."

Matthew shook his head. "But I was driving. I should have been more mindful." He let out a sigh of frustration. "Now two people are hurt, my buggy is ruined, and my best horse is out there lost or severely injured. I've made a mess of everything."

Colette gave him a look he remembered well. Her eyes were always so vivid and her expression so sure and steady. "You told me to trust you, and I do. Whatever you're going through, whatever Shelah is using to coerce you, I hope you'll tell me and let me help."

He glanced around. "Not here on the side of the road. Not like this."

Disappointment darkened her eyes. "Then let's see if we can make it to your folks' house. Maybe Sawdust is there."

Matthew helped her back onto Samson, glad she hadn't pushed him on his secrets. The air was frigid, so they needed to hurry. He didn't want to keep Colette away too long or after dark. The sun lent a fleeting warmth right now, but later the cold would be dangerous.

They didn't make it to his house. A large old oak tree had fallen across the only road to get there, and the snow in the forest was too deep to take a shortcut. In the end, they turned around and headed back to the inn.

They made it to the stables and dismounted from Samson, both cold and ready for a warm drink. He still wanted to talk to Colette about everything, but not finding Sawdust concerned him. The Amish depended on their horses to get them places and help with farming.

Levi met them coming up the stable alley. "Uh, new development. Shelah and Kathleen hired a cab to bring them back to the inn. Paid the poor man extra, but he did have snow tires. Matthew, Shelah is asking for you. And she's not happy."

Matthew glanced at Colette. "I'm sorry."

"It's all right. Go," she said. "We're back to reality now."

He hurried away, glancing back at her and wishing they'd had more time. He'd wanted to tell her everything, but instead he'd held it all inside. Again.

But he would tell her, and soon. He could only pray that Shelah was going to be okay. Physically okay, and okay with his decision.

CHAPTER TEN

Colette followed Matthew to the inn. She had to get supper ready. But she hoped to avoid Shelah. Though she was amazed at Shelah's determination, Colette also felt guilty about spending time alone with Matthew. Not that anything scandalous had happened, but Mamm would frown at her later, she knew.

Matthew gave her one last glance and then hurried upstairs to see Shelah.

Levi had left Jonah to take care of Samson and he'd walked back to the inn with them. Now he stared after Matthew. "This can't go on much longer."

"*Neh,*" she said. "I shouldn't have ridden out with him, but I did because he's so close to telling me the truth."

"But he didn't."

She shook her head and tugged off the layers of clothing now stifling her. "And we didn't find Sawdust. There is a huge oak down on the road to his house. I hope Sawdust made it home last night. I'm sure Titus and Agnes are concerned about both horse and man."

"They must have heard about the accident by now. I got word to my *mamm* and heard back they are all snuggled in and fine. Miriam trudged through the snow to get to them. She has become a big help to Mamm, and they are so close now."

"I'm glad to hear that," Colette said. Levi's *mamm* might be ill with a horrible disease, but she was holding her own and following the doctor's orders. And Aenti Miriam had found a cause that had softened her bitterness.

Levi gave her one last glance. "I'm going to help Jonah secure the stables and make sure all the animals are warm. Even Big Red and those pesky hens."

"I'll be here preparing supper. We should all eat at the inn, too. Saves energy, and it's rather cozy."

"Eliza and I might take you up on that, but Jonah said he and Abby are going to stay in for the night. Jon seems to have a bit of a cold."

"So I have Eliza and you and maybe Mattie to help me with the supper crowd."

"And me."

They turned to find Mamm standing at the back door, all bundled up.

"What are you doing here?" Colette asked. "You should have stayed inside where it's warm."

"And you should have done the same," Mamm replied in her serene tone. But her eyes held a hint of worry and disappointment.

Levi suddenly had to go. "I'll . . . uh . . . just leave you two alone."

Colette turned to her mother after Levi practically ran from the room. "I know you're angry with me."

"It's not that I'm angry," Mamm replied. "Colette, you yourself said you couldn't be seen alone with Mattie, and then you go off riding Samson together? What were you thinking?"

"I wasn't thinking," she said with a shrug as they walked together into the kitchen. She stopped at the potato bin. "Mamm, I just needed some time alone with Matthew, and I'm glad I took this one opportunity. He's so sad and confused. I should keep my distance, but that would feel like I'm handing him over to Shelah. He does not love her, and he shouldn't be forced to marry her."

"I agree on all accounts, but Colette, you have to be the one to take the high road. You can't afford to make mistakes or find yourself in a compromising situation. Can't you see that Shelah is trying her best to put Mattie in that kind of situation? Or are you trying to outdo her and win him over by force, too?" Colette shook her head, then grabbed a big pan and dumped potatoes into it. Why did it seem that every meal required potatoes?

"I'm not sorry I went with him today. He's worried about the accident, and about Shelah and Kathleen. He wants to find Sawdust. I thought we could talk, really talk, about all that's happened since he returned. And he was so close to telling me, but something stopped him. I'm beginning to think the worst, that maybe he has to marry her for obvious reasons, and he's holding off on telling me the inevitable."

Mamm started heating up the stew stock and added onions and carrots to finish the pot roast they'd cooked all day. The tender meat fell apart as she shredded it and dropped it into the pot. Colette attacked the red potatoes with a peeling knife, and then tackled the carrots.

They worked in silence for a few moments. Colette made fast work of the potatoes and chopped the carrots in record time.

Turning back to Colette, Mamm said, "If their marriage is meant to be, then you need to let it go. If it's not, you need to stay out of the way and let nature take its course. I believe this will all work out in your favor, but you have to be cautious and mindful of how to act. You can't fall into a trap just because you want to prove your point with Shelah."

"I understand," Colette replied. She tossed the vegetables into the pot. "Once these are cooked through, I'll heat up the biscuits I made earlier."

Mamm nodded. "We will discuss this further later. I'm on your side. Meantime, keep working on that quilt your sisters have suggested. You need to stay busy. The scholars' Christmas program is coming up soon and you should volunteer to help Maggie. She's got her hands full."

"So I'll stay out of trouble?" Colette asked.

"Precisely," Mamm replied with her famous smile. "We'll be quilting tomorrow, snow or no snow. And Maggie has plans to meet with Linda Gaber to plan out the scholars' Christmas program. I expect you to attend that meeting at the school. Maggie is expecting you to help. Remember, we agreed to host the whole thing this year because the schoolhouse is too small. Last year, some of the parents had to stand in the back and out the door. We have plenty of room here."

Maggie was a friend of the King family who worked in the kitchen part-time now that she had two children. Jonah and Mamm had helped her when she went into labor right here in the employee room.

"*Kumm* snow or no snow, it will be held here, and I am to help put it together?" Colette asked, smiling back at her mother.

"Now you are understanding." Mamm turned and hurried to get the pecan dump cake they would serve for dessert. Easy to dump everything in one dish and mix and bake. "And I hope we only have a light dusting, not a white-out."

When she came back, Colette glanced over at her. "I'm sorry, Mamm."

Mamm opened her arms. Colette ran to her mother. "I just . . . still love Mattie so much it hurts. We only had a short time together, and now I have to let him go. I've tried. I told him we were done, but we're not. I can't let this happen."

She sobbed against her mother's blue wool dress.

"It is not up to you, *liebling,*" Mamm whispered as she kissed Colette's brow. "*Gott*'s will. Remember that and take comfort. You will get through this difficult time. We will all get through it."

Mamm patted her back and held her tight, warming her, assuring her. Comforting her.

She knew Mamm was right and on her side. But she also knew her parents would advise caution to protect her. She'd never have a minute alone with Matthew now. Mamm would watch her like a hawk. Or, worse, consult Daed about things. Suddenly, Christmas seemed bleak instead of joyful. And yet, she held her *mamm* tightly and remembered, *Gott*'s will.

Matthew sat in a high-backed side chair in the living area of Shelah and Kathleen's suite. A fire roared in the fireplace and a serving table held fresh bread and cookies, along with a thermos of coffee and another full of hot chocolate. The room held beautiful Queen Anne furniture and smelled like cinnamon spice. The King sisters always placed candles in each room.

Across from him, Kathleen sat with a small bandage on her temple and another one on her arm. In the big bedroom, Shelah lay waiting to talk to Matthew.

Kathleen lifted her cup of hot chocolate and took a dainty sip. "You weren't here to greet us."

"I didn't know you'd be leaving the hospital today," he replied. "That was dangerous."

"We were fine," Kathleen said. "I found a driver who had a sturdy vehicle with the proper tires. I don't know much about automobiles, but I do know they can be driven over snow with special tires. So I made sure this driver could do that. And I paid him a hefty tip."

"I'm glad you made it back safely." Matthew waited, knowing Kathleen was about to give him a good talking-to.

"But you were off galivanting with Colette King."

"I wouldn't call it that. We were searching for my horse. I'm afraid he might be hurt or dead. He's my only means of transportation."

Kathleen put her cup down and folded her hands over her black apron. "Yet you took Colette out with you, instead of one of the men."

"I did," he said, tired of having to answer to Shelah and Kathleen. "I stand by what I've said all along, Kathleen. I have not committed to Shelah. I'm trying my best to do what's right, but I'm not sure I can marry her."

"So you rode out with Colette, maybe hoping you'd be forced to marry *her*?"

He stood and paced. "I rode out with Colette because I wanted to do so. I wanted to have some quiet time with her. There is nothing forced between us." Then he turned to stare at Kathleen. "I do not answer to you or Shelah. Now I'd like to see her and find out how she's doing, and I also want to tell her she needs to go back to Missouri. I will stay here through Christmas to help my folks. After the new year, I will return to Missouri to find a foreman to manage the farm Saul left to me."

"And then?"

"And then I'll decide what needs to be done. But that decision might end in me marrying the woman I love, not Shelah."

Kathleen didn't respond. She only let out a sigh. "Go in, then. I wish you the best on that decision."

Wondering exactly where Kathleen really stood in this matter, he went in to see Shelah.

She lay upon several pillows, magazines and books all around her, and a heavy robe covering her even though she was under a diamond-patterned quilt. Her face was bruised, and she had a big bandage on one side of her head.

"How are you feeling?" he asked, glad she was alive. Despite everything between them, he didn't want Shelah to come to harm.

She held her hand to her throat. "I have a mild concussion, so I must take it easy for a while. And my ankle was twisted. I find it difficult to walk, but it's getting better."

Kathleen came in and took a chair. Always the chaperone.

"I heard you wanted to talk to me," he said. "I'm glad you're okay. What did the doctor say?"

"He said to stay in bed for a while, stay out of the cold and snow. He wants me to gently try to walk on my ankle with help." She gave him a petulant pout. "I'd thought maybe you'd *kumm* to the hospital to see how I was. Do you even care?"

"Of course I care," Matthew replied. "But the roads were closed earlier today. The snow made it hazardous. I did call and get an update."

Her dark eyes widened as if she couldn't believe what he'd just said. "An update while I lay there in pain. That was kind of you." Then she pushed herself up onto the pillows, wincing as she did. "I was concerned for you."

Matthew helped her straighten, then fluffed a pillow behind her. "There." He stood back. "Thank you for being concerned, but I'm fine. A little sore and bruised, but I'm okay."

He doubted she'd been too worried about him, except that she needed him alive if he was to become her husband.

"You should have known that I wanted to see you, Matthew. You've changed since you came back here."

"I'm still me," he said, wishing he could understand what she truly wanted. Reminding himself of what she'd been through, he tried to show compassion. "I'm glad you're here and feeling better."

"I'm glad I'm alive," she retorted as she tugged on her *kapp* ribbons. "You know, you have money now. That buggy was old and too open for this kind of weather. I suggest you buy us a new one that has a sturdy winter cover. A bit more room would be good, too. And get the proper equipment."

Kathleen let out a sigh. "That was Matthew's work buggy, Shelah. He does not need a fancy buggy to get to work."

"He doesn't need to work," Shelah said, slapping a hand down on her quilt. "I do not understand this at all."

"No, you don't," Matthew said, anger simmering in his veins. "I've lost my buggy and possibly my horse. My folks used Sawdust with their buggy at times, too."

"Again, you have the power to take care of that. Saul

has a half dozen horses in the stable and can buy that many more."

"I'm not Saul," he said. "I never wanted any of this."

Shelah stared up at him. "Do you even care that I might not have a home, that Kathleen and I might be forced out on the street?"

"That won't happen," Matthew replied. He sat down on a chair by the window. "I know you found a better life with Saul. He allowed you and Kathleen to live in his home. He left you a small allowance, and maybe that wasn't fair. But you won't be homeless ever. I can promise you that." He reached out and took her hand. "I don't want to hurt you, but you need to go back to Saul's place. Let me have some time to mourn him and to digest what has happened."

"And time enough to marry Colette?" she asked. "That's what you really want, and you want me out of the way before you do it. Did you hope the buggy accident would do me in? Is that why you were with her today?"

Shocked, Matthew dropped her hand and sank back onto the chair. "I don't want you out of the way, and if you think that, then you don't know me at all. I truly want you to be happy. Neither of us is ready to rush into marriage. We barely know each other."

Shelah ignored his every word. "I could have died. That would have made things so easy for you."

"Nothing about this is easy," he replied, trying to control his temper. "I want you well and able so you can get on with your life. You only think you want to marry me because you're afraid you'll be left alone or thrown out of Saul's house. That won't happen. You and Kathleen can stay in the smaller home on the property." Saul had rented it out, but that couple had moved away after he passed. "I can fix it up for you."

"So you'll have her here and me there?"

The way her eyes lit up at that notion only reinforced his certainty that he could never fall for Shelah. She disregarded everything they'd been taught and thought only of herself. That she would even consider such a setup was beyond belief.

"*Neh*," he said, weary, "I want you to have a roof over your head and you'll have free room and board. You can consider finding a man you really love. I don't plan to live there year-round."

"What? But it's yours now."

"That doesn't mean I need to be there all the time."

She gazed at him, her eyes narrowing. "You seem to forget what Saul told you, what he expected of you."

Matthew leaned over the bed and lowered his voice. "I have forgotten nothing, but I'm going to tell Colette and my family the truth, right after I tell the bishop the whole story. So if you want to tattle your secrets, go ahead. Then no one will want to marry either of us."

"We'd still have each other. Think on that, Matthew. You'll still have Saul's farm, and if no one else wants you, I'll be there to make you happy."

And she'd be there to go through the money in Saul's bank account.

"I have to go," he said. "You need to rest and you're in a *gut* place to do that."

"Could we have supper together?" she asked, her brown eyes misty. "I'm hungry for that stew I heard . . . the kitchen staff is making."

She knew very well Colette was the head of the staff today.

"I need to check on some things. I'm not sure when I'll be eating. You go ahead. You need your nourishment."

She made a face and fell back on her pillows.

Matthew gave Shelah one last look, then turned to leave.

"I'll walk out with you," Kathleen said, following him and then shutting the door to the other room.

Wearing her shrewd face, she asked, "What was she talking about just now? What does she know that could ruin you?"

"That's between Saul and me," he said. "She thinks she knows the truth and she thinks that can sway me. But I have much to discuss with my family. I will not rush into marriage with anyone. Colette has every reason to hate me and Shelah thinks she loves me. I'm going to change all of that by confessing things myself. Best to get it all out there and suffer the consequences."

"Do you need to confess anything regarding Shelah? Were you two intimate?"

Matthew shook his head. "Never. Shelah kissed me once, but I stopped the kiss and told her it wasn't proper."

Kathleen relaxed. "I believe you, but I had to ask."

"Everyone must think the worst," he replied. "I wouldn't do that to Shelah, and I sure wouldn't betray Colette."

Kathleen nodded, her lips pursed. Then her stern expression softened. "Matthew, might I make a suggestion?"

"I'm listening," he said, wishing for any answers she might have.

"Once she's feeling better, I think Shelah needs to attend a youth frolic or two. A frolic where other young men might be."

Surprised, he stared at the prim older woman. "Whose side are you on, Kathleen?"

"I'm on Shelah's side, of course. And right now she's only worried about one thing—keeping her status within Saul's household. She went after you the minute she realized you'd be controlling her future. And if you were to marry that girl, she'd try to control you. She had a horrible, lonely childhood until I came along, so I understand her fears. But that doesn't mean she should make a *gut* man miserable. Maybe if she's introduced to other young people, she'll settle down and enjoy being young and free. And she might find someone she can truly love. That would let you off the hook."

Matthew liked that idea, but he had a feeling Shelah wouldn't be at all happy if she knew he had anything to do with it.

"Can I also make a suggestion?" he shot back.

Kathleen nodded. "What is that?"

"Will you ask Sarah, Colette's *mamm*, to bring this up to Shelah while you're with her? It will seem more proper if you approach Sarah with this than if I do the asking."

"I see, and I understand," Kathleen said. "Consider it done." She walked him to the door and said, "I appreciate your offer to let us take the smaller house on Saul's land. I have always loved that little house. It has three bedrooms, and that's more than enough for Shelah and me. The big house would be so lonely without Saul there."

"The guesthouse is yours," Matthew said. "I have to get through all the legal stuff and sign a lot of papers, but you can live there free of charge for as long as you like, with or without Shelah."

Kathleen's eyes watered. "You are a kind person, Matthew. Saul was kind, but he could also be bitter and angry at times."

Matthew knew the reason for that, but he couldn't say anything to Kathleen, because he didn't know how much Shelah had told her. "Did you care for Saul?" he asked.

Kathleen nodded. "I loved him, but he couldn't return my love. There was nothing between us but an abiding appreciation and a tentative friendship. I had to take care of Shelah, for the sake of her departed mother. My favorite cousin, Tricia."

She lowered her voice. "Tricia and I grew up together in Ohio, but she married and moved to Missouri with a man who worked for Saul. When they were both killed in a horrible buggy accident, Saul was concerned about their little girl, three-year-old Shelah, and wrote to us. None of our family even knew Tricia had a child. We searched until we found Shelah with her *daed*'s folks. They'd been passing her around for two years without letting Tricia's side of the family know anything. It took two more years for Saul to gain guardianship. When I found out where she was, I went to visit Shelah. Saul was so glad to see a relative of hers, he offered me the job of taking care of her. I was a widow who needed work and I knew this would be perfect. That's how I wound up in his home."

"I'm sorry for all of this," Matthew said. "But maybe your idea will help Shelah see she has options."

Kathleen patted his arm. "Go and get some supper. I'll make sure Shelah has a tray brought up here."

"*Denke*." He hurried down the winding stairs and turned toward the kitchen. When he heard laughter in the employee room, he went down the back hallway and headed there.

Everyone who worked at the inn or lived here had gathered to have a meal.

Jonah spotted him first. "Hello, Matthew. I wanted to let you know Levi and I didn't find Sawdust, but we did ask around and several people think they saw him."

"*Denke,*" he said, relief washing over him. "I'll look more myself tomorrow."

The room went quiet again.

He stood there, feeling like an outsider, until Abe looked at him and said, "Matthew, please join us. We all thought we'd stay in our homes tonight, but we also wanted to be together. If you stay, I'd appreciate your help making sure we get back to our own homes, or at least into a bed here safely, but right now we will eat."

Matthew glanced at Colette. She nodded and sent him a soft smile. That was invitation enough for him.

CHAPTER ELEVEN

Colette couldn't eat. She kept thinking about Matthew going upstairs with Shelah. What had they discussed? Did he feel sorry for Shelah? Had he changed his mind about everything? Mamm took over, giving her time to adjust her attitude.

"How is Shelah?" Mamm asked, her gaze on Matthew.

Matthew put down his second biscuit. "She's much better. She has a slight concussion, which Kathleen is monitoring, and some bruises. Her ankle was sprained, but she says she's walking better now."

"I have crutches if she needs them," Eliza said, reminding them of how she'd broken her leg last year. "They aren't fun, but it takes the pressure off the injured foot."

"That's kind of you, Eliza," Mamm said, giving Eliza her usual soft smile.

Colette almost snorted. Eliza wasn't being kind. Those crutches took the romance right out of a relationship. Not that she thought Matthew would get romantic with Shelah. Or, rather, she refused to think in those terms.

"I'll let you and Kathleen decide about that," he said

to Mamm. "She did want to speak with you about some things."

"I'll check on them first thing tomorrow," Mamm replied. "I'm glad Kathleen wasn't hurt badly. She seems like a reasonable person."

Matthew nodded. "She is that. We had an interesting visit after I talked to Shelah."

"*Gut.* I'll look forward to visiting with her tomorrow," Mamm said. "My children talked me into leaving my warm living room to have supper here, and now I'm wishing I'd asked them to bring me a plate instead."

Matthew glanced around. "I think this is nice. I've missed our get-together meals here."

Daed gave him a quick glance. "Then eat some more. I think Colette made enough to feed the whole community."

Colette smiled. "I did feed most of the community. Aside from our guests, several locals traipsed through the snow to get a warm meal because they have no power."

"None of us have any real power," Mamm reminded them. "We are grateful to *Gott* for our ability to provide."

The conversation moved to the snow and several power outages in the area. The inn had been blessed to have electricity, but they were prepared to run it by candlelight if needed. The stoves and refrigerators worked on propane, so that wouldn't be a problem.

Colette listened, her mind moving from keeping the inn running to everything she needed to prep for tomorrow's menus and then back to Matthew and Shelah. She wanted things to be perfect again, but if Matthew wouldn't open up to her, she'd have to walk away and get on with her life.

Tomorrow, she'd continue working on her quilt panels,

and she'd also do as Mamm had suggested. Colette would keep busy and bide her time. It would be up to Mattie to make the next move.

Later as she was finishing up in the kitchen, Matthew came in. "I'm staying here again tonight since that tree is still blocking the road. Henry said he'd get word to one of the phone booths on our road so my parents will know I'm here."

"That's for the best," she replied, tired and ready to go home. "I'm finished for now. I'll shut everything down."

"Not by yourself," he said. "I'll walk you to the cottage, and I'll sleep in the carriage *haus* room."

"But we're already in trouble for going out together earlier. I know the way home, Matthew."

"I promised Abigail I'd be a perfect gentleman and walk you home, Colette. And that's what I'm going to do. In return, Abigail distracted your mother so she didn't see me loitering about waiting for you."

Colette didn't protest, but she was surprised Abigail had agreed. Or maybe Mattie had been persuasive. He had changed over the last few months. Gone was the shy boy who seemed afraid to talk to her or flirt with her. Now a man stood before her, confused and trying to make the right decision. He'd been handed a big burden that came with extra pressure. But he'd matured and now had a voice of his own. She knew he'd make the right decision. He'd always had a logical mind and great instincts. She had to keep reminding herself he was a *gut* man and because of that, he was caught between two worlds right now. Mattie never wanted to hurt anyone. Probably he was the one in the most pain right now.

They finished up the last of the chores in silence, much

like the old days. The night crew would remain on-site to help guests. Henry was staying over again.

Colette and Matthew bundled up, and he held her arm while they walked toward her home. But when Colette turned on the porch to tell him good night, she saw a silhouette in the window of the big suite on the inn's top floor.

Shelah, always there in the shadows. Always lurking and waiting like a spider to snare her catch.

Colette would behave, but she would also fight to save Mattie from that horribly misguided woman. She watched as he trudged back along the path the men had cleared earlier. Watched and prayed in this quiet, snow-covered world.

"Your will, Lord. Not mine."

Colette turned and went inside, her heart heavy but her faith strong. She prayed for Matthew, and she also prayed for Shelah. There was a reason Shelah was so needy. She'd been left without parents at an early age. Colette decided she'd have to remember that and pray for a solution that would serve all of them.

It was three weeks until Christmas and the snow had melted to mush on the roads but still blanketed the woods. Colette sat in the quilt room and stared at the panels she'd made so far. She hadn't yet shared her work with anyone. With all the other things going on, she liked her quiet time in her room, working away at her panels. But she needed advice from here on out. Which was why she'd lugged all of her quilting materials down the hill to the inn's big workroom.

Eliza and Abigail came in with their own materials.

"We got here early so you can show us what you've done," Abigail said. She placed her handiwork down on a chair.

Eliza did the same and then turned to face Colette. "We also want to hear about your ride with Matthew the other day. We've been so busy cleaning up after the storm, we haven't had a chance to discuss that."

"I didn't know it needed discussing," Colette said, giving them a mock grin. Then she turned serious. "It was *wunderbar gut* to be with Matthew again." She shrugged. "It felt forbidden, but right."

Abigail nodded. "I know that feeling. Jonah was certainly forbidden to me, but now—"

"Now he is yours forever," Eliza finished. "The same with Levi. It felt wrong, but it also seemed right. Is it the same with you and Mattie?"

"It is," Colette said on a whisper. "But we have one too many people in our relationship."

"Shelah," her sisters both said at once.

"She is demanding," Eliza whispered. "Always calling down for trays and books and whatever she can think of. Always wondering where Mattie is. She's even got Henry in a mood, and we all know Henry is always happy and pleasant."

"Enough about her," Abigail said. "Show us what you've done so far."

Colette pulled out the panels she'd been working on. The first one, done in red, green, and brown, showed two faceless Amish children sitting in the grass.

"You and Mattie as toddlers," Abigail said, nodding.

Then the next one. Two older children walking together with lunch buckets, fall leaves all around them.

"Going to school?" Eliza asked. "Now that I think

about it, Matthew always liked to meet you at the end of the school lane."

Colette nodded. "I want to do several panels that show us working in the restaurant, maybe with a table behind us. Cakes, pies, all types of food."

"I can help with that," Abigail said, lifting her sketch pad out of her quilting bag. Then she leaned close. "Before I forget, Mamm met with Kathleen today. I wish I could have been a fly on that wall."

"I see you three are discussing current events," Mamm said from the doorway.

She had an uncanny way of sneaking up on people.

"What did you and Kathleen talk about?" Colette asked, skipping right past the part where they pretended to be innocent of any gossiping.

Mamm shut the door of the big quilting room, a sure sign that she had some sort of news. "Well, there has been a surprising turn of events."

They waited. Colette held her breath and tried not to fidget. Had Kathleen convinced Shelah to leave, or had she convinced Matthew to go with them when they did leave?

Mamm sat down and sighed. "It seems Kathleen has the same idea as you girls. She wants Shelah to attend some youth frolics to meet other men."

"What?" Colette had not expected that. "I thought she was all for Matthew and Shelah marrying."

"Not exactly." Mamm unfolded material and turned to the quilt stretched out over the main table. "Kathleen knows Matthew was spoken for before he went to Missouri, but Shelah managed to convince Saul that Matthew should marry her. Kathleen thinks Saul got confused and agreed because he cared so much about Shelah. But she also says Shelah hasn't had much practice with social events and meeting proper suitors. Saul spoiled her, but also held her back from a lot of things socially. Apparently, he didn't trust the local boys or Shelah."

Colette nodded her head. "That all makes perfect sense. Shelah is desperate and she's using Mattie because he's the first real man her age she's spent any time around. I know Mattie is a *gut* man and would make a *wunderbar* husband, but he's being used in this case. She also knows a secret Mattie can't share. Did Kathleen have a clue what Shelah might be holding over Mattie's head?"

"*Neh,*" Mamm replied, her tone low. "She only believes Shelah is looking for security and love, two things she missed out on when her parents died so young."

Colette nodded. "I've been praying for her, believe it or not. That's a horrible childhood, being moved around and finally landing with Saul. He did take care of her, but it was an odd arrangement. Kathleen is kind and understanding at times, and like a mama hen at other times. But I think she'd be content with finding Shelah a suitable man who isn't already spoken for. And I'm sure she'd rather find that man closer to Saul's place, where she and Shelah want to stay."

"If we can convince Shelah of that," Mamm said. "Kathleen and I are planning a Christmas frolic for later this week."

"That is a big step," Abigail said. "But necessary."

They all agreed. "I'll keep you updated," Mamm said. Then she asked about Colette's quilt squares.

Colette showed the first few. "I'm not the best at this, but Eliza and Abby are helping. I think next I'll put the fall festival on. Matthew and I behind a produce table. Or holding a basket of apples. We love apple-picking."

"I like the Christmas theme," Mamm said. "You could do a simple evergreen and put red berries on it."

"I like that," Colette replied. "I wish I had current memories."

"You do," Eliza reminded her. "You and Mattie rode out on Samson. Show that."

"Oh, *ja*, that will work. Abby, can you draw that for a panel?"

"I certainly can," her sister said, jotting down Colette's suggestions.

"And you and Mattie talked in the employee room—after I locked you in, I mean. You could show that. Some flowers on the table and the food you never ate."

"How very romantic," Mamm said. "That would be a nice panel, though."

Colette thought about the cookies she'd made and taken to Matthew. She'd create that scene, complete with a woven basket of cookies.

Abigail made notes and did a quick sketch. "Now we'd best get busy. The inn is filling up again now that the weather has improved and Christmas is getting closer. I hear you'll be meeting with Linda again about the scholars program tomorrow, *ja*?"

Colette smiled. "The first meeting was to go over the program and any costumes the scholars will need. Their mothers are stitching and sewing as we speak." She ran a hand over her panels, satisfied with her work and the new memories she'd add. "Tomorrow, we have the prop crew coming to the school to decide what to build for the background." Laughing, she said, "Mamm is finding ways for me to stay busy and away from temptation."

"I am certainly trying to keep you out of trouble," Mamm replied. Then she smiled. "Right now, I cherish this time alone with my girls. I'm glad we didn't have an open quilting session today."

They all nodded at that and began to stitch away.

Colette thought about what Mamm had told them. Maybe there was hope for her and Matthew yet. She'd keep praying on that account. And for Shelah, too.

While Colette was quilting with her mother and sisters, Matthew hurried to the stables to talk to Jonah and Levi. After he got there and stamped the snow off his boots, he looked up to find Abe sitting on a bench all bundled up, watching them work.

It looked like he'd be talking with all three of them. Best get this over with and told all at once.

Abe looked up, his bushy brows lifting like a raven's wings. "Young Matthew, what brings you out of the kitchen?"

"You three," Matthew said in a firm tone.

Jonah chuckled. "Too many cooks in the kitchen, or too many females in the kitchen?"

"A little of both," he admitted. "The King sisters and Sarah are quilting. Shelah is in her room with an aching ankle. I need advice."

Abe nodded slowly. "That you do, son, that you do." He pointed to a milking stool. "Drag that over and let's have a discussion."

Matthew grabbed the stool and a cup of coffee Jonah poured out of a huge thermos. "You all know most of it. Shelah talked to Saul about me before he died. She somehow convinced him we were in love and asked him to bless the marriage. She also asked him to tell me I needed to marry her, which he did. I'm not sure how much he knew, but the man was not coherent. Shelah filled in where I didn't understand."

Jonah rubbed his face and squinted his brow. "So technically, Shelah did most of the talking on Saul's behalf?"

"*Ja*, but he did finally take my hand and tell me I should marry her."

"Are you sure he said that?" Levi asked, his hand running over Samson's nose.

"I had to lean close," Matthew said. "But he told me that, and something else."

"Does this something else have anything to do with Shelah?"

"*Neh*, but it has to do with me." He lowered his head. "I always wondered why my *mamm* and *daed* weren't close to Onkel Saul. I know why now."

Jonah shot Levi a silent glance. Abe shifted on his chair. "Matthew, what you tell us here will go no further. You need someone to talk to? Is this a confession of sorts?"

"It's the truth," Matthew said. Then he looked up at the three men he admired almost as much as he admired his hardworking *daed*. "The truth I need to tell everyone, especially Colette." He glanced up at them. "The will confirmed what Saul whispered to me."

"Is Shelah with child?" Abe asked. "I have been assured that is not the case. At least, Colette believes it is not."

Matthew jumped up off his stool to pace. "*Neh*, I have not touched her. She kissed me once and it didn't go very well. But she is not going to have a *bobbeli*." He pushed at his hair. "At least, not with me."

"Then what?" Levi asked, his hands on his hips. "What is so bad and such a secret that you can't tell any of us?"

"Saul was my father," Matthew said, letting out a groan of relief as the words left his mouth. "It was there in the will. That's why he left me his estate. That's why he agreed with Shelah that she and I should get married. I'm his son and she is his ward. So that would make it perfect in his mind."

Jonah crossed his arms over his chest and let out a breath. "That does make a messy situation even worse. So this is why you came home with Shelah?"

"Shelah got on the bus and wouldn't get off. I was going to come to the wedding alone and explain to Colette, but Shelah insisted on coming, too. She knows about Saul's secret. She's been holding that over my head. My parents don't know what I found out, and I can't bring myself to upset Mamm by asking the truth."

"Your parents have no idea?" Abe asked, his eyes full of compassion. "Your *mamm* has to know, of course. But have you told her what you've found out? She needs to know, and maybe she can explain more of this to you."

Matthew shook his head. "I don't want to hurt my parents or shame them, and I'm honestly not clear about who knows what at this point. This could be why my *daed* and Saul were not close. I fear Shelah will tell them sooner or later that I found out the truth. I do not love this woman. I love Colette. So what should I do? Honor Saul's request and marry Shelah, move to Missouri? Or go to my folks and tell them what I know and stay here to try and win Colette back? I only know my *mamm* had a child with her husband's brother and kept it a secret all these years. She had no choice. Does my *daed* know? Did Mamm marry my *daed* to hide her shame? I have to decide how to handle this, and the sooner the better."

Abe, Jonah, and Levi stared at him and then they looked at each other.

Matthew almost wished he'd never told them the truth. Did they feel pity for him? Anger at him? Would they question him and force him to go to his parents?

Abe finally spoke. "Matthew, you were already engaged to my daughter when you went to Missouri, although you did not have a chance to make it official with the bishop. Do you love Shelah at all?"

"I do not," he quickly admitted. "I've told her that. She doesn't want me, Abe. She wants what she had living with Saul—security, and a *gut* home and lands for miles. Money. She was an orphan passed around, until Saul took in Kathleen and her. I think he was lonely and the guilt of what he did was eating at him, so he spoiled her, but he did not teach her right from wrong. Kathleen has tried, but Shelah is hard to tame. Now I have to take on the sins Saul brought to my family. I can bear that burden, and if necessary, I can even marry Shelah. But I will never love her in the same way I love Colette."

Abe stood and nodded his head, his long beard lifting with each nod. "I will need to consult the bishop on this matter, but it will go no further than that, as I've promised. Saul is gone; he can't confess to anyone else. But I suggest you talk to your *mamm* in private and find out how and when this happened. She might have a different story from the one you've formed in your head."

Matthew shook his head. "You don't understand. Mamm did not consent to Saul's attention. She . . . was forced. Saul put that in the will as his confession to me. I don't think my *daed* has any idea this happened, and I'm pretty sure he believes me to be his son." His head bent, he said, "If he doesn't know the truth and I tell him, it will destroy him."

"Is this what Shelah is holding over your head?" Jonah asked, his eyes flaring.

Matthew nodded. "It is. That's all she's got on me. But it is enough."

"More than enough," Jonah said, slapping Matthew on the back. "But you have us now. We will figure this out, somehow."

"I pray so," Matthew said. "I do pray so."

CHAPTER TWELVE

The next morning, Colette took the smaller buggy up the road to the big schoolhouse, her mind on the costumes, the hymns and songs, and the food. She'd leave the backdrop to the men, but she and Linda would get some of the women in to help paint.

The snow had mostly melted, but a definite chill was in the air. Winter had come to Shadow Lake Inn, so she'd bundled up and taken her time with Samson. The big horse loved clomping through the snow, but she held him steady. After getting him settled in the stable and throwing a warm blanket over him, she entered the schoolhouse, glad the potbellied stove nestled in the corner was burning wood.

She looked up, expecting to find Linda and a few of the others who'd volunteered to help. Instead, she found Matthew standing there smiling at her.

"What are you doing here?" she asked, wondering if Mamm had sent him to test her.

"I'm one of the builders," he said. "I volunteered since I want to stay busy. I've helped with the scholars' program just about every year, so I might as well help this year, too."

Did Mamm know this? Was her own mother playing her? Colette decided she should volunteer more often. She'd been missing out.

"Seems we had the same idea," she replied as she tugged at her scarf and cloak. "I heard the road is all clear and you've been back home."

"*Ja.*" His eyes held hers for a moment. "I tried to find you all day yesterday, but somehow you managed to avoid me."

"Mamm arranged that," she said, wishing she'd stayed home. If Mamm truly didn't know Matthew would be here, she wouldn't like this. "She is concerned."

"I understand that," Matthew said, "but, Colette, you have to know I'd marry you, scandal or no scandal. So if we get caught—"

She held up her hand. "That is no way to start a marriage, Matthew Mueller, and you know it."

"You're right. I was thinking with my heart, not my head."

"Well, that head needs to make up its mind and get on with things. Then we can discuss who you'll be marrying."

"I told Shelah I can't marry her."

His words stopped Colette in her boots. "And how did she respond to that?"

"Not very well," he admitted. "But Kathleen has caught on, and she has promised to discuss this with Sarah."

"She did," Colette told him while they waited for the others. "Mamm has planned a holiday frolic for Wednesday. Nothing fancy, just some singing with punch and cookies, at the inn. Weather permitting."

"I'll be there," he said. "But not because of Shelah. I want to sing and have punch with you, Colette. Only you."

Colette felt the heat of that declaration more intensely

than the fire in the stove. She wanted to run to him and hold him tight, but that would be wrong. Instead, she nodded and prayed for someone to come in and interrupt them.

He might have talked to Shelah, but Colette believed the determined woman would go to desperate lengths to keep Matthew and his inheritance—even if she had to compromise herself. No wonder Kathleen kept an eye on her both night and day.

Colette had to be careful. "Remember our plan to stay apart because we've ended things?"

"I remember," he said. "But I have hope."

Colette felt something shifting. Matthew acted as if he had more to say. She couldn't take that chance.

"I'll just set these refreshments Mamm sent out here on the table," she replied. But she gave Mattie a soft smile as she said it.

"You want to see me there at the frolic, don't you?" he asked.

A silence that held a lifetime of connection passed between them, and then was lost when the door flew open with a brisk wind behind it and two men from the community came in, laughing and talking. Maggie Yoder, who also worked at the inn, followed with more food. No one ever starved around here.

Saved by the volunteers, Colette thought. But how much longer could she resist the pull of her feelings for Matthew? And how much longer would he tolerate Shelah's unwanted aggressiveness? Somehow, she had to find out what Shelah was really up to and what she thought she had on Mattie.

* * *

Colette listened as Linda explained the props. "We only need a background that looks like trees in the woods. A forest, but a Christmas forest. Pines and spruces, maybe some firs. We'll want snow covering them, but not too much. And bright red in there—maybe cardinals and holly berries?"

"I like that idea," Colette said. She would put that same scene on her quilt. "That will make a nice backdrop for the singing."

Linda nodded. "*Ja*, and we'll do traditional hymns in High German, and maybe a few contemporary tunes for fun."

"I do a little woodworking here and there," Matthew said. "I think I can cut out the trees and shape them from plywood. That way you can keep them and use them over and over."

"That would be nice," Linda said. "I didn't know you liked to work with wood, Mattie."

"Neither did I," Colette admitted.

Maggie giggled. "He's always telling me about something else he's built for his folks. I think the man could whittle a full house if he had time."

It occurred to Colette that she didn't know nearly enough about the man she'd planned to marry. She only thought of Matthew Mueller in relation to the café and the kitchen at the inn. She had taken him for granted in so many ways, pushed him aside when other boys came calling, neglected to really ask him about his hopes and dreams. She'd still been on that path when he got called away.

It hit her hard—her failure to be a friend to him. A true friend. No wonder he might have been swayed toward Shelah, who seemed to adore him and wanted to be with him exclusively. But her reasons weren't much better. She wanted his inheritance.

Colette rubbed her forehead in worry. She wanted Matthew. She was certain of that now.

"What do you think about the food?" Linda asked, bringing Colette's head up. Everyone was waiting for her answer.

"I . . . uh . . . I think I'm getting a headache. Could you repeat that?"

Linda nodded. "Do you need to leave?"

Maggie and Matthew both gave her concerned glances.

"I can take you home," Matthew said.

"I'm fine. I have Samson and a buggy. I just have a lot on my mind. But food—I think finger sandwiches and cookies with the punch. Not too messy for the scholars. The inn will take care of that. It will be easy to set up serving tables, and the *kinder* can enjoy the bonfires and the pavilion after the singing is over."

"*Denke*," Linda said, relaxing. "It will be so nice and roomy there. Unlike this cold, small schoolhouse."

Colette imagined that everyone in the room expected her and Matthew to get in a fight. That would not happen. But they were playing a dangerous game, pretending they didn't still have feelings for each other.

"So we have a plan," she finally said, hoping Linda would end the meeting. She really did have a headache.

Linda bobbed her head. "Well, we've got the program figured out and we've planned a backdrop and what food to serve to everyone. We can meet again once the men have the backdrop ready. I expect we can all help paint?"

"*Ja*," Maggie said.

"Sure," Colette replied. She'd be near Mattie if she helped paint.

She left with a new purpose: to get to know Matthew better, to never take him for granted again. And despite her vow to stay out of his life, she planned to find a way to keep him in hers.

She'd definitely be at that frolic next week.

Colette King was not a coward. It was time she stopped acting like one.

After he left the school meeting, Matthew entered the house and looked around. Maybe he could have a moment with Mamm. Abe had suggested that he talk to his *mamm* first, to hear her side of this sad story. Matthew felt better now, glad he'd confided in the people he trusted. He still needed to explain to Colette, but he never seemed to find the right moment. Abe told him to wait on that. Family first, and then he could move on to telling everyone else the truth.

"Once you've done that, Shelah will have no power over you. You can refuse to marry the woman who tried to trick you into that union, understand?"

He did understand. Meantime, Jonah was quietly doing some background research on Shelah. He'd also spoken to Matthew about the blue vehicle that had caused the buggy crash. "A hit-and-run is a crime. The driver needs to be held accountable. I can ask around about any vehicle that might have been damaged that night."

"But it won't fix my buggy, and we have yet to find Sawdust. I fear we might not ever find him."

"If we find the culprit, his insurance will pay, believe

me," Jonah told him. "The buggy is evidence and the locals have taken statements and have a record of the accident."

Matthew prayed the blue car would be found. "There would be extensive damage on the automobile."

"Exactly." Jonah slapped him on the back. "You were wise to come to us. We all believe in you, and we want you and Colette back together."

"I want the same," he'd replied, hoping that could happen.

Now, he checked and saw his brothers and Daed out by the barn, working on a fence. "Mamm," he called out. "Are you here?"

"I'm back in my room," Agnes called out. "*Kumm*."

Matthew walked down the hallway and found Mamm in her hickory rocking chair—one of his first attempts at woodworking.

"Are you feeling poorly?" he asked, afraid to open up old wounds.

Mamm looked up at him with tears in her eyes. "I was thinking of Saul and how you inherited his place. That's a blessing for you, Mattie. But sometimes blessings *kumm* with great burdens, ain't so."

Matthew sat down on the stool near her chair. "The truth, Mamm. I need to know the truth. I think you understand why Saul left it all to me and not Daed or even Shelah."

She nodded, tears misting her eyes, a strand of grayish-brown hair slipping from her *kapp*. "*Ja*, I think I've figured it out. But I'm wondering if you have, and especially if Shelah knows, too."

"What did she say?" he asked, dread coloring his words.

"Enough to give me a hint," Mamm replied. "She

implied you had to do right by Saul and her. I thought she might be with child, but I was afraid to ask."

"It's not that," Matthew said. "But it is something that will be painful for all of us to bear."

"It's about Saul, then," Mamm said, making a statement rather than a question.

He nodded, swallowed the pain in his throat. "Did my *onkel* assault you? Or did something happen because you both wanted it? Did you love Saul more than you love Daed?"

His mother shook her head. "I hated Saul for what he did. Cornered me in an old barn when he found me out picking blueberries." She closed her eyes, and Matthew's gut wrenched when he saw a single tear falling down her cheek. "Your *daed* and I had been married about four months, but Saul didn't care. He'd flirted with me since the day we met, even at my wedding. Then he found his opportunity. Followed me through the woods." She rubbed her hands against her apron, as if trying to get rid of something. "I never went blueberry picking again after that." She sat silent for a moment. "I was so glad when he up and moved to Missouri."

Matthew came off the stool and kneeled in front of her. Taking her hands, he asked, "Does Daed know?"

She burst into tears. "I can't tell him, Mattie. He can't know. He and Saul got into a bad fight because Saul hinted that I'd flirted with him, trying to cover his tracks. Saul had warned me he'd deny everything, claim that I pursued him." She kept shaking her head. "I told him to leave and I'd never mention it. A few weeks later, he left. But he was bitter and angry. He actually thought I'd leave your *daed* for him. Even after that day . . ."

Matthew thought he might be ill. How could Saul have

been so kind to him and so horrible to his mother? Now he had to wonder if Saul had given him the inheritance out of guilt instead of love. But did it matter? It was tainted.

"Even after the fight, you never told Daed?"

"I couldn't. I was afraid he'd go after Saul, or he'd always wonder which one of us was telling the truth." She wiped her eyes with her apron. "He told Saul he didn't believe I'd flirted with him, and to leave and never *kumm* back here. I told Saul the same. I told him if he'd leave, I'd never accuse him." She glanced out the window to where Daed stood laughing with Aaron and Timothy. "Since we both wanted him gone, he did leave. And we rarely heard from him."

Matthew's heart broke into pieces. He felt physically ill. "So Daed truly didn't believe you were flirting with Saul?"

"*Ja.*" Her revelations grated at Matthew's soul. "He told me Saul had always been a womanizer and a ladies' man, but he knew me, and I would not have done that. He teased that I'd barely flirted with *him*. We got past it, and a few weeks later, I found out I was with child."

Matthew's brain went to work as hope entered his heart. "So, I could be Daed's son?"

"*Neh.*" Another whisper. "I was so . . . frightened and ashamed, I didn't want to be with your *daed* for a while. I wasn't afraid of him, but afraid of how I felt—broken, abused, humiliated. I pretended female problems, but I think he became suspicious. He'd hold me and tell me he loved me, and slowly, I began to trust again. When I told him I was with child, he assumed *that* was the female problem I was having." She finally smiled. "After you were born, we moved on because we loved you so much.

Then we had your brothers. We had—we still have—a *gut* life. I can't ruin that for your father now. Saul is gone. It's over. I won't break your *daed*'s heart over it."

"But, Mamm, Shelah knows Saul is my father. And she's threatening to tell."

His mother lifted her head in shock. "Is that why you are considering marrying that girl? Mattie, I can't let you do that." She stood up and looked out the window toward the barn. "I won't let you do that. You belong with Colette, and somehow we will face this, no matter the outcome with your *daed* and me."

"If we tell him, we do it together," Matthew said, standing behind his *mamm*. "We'll be the ones to tell Daed, not Shelah. And the boys need never know."

Mamm lifted her chin high. "I was against confessing to Titus, but now I see I have no choice. My sin has caught up with me."

Matthew turned to face her there at the window. "You did not commit the sin. Saul did. And he's paying for it now. But the truth can help all of us here on earth to heal and get past this. *Gott*'s will—isn't that what you've always taught me?"

Agnes put a hand on his jaw. "I think we've taught you a lot more than that. I have never been prouder of you, Mattie."

Matthew placed his arm over her shoulders. "I need a little more time to win Colette back. Then we will talk to Daed."

Agnes lifted her head and smiled. "I hope you succeed. I have always loved those King girls. Especially Colette."

"Me too," he said. Then Matthew noticed Daed and the boys running toward something. Fearful, he nudged Mamm. "What's up?"

They both hurried out onto the porch.

"It's Sawdust," Mamm said, tears in her eyes again. "Your horse is home, Mattie."

Matthew kissed his *mamm* and ran out to where Sawdust stood, looking the worse for wear but happy to finally be safe at home. Matthew breathed a sigh of relief and thanked *Gott* for this one *gut* thing. He felt the same.

CHAPTER THIRTEEN

People were arriving for the frolic, so Colette hurried downstairs and grabbed her cloak. She needed to get to the pavilion to greet people. The day was sunny but still chilly, so they had fires going around the sturdy covered structure and they'd sectioned off part of the inn's dining room for refreshments and snacks. They planned to make s'mores and serve hot chocolate, and grill hotdogs with crisp french fries.

Samson was already hitched up and ready to take people on a ride through the snowy woods.

They'd scheduled the frolic for a day when the inn wasn't too busy, so Edith and Henry were there to help, along with Jonah and Abigail to act as chaperones. Eliza and Levi planned to make an appearance, too, but they were busy moving things around in the cottage and sending what Mamm and Daed wanted to keep to the *gross-daddi haus*. By Christmas, both households should be settled and ready to celebrate the holidays.

Colette flew through the cottage living room and saw Eliza in the kitchen across the way. "I'm stuck here," her sister said. "I'm rearranging things so the kitchen will be more efficient. I hope Mamm won't mind."

"It's your kitchen now," Colette pointed out. "And you have Levi to help you rearrange."

"But I will always think of it as Mamm's," Eliza said. "I love this house, and I'm glad Mamm and Daed decided it was time for them to move into something smaller. But that means they are getting on in age. I don't like that part."

"None of us do," Colette said as she adjusted her winter bonnet. She'd put on one of her best dresses, a deep green wool that would keep her warm. She had on sturdy high-topped black boots to keep her legs covered. Would Matthew notice she'd tried to dress nicely?

She hadn't talked to him much since the meeting at school. He'd been busy helping his folks repair some things and he'd been working on the backdrop for the scholars' singing. She knew he had a lot of paperwork to complete and send back to Missouri so he could properly take over Saul's estate after Christmas. A busy man.

She had noticed he seemed quiet again and almost melancholy. Was he thinking about what might happen after Christmas? Just as she was?

She'd also seen him talking to Shelah now and then. Shelah had managed to get herself downstairs so she could sit in the inn's parlor and call out to Matthew if he went by. Henry had begun to call her the Table Lamp Girl since she sat there like a lamp most days and only lit up when Matthew was around. Kathleen had become close to Mamm, and Mamm had reported that Shelah didn't have anywhere else to go until things were settled with Saul's estate. They'd been offered the guesthouse on Saul's property, which Kathleen thought would suffice, but which Shelah thought beneath her.

"We must show them grace," Mamm had said. "They

are homeless for now because they won't go back to Saul's big house alone. Matthew has promised them a small property on Saul's land. It's a nice three-bedroom ranch style house that has everything they need. Shelah refuses to leave, however, until Matthew goes back too. Due to the needs of his family, he can't get back there until after Christmas. She seems to be waiting for Mattie to fall in love with her."

Colette let out a sigh, thinking that her mother knew more about Matthew's life than she did. She shrugged at Eliza now. "I sometimes wish we were still young. Growing up seems to be a painful process."

"That's a part of growing up," Eliza said, her eyes as dreamy as ever. "I hate the time I wasted being angry at Levi, but we will make up for that."

Colette had to close her eyes. Too much happiness burned at her soul. She was so glad for her sisters and their happy homes, but she'd been planning the same dreamy things, and in the blink of an eye, her life had been turned upside down. Well, nothing to be done about that now. She'd certainly had an epiphany at that scholars meeting the other day.

She needed to stop being so self-absorbed and really listen to people. The Mattie she thought she knew was a completely different person now. She wanted to know all the things about him she'd taken for granted or had ignored.

She didn't really want to be at this frolic, except to show up and listen to anything Matthew had to say. She'd concluded that he might care for her, but he didn't trust her to help him through this mess. Matthew never kept secrets, but something besides Shelah was gnawing at him. She had to win his trust in order to win him—again.

But first, she'd have to find out what Shelah was using as leverage against Matthew.

Matthew walked toward the pavilion, wondering why he'd come here today. Well, Henry had suggested it in case they needed him, but Matthew knew he'd really been invited because of Colette. He had to pretend he didn't want to be here, but he and Colette knew the truth. They could hang out without anyone commenting as long as they avoided being alone together. He'd also have to endure Shelah, since she'd been convinced to attend with the promise of meeting new people. Would she find new friends? From what he'd seen, Shelah ran friends away with her complaining and negative, demanding attitude.

He could deal with Shelah, but how would he and Colette avoid each other when people kept inadvertently bringing them together? Shadow Lake was a small community; it was hard to hide from anyone.

After his talk with Mamm and Sawdust's return, he'd been busy helping Levi. Sawdust had some bruises and cuts, but his legs were healthy and sturdy. A few good feedings would fatten him up again, and a treat every afternoon, courtesy of Eliza, who pampered him when he came to see Levi, would put Sawdust right. Neither Levi nor Jonah had mentioned what he'd told them. He didn't like asking his friends to keep secrets, but what other choice did he have? He knew he could trust them, and Abe, too.

Now Matthew thought over all his reasons for postponing his return to Missouri and for postponing his confrontation with Shelah. First and foremost was his desire to help his folks, and now he had the income to do it.

They'd been gently trying to guide him as he shouldered the enormous responsibility he'd been given. But each time he saw Mamm and Daed together, he wished he didn't have to mess up their lives with the truth. Mamm was fidgety, but Daed didn't seem to notice. Or maybe he did notice and just didn't let on. He loved Agnes so much. Enough to forgive her for keeping the truth from him? Matthew hoped so. She had done no wrong.

She'd opened up about Shelah, however.

"She won't go away," his mother had told him in a firm tone just this morning. "That girl has it in her head to win you over and become the mistress of Saul's estate."

Shelah and Kathleen had visited Mamm after Mattie left to take Sawdust to the vet and then to Levi for new shoes.

"She brought what she thought was pumpkin bread. It tasted more like Sawdust's feed. And she insisted on helping me fold the laundry—which she did all wrong. The girl has not been trained to run a house."

He had to grit his teeth. If Mamm was criticizing Shelah's work, it must be really poor. His mother was always kind to anyone who visited her home.

But this woman would always be a reminder of what had happened between Mamm and Saul. Shelah would use that information whenever she had the opportunity. He wouldn't let her do that. She could threaten him all she wanted, but not his sweet, hardworking, loving *mamm*.

He'd decided after the horrible buggy accident that he intended to make those dreams he and Colette had talked about come true. He prayed that *Gott*'s will would help him along.

He walked toward the group gathering by the firepits

near the pavilion. Underneath the structure, benches and tables had been set up and a hot chocolate table held a coffee urn full of already mixed cocoa, along with sugar cookies and red velvet brownies covered in a clear removable plastic dome they used a lot in the inn's kitchen.

The air smelled of woodsmoke and evergreen trees, with just a hint of burnt marshmallows. The snow decorated the trees like a necklace on a woman. He glanced around, looking for Colette, but his gaze landed on Shelah. She wore a dark burgundy cloak with a heavy collar and a matching bonnet. She was a pretty woman, no doubt about that. Seeing him, she hurried toward him. At least her ankle had healed and her headaches were better.

A noise behind him caused him to turn. Colette was laughing with some of the young folks they both knew.

He heard, "Hey, Colette. I hear you're on the market again? Do I get to sit by you during the singing?"

Matthew's jealousy spiked. Mark Yoder had always been a flirt. He was Maggie's younger brother-in-law, and a troublemaker at that.

Colette shook her head and kept walking, but she did look back and smile at Mark.

Then Stephen Goyer stopped her. "Sorry to hear about you and Matthew. You deserve better than him." The man actually glared at Matthew, causing Colette to turn and spot him there.

Matthew wanted to pivot and leave, but someone grabbed his arm. "There you are," Shelah said, her smile sweet but her eyes like steel. "I think we'll have fun today. We can finally walk out together."

Matthew was about to tell her he couldn't do that when he looked up and saw Colette still staring at them. He expected her to throw the platter of brownies she carried at them, but instead she managed a smile.

She placed the brownies on the table and covered them with another cake dome, then marched right up to the two of them. "Mattie, I'm so pleased with the backdrop you made for the scholars. I can't wait to help paint it. What a great Christmas singing this will be. I'll see you at the painting party tomorrow." Then she gave Shelah a quick glance. "Hello. I hope you're feeling less frail today."

Shelah looked confused and mad all at the same time. "I'm fine. In fact, I'm feeling so much better, I hope Matthew can take me for a nice ride soon. Perhaps tomorrow. I need some fresh air. That old inn smells like stale cooking oil mixed with too-ripe lemons."

"Maybe that's just your room," Colette replied. "You might try airing out all those dresses you packed into the closet."

With that she twirled around and headed to the refreshment table, where she laughed and talked to several more friends.

She was either putting on a very *gut* act, or she'd finally given up on him. Matthew could never be sure of Colette. And that had been true for most of their lives. He could see it clearly now. Even after they'd declared their love, he was still in awe of her and doubtful. Had his uncertainty factored into his being so considerate of Shelah, who gave him all her attention? *Neh*, he loved Colette, no matter what.

Which only made him stare at her with a longing that burned hotter than the firepits around them.

Shelah let out a huff. "I don't know what you saw in her. She's so obvious."

If he hadn't been so angry, Matthew might have

laughed out loud. "Really, I haven't noticed her being obvious about anything. She is my friend."

Shelah gave him a little cough of a laugh. "And why would you notice? She's had you fooled for most of your life. You told me how you pined for her and then she suddenly decided she wanted to be with you, but that's all over. You owe me even more now, Matthew Mueller. I could have died in that accident."

Matthew took in a breath. "Well, I'm thankful you didn't. Now, do you want to have fun? Or do you want to lament and argue all day?"

"Fun, please," she replied, her eyelashes fluttering. "You've been so patient and kind. I hope you're beginning to see the merits of us teaming up. It's in our best interest, don't you think?"

"I'm beginning to see the logic," he replied, almost choking on the words. Because there was nothing logical about any of this. Shelah had never declared her love for him, and he'd tried not to lead her to think he loved her.

"*Gut*, because that buggy accident scared me. That horrible accident that could have killed all of us. Let's not forget that."

She'd mentioned the accident in passing several times over the last few days. What else would she find to hold over his head? She thought he'd cave and marry her. But Shelah always stopped at actual extortion, confining herself to veiled threats. He'd never known someone so pretty and sweet-looking could be such a manipulator.

And what about Colette? He knew her well enough to see she was up to something. That could be good or bad. Either way, he was here to stay, and he planned on talking to Colette today. If he could pry himself away from Shelah long enough and not get caught.

He was about to try to slip away when Shelah let out a gasp, her gaze fastened on a newcomer across the way.

"What's wrong?" Matthew asked, curious. Then he spotted a man he'd not seen around the inn before, dressed Amish but with what appeared to be an *Englisch*-style haircut. Shelah's reaction to the man was odd. "Are you all right?"

"Nothing's wrong," she said, taking his arm. "I thought I saw Kathleen spying on us."

But her gaze was on the stranger watching them.

Matthew studied the tall man with the dark hair. The newcomer seemed familiar to him, and Shelah's hand on his arm trembled with awareness. Did she know this man?

Colette watched the way Shelah held on to Matthew and wanted to throw up. Her nerves were all twisted, and Mattie kept staring at her as if she'd done something horrible. Was he jealous that other men were actually talking to her? He was staring at her more than he was paying attention to Shelah.

Her family and friends were right. She couldn't be engaged to Matthew while he was walking around with that person stuck to his arm. Until she had an opportunity to talk to Matthew, why not try to have a nice time?

She'd enjoy herself and be friendly with people she wanted to get to know better. So she started conversing, and she accepted some hot chocolate from Simon Gaber, then she took some cookies from Abel Sawyer. She'd agreed to stand by James Donner during the singing. She was really trying to have fun. She'd forgotten how mingling with friends her age could fill an afternoon. She caught up with other women friends and took a couple of them into the quilt room to see what she and her sisters had been working on. She'd left her quilt pieces at the cottage, however. No one needed to see that story. Yet.

Later, when the food started getting low, Colette hurried toward the kitchen to bring out more orange-cranberry bread and cheese.

But when she heard voices around the corner, she looked up and found Matthew face-to-face with a man she didn't know. It looked as if they were arguing. Setting down the baskets she'd planned to refill, she moved closer to listen.

"You need to leave," Matthew told the other man. "You've upset Shelah."

"I came here to see Shelah," the man replied. "She knows me, but we had an argument."

Colette's ears perked up. This was getting interesting. What was this man up to? What was Shelah up to? Colette searched and saw Shelah standing alone, a look of fear on her pretty face. Was she running from this man? Expecting Matthew to protect her?

"She does not want to speak to you," Matthew said again, moving closer to the man. "She told me how you met in town. But she did not invite you here."

"I didn't mean to interrupt but wanted to visit with her. To explain some things." He stared over at Shelah, his whole demeanor full of frustration and anger.

Shelah spotted the two men talking, then pivoted and ran away.

Colette stayed hidden behind the bushes, listening to Matthew. "You need to leave. There is nothing to explain. Shelah likes to talk to strangers, but you've overstepped. So please leave."

"Okay, I'll go," the man said, speaking *Englisch*. "But you're wrong. Shelah didn't think I was overstepping last time we talked."

Matthew glared at him. "I don't want to see you here again."

Matthew sure seemed jealous for a man who claimed he didn't care for Shelah. Perhaps he was only trying to protect her. Colette would never understand their relationship.

The man shot Matthew a sinister grin. "I'll see you around. If you think to marry Shelah, you might want to reconsider that notion."

Colette held a hand over her mouth to silence her gasp. What did that mean? A threat to Matthew? Or a warning?

She watched as the stranger stalked away.

He looked Amish and was dressed so, and he had spoken a bit of Pennsylvania Dutch—the Low German most Amish used to speak to each other. But something about his demeanor was off. How had he wound up here? Shelah could have invited him just to irritate Matthew. But what had Shelah done to this handsome man to make him so angry?

She watched as Matthew stood there glaring at the man's back. She so wanted to rush to him and ask questions, but they couldn't be seen together. So she gathered her baskets and slipped into the kitchen by the side door. When she heard a car cranking up in the nearby parking lot, she ran to the other side of the kitchen and watched out the window as a small blue vehicle sped away.

A blue sports car with a dent in one of the front fenders.

CHAPTER FOURTEEN

Over the next few hours, Colette didn't have time to think about the stranger. He'd left in a car, so that meant he wasn't really Amish. And he looked too old to be on his Rumspringa. She searched for Matthew to tell him about the car. When she spotted him off by himself, she grabbed a cup of hot chocolate and hurried toward him.

"Matthew?"

He whirled to face her. "Hi. Nice of you to find time to speak to me."

"I don't have much time. I need to tell you something."

She handed him the cup and quickly glanced around.

"What is it?" He seemed as on edge as she felt, his eyes darting here and there.

"The man—"

"Matthew, there you are."

Shelah.

"Are you two hiding out? That's not proper. Matthew, you promised me a hayride. It's getting late—can we go now?"

Matthew turned back to Colette. "Is this urgent?"

"Everything is urgent with her," Shelah said, her hand on his arm.

Colette knew if she blurted this news out in front of Shelah, the other woman would twist her words. She'd have to find another time to explain to Matthew. "It was nothing. Just wanted to say hi."

Shelah gave Matthew a demanding glance. He looked at Colette, his frown full of questions and regret. "*Denke* for the hot chocolate."

Shelah clung to him. The other woman looked shocked and frightened. Perhaps because of that strange man.

Colette rushed back inside the inn, her mind whirling.

Jonah walked by while she was refilling a cookie tray. Mamm and Kathleen were sitting in the big lobby by the fire, talking to Aenti Miriam, who'd taken a day off to visit. Colette could hear them chattering and laughing.

Jonah scanned the room. "Why do you have that stern look on your face?"

Colette nodded toward Matthew and Shelah. "That. She is too touchy-feely, ain't so?"

Jonah glanced out to where Matthew was helping Shelah up on the hayride wagon full of other young people. "You could say that."

It irked her soul to see them together, but she had no choice but to stay away from Matthew. And because she couldn't warn Mattie about the man and the blue car, she felt angry and sad.

She grabbed her brother-in-law's jacket sleeve. "I need to tell someone what I saw today."

Jonah looked down at her, a touch of panic in his eyes. Men never liked drama. "And I'm guessing that would be me?"

"You're the former detective," she pointed out. Then she told him about the mysterious man who'd implied he knew Shelah. "He told Mattie he needed to talk to her, but she ran away like a hen running from becoming Sunday dinner."

"Interesting," Jonah said, his dark blue eyes burning with curiosity. "Describe the man."

She gave him the details. "He had a fresh haircut—an *Englisch* style, but he knew some of our language. Stood out like a pigeon hanging out with doves."

Jonah rubbed his beard. "Maybe she met him since she's been here? She did sit in the lobby by the fire a lot all week. Or at the hospital?"

"I wondered the same, because there is no way she's had time to meet him anywhere else," Colette admitted. Then she whirled to face Jonah, almost taking the cookie tray with her. "Jonah, Matthew said he remembered a light blue sports car hitting the buggy the other night."

"*Ja*, he did say that. What's that got to do with this man?"

"He drove off in a small fancy blue car. A car with a big dent on one of the front fenders."

"Now we're getting somewhere," Jonah said. "So you think this man you saw today could also have been the person who struck Matthew's buggy that night?"

"That's what I'm wondering," she said. "He'd be stupid to keep driving that car, but if he's desperate to see Shelah, he might not care."

"And he probably doesn't realize who was driving the buggy he sideswiped or that anyone was in the covered back seat."

"That's possible, too." Then she bobbed her head. "See, that's why I'm telling you. Your instincts are usually *gut*."

Jonah lifted his chin. "Appreciate your confidence."

Colette went on, hope soaring inside her. "You need to

talk to Matthew to see how he describes the car, but I'm sure it was the same one. We don't see that kind of car around here every day." Then she went back to the window where she'd seen the car. "He did park it away from the main parking area. Over by the side of the house, near the kitchen. If I hadn't heard him starting it, no one would have seen it or known he'd driven it here."

Jonah's brow furrowed. "If it was a sports car, it probably was lightweight and wouldn't have great traction in the snow and ice."

"And that would make it fishtail toward the buggy," she added, her heart pumping. "Jonah, what could Shelah and that man possibly have in common?"

Jonah crossed his massive arms. "One thing, my little sister. Only one thing. Money. Or the craving for money." He studied the surroundings again, then looked back at Colette. "It could be that car hit the buggy on purpose. Like I said, money."

"You mean such as money from an inheritance and a big estate." Colette put a hand to her mouth. "Mattie could be in danger." She started toward the door. "We have to warn him."

Jonah tugged her back. "Not you. Me. You stay away from him. If this man is dangerous, all the more reason for you and Matthew to stay apart."

Colette didn't like that notion, but she'd do anything to protect Matthew. "Find out for me, please."

Jonah touched her arm. "I'll do my best." Then he leaned in. "Meantime, do not mention this to anyone. The more people who know, the more danger for all."

Colette couldn't speak, so she only nodded. Was this how Abigail had felt when Jonah had regained his memory and told her his true identity? Helpless, scared, confused, worried, and hopeful all at the same time?

She sank down on a counter stool and caught her breath. Jonah marched back outside, and then with shaky hands, Colette took the tray of warm cookies out to the few people still remaining. Their plans to introduce Shelah to several young men had failed, and Colette had witnessed something much more concerning.

Someone Shelah already knew had crashed the party, and Shelah had not liked that at all. This could be the start of finally finding out the secret she held over Mattie's head. Despite the danger involved, there was hope on the horizon.

As fate would have it, Colette ran into Shelah when she went back outside to help clean up. Though she'd had a nice time initially, now she only wanted to go up to her room to work on her quilt. But she had to get past Shelah first.

The other woman came hurrying toward her like a big burgundy moth. "Colette, have you seen Matthew?"

Colette stared at Shelah. Didn't she realize Colette was the last person she should ask about Mattie's whereabouts? But Shelah shifted on her boots and waited, her expression bordering on frantic.

Which caused Colette great concern. Where was Matthew?

"I saw him around earlier, but I have not talked to him since I brought him the hot chocolate," she replied. Keeping the panic out of her voice, she added, "As you well know, we have parted ways."

Shelah's expression showed genuine concern, causing Colette to wonder if she was worried for Matthew's sake or her own. "I need to talk to him." Shelah grabbed Colette's hand. "I know he still cares for you, and earlier I thought maybe he'd tried to speak to you, even though you are no longer together."

"*Neh*, I saw him alone and I sought him out—but just to say hi and give him a drink. Nothing more."

Shelah did some serious hand-wringing, and she had a look of fear and desperation in her eyes. Maybe if Colette listened, she could learn some useful information to help Jonah find the truth. "What's wrong?"

"I think he's avoiding me," Shelah said. "I can't find him anywhere."

"But you two seemed to be enjoying the frolic. I saw you leave together for the hayride."

"We did, but he barely talked to me. I was forced to find others to have a conversation with, and it was cold and dreary. I would have rather been alone with him. I thought we'd made progress and then . . ." Shelah stopped and sank down on a chair by one of the still-smoldering firepits. "Matthew got jealous earlier because one of the boys attending the frolic wanted to talk to me in private."

"Oh, I see." Colette went along with her. The man she'd seen was no boy. "You mean on the hayride?"

"*Neh* . . . before. A man I talked to briefly one day when Kathleen and I were in town."

"You and Kathleen went to town recently?" Impossible, since Shelah had been in the hospital and then an invalid confined to the inn. But who was Colette to question her? "So you talked to a man there?"

"*Ja*, while we were in a department store."

Hmmm. The nearest department store was miles away, and what man would have been hanging around a department store? "I see. Was it that tall man with the short haircut? Did you invite him here?"

"Oh, you saw him?" Shelah actually blushed. "*Neh*, I did not invite him here, but he showed up today, hoping to visit with me."

The woman was lying. Colette knew this, but she had to pretend to accept the explanation. Gritting her teeth, she sat down beside Shelah. "Do you care about this man?"

Shelah's gaze lifted and then went down and to the right. "I don't know him that well. He meant no harm coming to find me, but I did not invite him or expect him today. I don't want that man and Matthew to come to blows." She heaved a dramatic sigh. "Matthew and I make a perfect match. Saul saw that."

"Did he now? Did Saul call Matthew to his side to bring you two together?"

"I believe so." Shelah bobbed her head so fast, Colette expected her neck to pop. "I mean, once I explained to him how compatible we were and that we were growing close. You know—"

"I'm beginning to understand," Colette replied.

Shelah hadn't just approached her to ask about Matthew. She also wanted to make a point with Colette.

Colette pasted a smile on her face and gave Shelah what she hoped was a neutral glance. "Matthew is not the jealous type." Even though Colette had enjoyed seeing him squirm while he stared at her each time she had talked to other men today. "He is kind and considerate, but he won't back down from anyone, as you well should know."

Shelah stared at her. "I haven't stopped to consider his temperament. But I am worried."

"About Matthew, or about this man?"

"Both. I'd never do that to Matthew. I want to marry him."

"Do what, Shelah?"

Again, a blush and a sigh. "Uh, flirt with others. Entice other men, you know. I only have eyes for Matthew."

"So we've all heard and seen. Shelah, that's just what happened to Matthew and me, don't you see? You enticed a man who was already committed to another woman."

That ended the conversation. Shelah stood and shook out her skirt. "I am cold and tired. I hope Matthew will visit me before he goes home. If you see him, please tell him that."

"Oh, I will," Colette replied, anger making her want to stop this woman in her tracks. "I'll make every effort to find him."

Shelah's expression changed from fear and worry to a shrewd, hard glare. "He brought me here for a reason, and you should accept that. We will be married."

"If you say so," Colette replied, her fingernails cutting into her palms as she held herself in check. "And if it's *Gott*'s will."

Shelah huffed. "Sometimes, we have to follow our own will."

Colette watched as Shelah lifted her skirt and hurried toward the inn. Once she was out of sight, Colette dropped what she was doing and went in search of Mattie. What if he was hurt or worse? She had to find him. If she told him what she'd seen and heard today, she would look like a jealous ninny. But he should be aware of Shelah's shenanigans.

She only wanted to make sure he was safe. So she left the tablecloths she'd gathered and started searching.

When she heard men laughing from the direction of the stables, she followed the echo toward the back of the barn and found Jonah, Levi, and Daed gathered around a makeshift firepit.

"We're in trouble now," Jonah teased. "A female has entered our secret spot."

"It's hard not to find you all," she retorted. "I heard you all the way up the alley."

Daed gave her a soft smile. "Colette, you have fire in your eyes."

"I was looking for—Mamm," she replied. "I thought maybe she and Kathleen had taken a walk to see the horses."

Jonah, who was sensitive to the undercurrents around him, stared at her. "I think Kathleen is back at the inn and Sarah walked home with Abigail and Eliza. I'm on my way home. I'll walk with you."

"Denke," she said. "I want to go inside and get warm."

"I'll get Abe home in a bit," Levi said as if he understood.

"Denke."

Jonah nodded to Levi; he and Daed were silent as they watched Jonah and her walk away from the stables.

Had Jonah told them what she'd seen today?

CHAPTER FIFTEEN

"What's up?" Jonah asked, glancing back toward the barn and stables. "Did you find out something else?"

Colette looked up at her brother-in-law. "Did you tell Daed and Levi about what I saw?"

Jonah gave her a look that almost became an eye roll. But he shook his head. "I'm not telling a thing until I have proof. I don't want rumors to get started, or Shelah to find out we're checking up on her friend."

Jonah knew how to keep secrets. It had once been part of his job. She wondered now how much he'd already figured out regarding Matthew and Shelah.

"She knows him," Colette said. "She came looking for Matthew, and after I questioned her, she admitted she knew the man but didn't want him here. She claims they met in town at a department store. I don't believe that at all, since the township docsn't have what I'd call a department store. The man can't be Amish, because he's driving that fancy car. Or maybe he's left for the outside world and wants her to be with him? Have you seen Matthew? I think he's upset about the confrontation they had earlier. Shelah hinted that he was jealous, which is ridiculous."

Jonah absorbed that revelation in silence. "He left a little while ago. Said he wanted to check on his *mamm*. She wasn't feeling well this morning."

Jonah guided her over a patch of snow, but Colette stopped and waited for him to continue. "He did seem down. Looked weary. I'm sure he wants this burden off his back."

Colette bobbed her head. "The inheritance or Shelah or both?"

"I'd say both. Great wealth may be a blessing, but we know most Amish are not wealthy, and if they are, they tend to keep it to themselves and serve the community. His *onkel* could have left Matthew with more than he bargained for. If Shelah knew of something Saul was doing illegally, that might be what she's threatening Matthew with. Marry her or she tells all."

Colette let that possibility soak in. "A form of blackmail that would leave Mattie in shame if word got out."

"Exactly."

"Why not just ask him for money and then go her merry way?"

Jonah's expression darkened. "Oh, she won't stop at money, Colette. She wants it all. And it may be that the man she claims to have just met is her partner in crime."

Colette let out a huff of shock. "You think they already knew each other back in Missouri? And they are working together? That's too devious for words."

"I fear Shelah is using her Rumspringa for more than walking out with boys."

Colette lifted her head, wondering how much Jonah really knew. "I should go and visit Agnes. I haven't been over to their home in a long time. I'll go tomorrow and take food as an excuse. Maybe she can shed some light on this situation. I know for a fact Shelah goes to visit there often, trying to spend time with Matthew." She stopped and put her hands on her hips. "If she is lying and trying to win him over to gain access to Saul's bank account, I will fight her." She started walking again. "I should warn Mattie."

Jonah looked up as they reached the cottage. "Do not repeat what you saw or heard. These two could be dangerous to both Matthew and you. If she's aiming to marry him and swindle him out of his inheritance, this could turn very ugly, very quickly. It's best that Matthew knows nothing right now. If he confronts Shelah, she might run to her friend, and that could make things worse."

"But how could she gain the inheritance if they're married?" Colette asked. When Jonah didn't say anything, she gasped. "She'd become a widow one day?"

He nodded, his expression grim. "I'm afraid so. But we have no proof. So do not get Matthew involved in our conspiracy theories for now."

"Get proof," Colette said, shivering. "Whatever you need to do, Jonah. I know you have friends in the *Englisch* world who can find out the truth, right?"

"I will do my best." Then he shot her the Jonah frown. "Do not do anything on your own, Colette. There could be more to this than any of us know."

"I won't." Now she felt certain sure Jonah knew something she didn't. But she wouldn't try to force it out of him. He was one of the few people who could discover the whole truth.

"*Gut*, because your sisters and Sarah and Abe would have my hide, understand?"

"Got it. I won't do anything. How could I? I don't have your expertise or connections."

"And that's what scares me the most," Jonah replied in a wry tone.

He watched her open the door into the house, then turned to go home to Abigail and Jon. Colette walked to the front window and stared up at the inn, toward the big corner room occupied by Kathleen and Shelah. Did she plan to marry Mattie and then do him harm so she could take over Saul's estate?

Colette stood, her hand touching the glass, her eyes on the lamplight coming from that room, her prayers silent but steady. When she saw a dark shadow passing by the window, she stepped back.

Not out of fear. But because she wanted to catch this woman in her web of lies. And she'd do some serious praying for *Gott* to show her the best way to do so. Because she had not *promised* Jonah she'd stay out of it.

If she heard or saw something, she'd act.

Matthew walked in to find his *mamm* mending shirts. How many times had he come through the door to find her in her favorite rocker, stitching up tears and patching up pants. Now that he'd inherited a vast, thriving property, she wouldn't need to mend anymore. But he couldn't say that to her.

It was Saul's property, and Saul had not been the kind man everyone in his community thought. He'd tried to pay his way out of answering for his sins.

"*Gut*, you're home," Mamm said with a tired smile. "Daed and the boys are finishing up chores. I've warmed up some white chicken chili for supper."

"I'll go help," he said, too tired to think about everything.

"Stay with me," Mamm said in a tone that brooked no protest. "We need to talk."

"Are you feeling better?" he asked as he warmed his hands by the stovepipe.

"I haven't felt well since the day you and I talked about Saul," Mamm said. "We need to tell your *daed*, Matthew. It's the only way we can move forward."

"Not yet, Mamm," he replied in a low voice, planning to make everyone think he and Colette were finished. "I know that would stop Shelah's demands, but not yet. Today Colette made it clear she wants nothing to do with me, so maybe I should just marry Shelah and take over Saul's place. I can send money home—"

"*Neh!*" His mother dropped her sewing. "I will not take a dime of that man's money. He came close to ruining my life and my marriage. Even in death, he haunts me. I won't have it."

Matthew went to her. "I'm sorry. I never considered how this must make you feel. Saul had everything and yet he strayed from his faith. He gave to the community to clear his soul of sins, but he refused to confess his sins. He never had what we've had though, Mamm. He didn't have a family; he never knew real love. He just grabbed the first person he found who needed a family—Shelah. He used her as a shield to prove he was a *gut* man, and yet he treated Kathleen like a maid and never once taught Shelah the ways of our beliefs. He sheltered her and let her run wild. That is why she's so broken and difficult today."

Tears misted Mamm's eyes. "And you—look at you today, my son. A *gut* man who has always had a kind heart. Your *daed* and I raised you and your *bruders* with the Old Order teachings. You've never once strayed. You could have taken advantage of Shelah, as Saul took advantage of me. But instead, you are caught between duty and love. Saul accounted to no one, but you are trying to appease everyone. Let it all go. We will tell your father."

"I will, I promise," Matthew said. "But if I can get Shelah to leave, we won't need to tell him anything. He need never know."

"But I'll know," Mamm said. "That is my sin—not being honest from the beginning. I let Saul manipulate me and control me and he did this one last thing, knowing it would ruin our lives. From the grave, that man taunts me."

"I'll figure this out," Matthew said. "I've spoken to Abe, and we are to talk to the bishop. Wait for a while longer and try not to worry. I'm going to find a way for us."

Agnes smiled at her son. "I believe you will, but you let me know the day you are ready. I will be there, and I will tell Titus what happened so long ago. Saul did give me one *gut* thing, Matthew. And that is you."

"I love you, Mamm," he said, his own eyes burning. "I love you and Daed and my annoying *bruders*, too. Always remember that."

Mamm smiled and wiped her eyes. "Get on out there, then, and help. I'll have corn bread ready with the soup."

Matthew stood and swallowed the lump in his throat. "I just hate what I've had to do to Colette."

"Maybe you should start with her," Mamm suggested. "Go to her and be honest, son."

"I'm going to try. If she'll listen."

Matthew went out to the barn to help finish the chores. Daed gave him a quizzical glance, then told the boys to put away the shovels and buckets.

While the boys put their tools away, Matthew helped his *daed* finish the feedings and make sure the animals had clean straw. They worked in silence. Daed had never been a big talker. So different from Saul—the man who'd sired him. The shock of that still hit Matthew with a lightning-bolt clash each time he thought of it. Nonetheless, the man working beside him now was his true father. And he had *Gott*. He sometimes wished he'd never found out the truth of how he'd been brought into the world. A horrible act, an assault on his married mother. How she must have suffered. He wanted to punch something, but he had to remind himself Saul was dead and gone now. And thankfully, Matthew had been taught to respect women.

"Is Mamm feeling better?" Daed finally asked. "She's been quiet lately."

Matthew couldn't lie to the man he considered his *daed*. "I think she's worried about me and what I plan to do. Shelah thinks it's time for us to go back to Missouri."

Daed gave him a narrow-eyed stare. "Is Shelah making your decisions these days?"

"*Neh*. I have told her I won't go back until after Christmas. I need to help out here, and the inn is so busy these days."

"You do know you don't have to work there anymore, don't you?"

Matthew glanced over at his *daed*. Titus stood ramrod straight, one foot pressed against the wooden door of Sawdust's stall.

"I'm not sure what I know," he finally said. "I thought Colette and I would be planning our marriage by now, but that's not going to happen. Now I've inherited a house too big for one person, and too far away to take care of from here. I could give it to you and Mamm, but she wants to stay here. You all belong here, same as me."

Daed studied Matthew, his dark eyes searching. "What if you took Colette there?"

"I don't think she'd go. Even if Shelah won't be living in the big house, she'd be on the property. I don't think Colette would handle that very well. Nor Shelah."

"My brother—always boisterous and underhanded. He was a ladies' man, but he never married. Yet he takes in this young girl and lets her live in his home most of her life." Daed shook his head. "Do you think she could be his child?"

Matthew almost choked, but he cleared his throat. "Kathleen said she belonged to friends of his—a couple he'd been close to and cared about. When they died, he was worried about Shelah, who was only a few years old. For some reason, he took her and Kathleen in, or they might be living in poverty."

"And Shelah wants to keep her fancy way of life?"

"I think so," Matthew admitted. "I've been holding off on going through with the marriage for that reason and, well, because I love Colette. She wants the place and the money and her position in life more than she wants to be with me." He shrugged and looked back at his giggling brothers chasing a barn cat. "She does not love me."

He almost told his *daed* about the man who'd crashed the frolic today, but something held him back. He didn't want to involve his parents in his problems any more than necessary. Shelah was a pretty girl, so maybe the stranger had thought he'd like to get to know her better. It could be that simple. Shelah did like to flirt, but Matthew had a bad feeling about the situation. He had to wonder what was really going on between that strange man and Shelah.

"What do you think I should do?" he finally asked. "I'm not sure I want that much money or obligation. I was content before this, and I can be content again." Then he pivoted and leaned against the stall so he could face his father. "This should be your inheritance anyway. You are his only brother."

"*Neh*," Daed replied with almost as much animosity as Mamm. "Saul and I never got along. He was five years older than me, and he liked to push me around. We had twin sisters, but they died at birth."

Matthew stared at Titus. "I never knew that."

"We didn't talk about it much. It almost killed our sweet *mamm*. She never got over it and never had any more children. And I'm afraid Saul and I didn't measure up to her hopes. But she tried to love us." Daed let out a sigh. "I do believe that loss might be why Saul took to Shelah so much. He wanted to make up for losing our sisters. He could be so kind at times; other times not so much. He lived here for a while, but after our parents both died, and he and I had a few disagreements, he moved on. We just never mended our fences, so I can't accept his fortune. He was wise to pass it to you, son. You'll do well by Saul and us, I know. I don't need his money. You can put it to *gut* use."

"I never knew about the twin sisters," Matthew said again. "Saul never mentioned them." But then, he'd never known his *daed*'s side of the family either. His paternal grandparents had both passed on a few years apart from each other, not long after Matthew had been born.

"We didn't talk much about Beth and Becky," Daed said, his tone low. "My *mamm* couldn't deal with it. I think she and Saul had some of the same traits. She was bitter and what we'd call depressed after that horrible loss. But she loved your *grossdaddi* and tried very hard to love Saul and me."

"I'm sorry to hear this, Daed," Matthew said. "It gives me a better understanding of Saul's moods and his character. You must have taken after Grossdaddi, then."

Daed chuckled. "I could have. He was a quiet man, but he could be so funny at times. I'd like to believe I gained his kindness and integrity."

"You did, I believe. I understand why you can't take Saul's fortune. You have all that matters right here, ain't so?"

Titus nodded. "That is the truth of it."

While they had a sturdy home and a fair amount of security, Matthew could give his parents so much more now. This old barn needed repairs, and the house could be tightened up. Daed had built a strong home, a nice foursquare that Mamm loved. Matthew had never once compared their life to anyone else's before.

Now he'd had a taste of an easier way of living, but, oh, how he longed for the old way, for this home and his parents happy, his brothers laughing, and he and Colette walking hand in hand. That had been his dream, an inheritance he'd gladly take because he knew *Gott* had brought them together, finally.

But why had they been broken apart?

"Matthew?"

He looked up to find Daed staring at him. "I didn't mean to be unkind. You gave me a generous offer, but one I must decline. You will figure out why *Gott* brought you to this place, and you will understand that things happen in His own *gut* time, not ours. But no matter, all wrongs can be righted, and all sins can be revealed. *Gott*'s will, remember?"

Matthew got a feeling, a nudge deep inside his soul, maybe a message that his *daed* wanted him to hear without actually saying the words. "Are you telling me there is a reason Saul left everything to me? A reason that Colette and I have to be apart for a while, a reason why I'm so hurt and confused and overwhelmed when I only want to go and find my girl and tell her I have always and will always love her?"

Daed smiled a soft, bittersweet smile. "*Ja*, that is what I'm telling you. Secrets and lies tend to fester, and one day, they have to be attended to. Saul had a lot of secrets and lies, and I think, in his own way, he wanted them all to be attended to because he realized he was dying—dying a lonely, bitter old man with no wife or brother there holding his hand. I hope he prayed and turned back to the Lord before he passed on. I hope whatever secrets he held have now been cleared and resolved. You are the key to this, Matthew. And *Gott* will show you the way."

Matthew stood staring at his *daed*, his mind whirling. Did Daed know more than he was letting on? Was that what he was trying to say?

CHAPTER SIXTEEN

The next night, Colette studied her quilt again. She'd spread it out on the bed so she could see the overall view. In all the different scenes, her heart spotted the truth. She couldn't pretend she didn't care about Mattie. She would, always. So she must find out what Shelah and that man were up to, for Matthew's sake. His family could use the money from Saul's estate, and if she knew Matthew, he'd make sure Shelah and Kathleen were provided for, too.

Her visit with Agnes would have to wait. She'd seen Kathleen and Shelah leaving in one of the inn's buggies earlier. Henry had told her they were going to see Matthew's folks. She'd watched all day, but they'd only returned at dusk. Aggravated, she'd come into her bedroom to find some quiet time.

This quilt showed her love for Matthew, beginning in their growing-up years and stretching out into adulthood. Their love shined through each stitch. Her *mamm* and sisters had guided her hands on this one. She planned to put a pretty poinsettia panel in the middle. She and Matthew always set out the poinsettias every Christmas. The lobby and lounge of the inn were now full of them, and they'd put one in each room, some a creamy white and some rich red. It was frustrating to see everything she and Matthew had been through together, knowing they might not be together again.

Abby had helped her with a panel depicting the restaurant—two faceless figures in front of a brown buffet with a vase of flowers centered near the pies and cakes. She'd worked side by side with Mattie for years now. Why hadn't she seen what was right in front of her sooner?

They could have been married already.

She'd add the frolic, showing a lot of faceless men and women mingling, with one man off to the side, and one woman off to the other side. Their pretend breakup.

She stood there, thinking of Shelah and that strange man, wondering if Jonah's hunch could be true. Maybe if she befriended Shelah, the other woman would talk. She'd done that the other night after the frolic. Shelah needed a friend, but why did Colette have to be that friend?

To get to the truth, if nothing else.

She'd pray on that. Right now, she only wanted to study her quilt and cherish her memories. Memories she'd taken for granted for too long now.

Her bedroom door opened without a knock and in walked Abigail and Eliza, her two married, dreamy-eyed sisters.

"I didn't say you two could visit tonight."

"Do we need an invitation?" Eliza asked as she touched a hand to the quilt. "Oh, this is lovely, Colette. So festive."

"Festive? My whole crumbling life laid out in each panel, and you find it festive?"

"It has Christmas colors," Eliza said with a jutting lip.

"And anyone who has a brain can see you and Mattie belong together."

"How? His name is not on the quilt."

Abigail let out a huff. "*Neh*, but your style is all over it, and if a person knows you two, they'd see him, too, in these scenes. You've done a lovely job. That cinnamon bun panel looks delicious."

She stopped fretting and told her sisters about how she wanted to add a frolic panel.

"That's a great idea," Abigail said. "I'll make a sketch and we'll get busy on that. You need to have it done by next week. We can display it along with the other Christmas quilts."

"I'm not sure I want to display it," Colette said. "I'd rather keep it to myself. Or give it to Agnes."

"Like I wanted to give mine to Connie," Eliza reminded them. "But she insisted I keep it."

"And I still have mine," Abigail said. "These memories are so precious."

"Precious, *ja*," Colette replied as her sisters touched the quilt and smiled. "But for my eyes only."

"Matthew should see it."

"Shelah should see it."

"We should display it."

"Stop," she finally said as her sisters threw out comments as if pitching softballs. "I don't know why I started it. Mattie still hasn't told me what Shelah has on him. He'll probably do the right thing and marry her, and they can be miserable together the rest of their days."

"What a lovely story," Abigail said. "You know you don't want that."

"It's not about what I want—it's about what Mattie has to do."

"He's made it clear he doesn't love her," Eliza reminded her.

"And yet, she is still here." Colette moved away from the quilt and went to the window. "I think of him every night. Then I glance toward the inn and think of her." She twisted away and turned toward her sisters. "I'm going to befriend her."

Abigail and Eliza sent out speaking looks to each other that translated to *bad idea*.

"Do you think that's wise?" Abigail asked.

"I think that might involve harsh words and . . . a lot of dangerous complications," Eliza added.

"I'm not going to hurt the woman," Colette explained. "She chattered away to me last night, as if she'd never been a wedge between Mattie and me. The woman is desperate and lonely, so what better time to befriend her?"

"Ah, and find out what secrets she knows?" Abigail walked to the window and nodded. "I see. Are you sure you're ready for that?"

"I'm ready for whatever comes next," Colette said. "No matter what happens between Matthew Mueller and me, I want to find out the truth. If he loves her, I could deal with that. But if he's just doing his duty and is willing to give me up to marry her and live comfortably on Saul's money, it will be much harder to accept."

"Love is never easy," Eliza said with the wisdom of a now-married woman.

"That is the truth," Abigail added.

"You two are well and happy," Colette snapped. "I'm going to be bitter and alone, babysitting your children."

"You will find the truth." Abigail touched a finger to the quilt again. "Or display this and everyone will see the truth, right here. Mamm always says every quilt has a story, and we three should know that firsthand."

Colette wiped her eyes. "This quilt does tell the truth. But it won't matter if he is forced to do her bidding."

"You want him to fight for you, ain't so?" Abigail asked.

"I do," Colette admitted. "And I believe he is trying to do that in his own way. But I am sorely impatient."

"We've never noticed that about you," Eliza whispered.

They all smiled, and then they hugged each other, forming a circle.

Colette held tight and whispered, "I'm putting this moment on the quilt, too."

Then they all started giggling.

She loved her sisters. Maybe babysitting wouldn't be so bad after all.

The next day, Colette walked into the schoolroom and found the men painting the props they'd finished building. The plywood cutouts did look like trees, painted with brown trunks and bright green branches. Maggie had suggested putting a bright red ribbon cutout on top of each tree.

Colette could paint those and attach them to the trees. That way the ribbons could be used for other festive events, too.

Matthew came in a few minutes after she'd set out the muffins and coffee she'd prepared. He grabbed an oatmeal muffin and poured himself a cup of coffee from the big thermos she'd filled at the inn.

"This is looking nice," he said to the room. "We did *gut* work. Those trees look real."

Colette gave him a quick glance. His gaze hit her and moved on. Awkward, but necessary. Not a time to bring up her suspicions about Shelah.

Linda grinned. "*Gut*, because we only have a few days to finish. I don't know where this month has gone."

"I do," Colette murmured under her breath.

Matthew walked up behind her. "Talking to yourself?"

"Maybe." She kept painting while she tried to ignore his clean pine scent and his nearness. Once, she'd have turned and teased and tormented him. Now she didn't have the stomach for such frivolous play. "This has been the worst December of my life."

"Too much snow," someone said, misunderstanding her pain.

"Too much of everything," she retorted. "I have always loved a quiet, peaceful Christmas." She shot Matthew a glance on that note. "But this year has been chaotic and full of worry."

"Then you need to remember the reason we're here," Linda said, smiling. "Peace on earth; goodwill toward men."

"All men?" Colette asked with a hint of snark. Then she lowered her head. "I'm sorry. I shouldn't make light of the birth of our Lord."

"*Neh*, you should not," Linda's husband replied. But he did give her an understanding smile.

The talk moved to how blessed everyone was, and how the scholars would honor the Lord in songs and speeches. Colette prayed for clarity and that she wouldn't do harm. What else could she do—*Gott* saw her sins and knew her heart.

They painted in silence for a while. Matthew left her, his expression caught between a scowl and impatience. But that was the way of it for now. They couldn't appear to be together, and yet, they weren't really apart.

When they'd finished the scenery and put all the trees up as a backdrop behind the bleachers they'd brought in for practice sessions, Linda suggested a break for more muffins before they cleaned up and went back home.

Matthew came toward Colette. "I'm planning to talk to the bishop today."

"I see. Please explain to him all the things you can't explain to me."

"I plan to have a heart-to-heart with him."

"About time."

"You're enjoying this, aren't you?"

"Helping the scholars, *ja*."

"Tormenting me, just as always."

She pivoted to stare up at him. Why did he seem taller now, and when had his chest become so broad? Could a boy become a man over a few months? This one had. But he'd done it while he was away. Away from her. Had she been holding him back? Had he grown tired of her once he had Saul's estate and Shelah's attention? Had there been something between Shelah and him that Mattie was now trying to deny? Would she ever know the truth?

"I did torment you a lot, didn't I?" she said, her tone low and only for his ears. "I wasted years tormenting you and taking you for granted. My Mattie, always there right by my side, always helping me, hindering me, teasing me. Loving me."

She glanced up and realized the whole room had heard her words. Colette blushed and cleared her throat, her voice rising. "But all that is over now. We came here to help, so let's get this place cleaned up and ready. The singing is coming up soon, after all. And then Christmas. Like I said, December has been one long month."

Matthew began moving chairs and rearranging the bleachers so the backdrop could be seen. He came by with a stack of chairs. "You need to know, I loved your torments. I lived for you to see me, flirt with me, fight with me, or have *kaffe* and share a muffin with me. Because I knew all along that you cared. You were just afraid to show it. And you're afraid now. I understand that. But it's not over yet, Colette. Not by a long shot."

He finished placing the chairs, then turned and walked out the door.

Colette stared after him. Maggie came up and started putting away the food. "I always thought you two would be together. This news about your breakup is unsettling. I'd hate to see Matthew move away, and from what I've seen of Shelah, I can say without a doubt—she is not his type."

"*Denke,*" Colette replied, holding back tears. "As my folks keep telling me, *Gott*'s will, not mine. I have to let him go."

Maggie nodded. "I hope he comes to his senses before it's too late."

Colette didn't respond to that. But in her head, she screamed, "I hope so, too." And she hoped she'd be able to talk to him and tell him about the stranger and his sports car, so they could all rejoice and enjoy Christmas.

Matthew walked into Bishop Zook's home and waited in the big parlor for Abe to arrive. John Zook came in from the back and entered the parlor a few minutes after

Matthew. His wife Nan brought in cookies and hot apple cider, then left the men alone.

Matthew was too agitated to eat. He wanted to get this over with. He knew John Zook to be a kind man, but this was an unusual situation. A troubling situation.

John sank down in a big stuffed chair and nodded. "Matthew Mueller, I was wondering when we'd have this talk. Seems you've come home with a heavy load on your heart."

A knock at the door brought a short reprieve. Abe came in and nodded to them. Soon the three of them were seated and fed.

"Now, tell me everything," John said. "Start at the beginning and be honest with me. Completely honest."

Matthew hung his head. He dreaded this, but at least Abe was here for support. No matter. Matthew would have to do what the bishop suggested. He just prayed it would all come right in the end.

An hour later, Matthew and Abe walked out of the bishop's home, both lost in thought.

"I don't know how to explain this to Colette," Matthew said. "But John made his decision."

Abe glanced out at the horizon. "I had a feeling he'd tell you that you must honor your obligation to your biological father. But I was hoping he'd be lenient when he learned the truth."

"The truth is I'm Saul's only child, and he's left me his place. I must go back there and take care of it. Alone."

"And what will you do about Shelah?"

"I will marry her," Matthew said, the words sounding foreign in his head. "What else can I do?" John thought Matthew should honor Saul's wishes. And that both his parents needed to know the truth. *Honesty.* The family could heal with honesty.

Matthew didn't understand why Shelah had to be a part of that.

Abe stood tugging on his beard. "Colette needs to hear this from you."

"I know." But he didn't know how he'd tell her. The bishop had listened, nodded, listened some more, and then stated that he must follow Saul's will. And he had to be truthful with his parents, too. Because he and Colette had not officially announced their engagement, nor had they come to the bishop with a *Zeugnis* to show their good standing and clear any sins, Matthew couldn't now claim he'd planned to marry Colette. Matthew had a duty to do as Saul had asked. He must marry Shelah. He'd been in the same house with her all this time. With no letter of intent showing their good standings, the bishop could not agree to let Matthew continue on with Colette when he had a woman waiting in the wings because of a deathbed promise.

"I can't believe this," Matthew said, his heart shattered. "I must marry a woman I dislike, all because I didn't write a letter to the bishop announcing my intent with Colette." He fisted his hands and looked out at the bare trees. "I wish I'd never gone to help Saul. If I'd declined, none of this would have happened."

"You would still be his heir," Abe pointed out. "That's the way of it, unless the bishop deems it otherwise."

"Everyone knew I wanted to marry Colette."

"But you two did not make it official."

"Because I had to leave."

Abe stopped him at his buggy. "I know this is hard to

accept, but Matthew, for now it's the final word. Go home and consider what you've heard."

"*Neh*, first I must find Colette, before she hears this from somebody else."

Abe nodded, turned, and climbed into his own buggy.

Matthew stood in the cold wind and realized his life would never be the same. Because Colette would not be in it anymore.

CHAPTER SEVENTEEN

Colette worked on her quilt all day. Less than two weeks until Christmas. The scholars' singing was to be held next week, but the bleachers they'd stand on had been delivered so they could do one practice here in the inn. The quilt display would remain in the inn from Sunday through the new year. Matthew had to go back to Missouri to decide what to do with Saul's estate.

Shelah would go back to Missouri with him, Kathleen acting as chaperone. No doubt, Shelah would continue trying to make Matthew marry her. The trip had to be made one way or the other, whether Shelah won or not. And Colette needed to stay out of it.

But because she would not have an opportunity to speak to Matthew, she prayed Jonah would talk to him. She could still try to find out the truth from Shelah. Then she would be able to go to Matthew, not as a jealous woman, but as someone who cared and wanted him to be safe.

So she left her quilt in the quilting room, found some chocolate snickerdoodle cookies, and put them on a pretty plate to take upstairs.

After knocking on the door to the suite, she waited for

Kathleen to open it. But Shelah stood there instead, her dark blue wool dress prim underneath a black apron. Why the woman wore an apron at all confused Colette. Shelah had never done a true day's work in her life.

"Hello," Shelah said, looking behind Colette. "Did you come alone?"

"I did," Colette replied. "Why? Are you afraid I'll attack you or something?"

"I know how you feel about Matthew. You've been so obvious about it."

"And I know how you feel about him, too."

They stared each other down for a long moment.

"I brought freshly baked cookies. We give them to all the guests." *Even those who stay here too long.*

"That was thoughtful. Kathleen is actually in the kitchen with Edith and your Aenti Miriam."

"Oh, that sounds like someone cooking up trouble," Colette said, sweeping into the room. Just as she expected, Shelah was messy. A dress lay across an armchair, and a *kapp* was crumpled on the antique dressing table. Soiled dishes were on the bistro table by the window. "I thought I'd check on you. You weren't in your usual spot in the lobby today."

"I wasn't feeling well," Shelah said as she grabbed three cookies and shoved one into her mouth. She sat down, poured a cup of tea and handed it to Colette. Then she poured herself one. "I'm bored."

"I can see," Colette said, wondering what Shelah did all day. She took a sip of the tea and tried not to grimace. Shelah must have tried to make her own. "I have books if you enjoy reading."

Shelah looked confused. "Not much." She motioned to a stack of magazines on the coffee table.

Colette tried again. "Do you knit or sew?"

"No."

"Do you have hobbies?"

"Hobbies?" Shelah shook her head and took a long sip of her tea. Then she set the teacup down and put her hands in her lap. "I'm bored. I'm waiting for Matthew. He went to talk to the bishop about our marriage."

The woman could put a spin on everything. Colette pretended she didn't care, even though her heart had felt the sting of that pointed arrow. "Oh, I see. The bishop does have to be consulted on weddings. I never got that far, unfortunately."

"You mean because Matthew had to leave and go to Missouri."

"*Ja*, that exactly," Colette replied, her smile hurting her cheeks. "And then he met you, of course."

Shelah's smile reminded Colette of a cat waiting to pounce on a mouse. "I know it must be so hard for you to accept, but I can't help that Matthew and I fell for each other so quickly. And then when Saul blessed the union, I knew it was meant to be."

"I suppose so," Colette said, thinking maybe Shelah was correct. "*Gott*'s will."

Shelah nodded, happier now. "That's it—right—*Gott*'s will." Something she had denied the other day. The woman said what she thought people expected to hear. Never the truth.

"Did you pray about this marriage to Matthew? Have you had any frolics—you know—for household goods and things for your hope chest?" *Like I have*, she wanted to scream.

Shelah shrugged. "Saul's house is completely equipped, and he had a cook."

"He is dead."

"Are you saying I might have to cook? I can, you know. I cooked for Matthew's family, several times."

Colette had heard from one of Mattie's brothers that they all got sick, but she wouldn't repeat that.

"Like three times a day," Colette replied, nonchalantly. "And the wash. Never-ending, that. Then there are the vegetables—in the spring, summer, and fall. Canning, freezing, curing, cooking. A wife's work is never done." She let out a long sigh. "And the winters—always mending clothes, and washing them, and trudging through the snow for supplies and food, or just trying to get around with children needing your attention."

Shelah looked like she might pass out. "We will have a cook and a maid."

"I have never heard of an Amish wife who has a cook and a maid," Colette retorted. "That would be luxury—frowned on, of course—but so nice."

"I'll talk to Matthew about that. He'll understand we need to keep up a certain status."

"You know what might get you out of your boredom," Colette said, standing so she wouldn't burst out laughing. "You can come down to the kitchen and tell me about some of your favorite recipes. Or better yet, I'll tell you which dishes are Matthew's favorites. We've been cooking them at the inn for years, so I know most of them by heart."

Shelah's pout became more pronounced. "I'll come up with new dishes."

"Or your cook can, I reckon."

A stark silence followed, while Colette watched Shelah's many facial expressions in amazement. Pouting, denial, refusal, concern, worry, the quick flutter of an actual thinking process.

And finally, "I guess it wouldn't hurt to try some of his favorites. I can surprise him by fixing supper here with me."

"And Kathleen," Colette said with a smile. "*Kumm*, we'll tweak a few recipes and compare notes. I'll make new recipes, perhaps for a new fellow. Like that man who came looking for you the other day. He was certainly handsome. Have you heard more from him?"

Shelah's dark eyes flashed. Colette recognized the expression immediately, because she herself knew what jealousy felt like.

Shelah smiled. "*Neh*. That was just an admirer wanting to get to know me better. He's long gone."

"I reckon so, since he left in a fancy vehicle."

"He did?"

Colette shouldn't have revealed that. "I think so. I saw a blue car leaving a few minutes after I saw him talking to Matthew."

"I wouldn't know," Shelah replied. "I don't remember any cars being around."

Colette wanted to laugh. This woman had no clue what kind of havoc she'd wreaked by insisting that Matthew should marry her. She thought she had him on a string, even while she had another man waiting in the shadows for her. Her lies and games were beginning to catch up with her. Why didn't she just go back to Missouri?

They were in the kitchen, putting biscuits in the oven, when Matthew walked in from the back hallway.

When he entered the building, both Shelah and Colette

looked up from the mess of dough and other ingredients left after they'd finished making the biscuits. No one said anything, not even Edith.

He stared at both of them standing there, and Colette's heart dropped. His expression held a weary acceptance, a tired listlessness that showed he'd lost a great battle.

"What's going on?" he asked, his voice hoarse.

Shelah beamed. "Edith and Colette are teaching me how to make biscuits. So I'll be a *gut* wife for you. The first batch should be done soon."

Matthew did not look at Shelah. His gaze hit on Colette and held. Colette wanted to run to him and ask what had happened, but she couldn't move.

Edith took over. "Colette, go check on the wash. The sheets need to be put in the dryer."

Colette tried to move but couldn't. A sense of dread hit her in her stomach. She'd never seen Matthew like this.

Aenti Miriam came in from the storeroom on the other side of the kitchen, her shrewd gaze reading the room, her keen nose sniffing the air. "I smell biscuits. Burning biscuits."

She was correct. Shelah let out a screech and grabbed a pot holder so she could get the biscuits out of the big oven. But the pot holder slipped, she burned her hand, and the biscuits went flying all over the kitchen.

Shelah screamed in pain and then she burst into tears. Edith rolled her eyes and went in search of the burn salve.

Aenti Miriam took Shelah into her arms. "There, there, it's only a burn. And ruined biscuits. Nothing more." She waved Colette and Matthew away as she pushed Shelah toward the employee bathroom. Then she held up five fingers and mouthed, "Five minutes."

They had five minutes to either plan their life together or walk away from each other forever.

The scent of charred biscuits filled the kitchen. Colette would remember that later, in her nightmares. The charred, ruined scent of burned food and her dreams going up in flames.

Colette followed Matthew through the maze of hallways until they reached a small parlor near the lobby. The staff rarely came into this room, because usually guests liked to sit here to sip coffee and read. It had a wall full of windows that looked out onto the lake and a wall full of books on the other side. Colette and her sisters had read most of the books, and often while they were growing up, any one of them could be found hidden away here.

She stared at the rows and rows of books, the muted colors ranging from black to gray to yellow, blue, red, and green. Her world, her escape. Then she glanced out at the lake, puffy with frozen pieces of ice covered in snow, so beautiful, but so stark and cold and ominous. So deceiving.

Why did he have to bring her here?

"Mattie?" She swallowed, her hand going to his arm. "Mattie, tell me, please."

Matthew had been staring out the window, too, and when he turned, she saw the truth in his misty eyes. "You have to marry her?" Colette's heart raced, the bumping of it against her ribs like a bell tolling far away. A chill went down her spine. "Mattie?"

"I'm sorry," he said, his eyes dark and filled with

sorrow, deep with regret, deep with longing. "I've made a mess of things, Colette. I'm so sorry."

Colette pulled away, shaking her head, telling herself this was a bad dream. "I can't—I don't understand. We were to be married."

Matthew stood silent for a moment. Then he gazed into her eyes. "But we didn't go to the bishop; we didn't get it all settled and clear; there was no official announcement. Bishop Zook said I must honor Saul's wishes."

She kept shaking her head. "Why?"

He reached out to her, but she backed up. "Why?"

Matthew hesitated and then whispered, "Because I now have what was once his, because she was there, and because we were in the house together."

"That makes her sound like a piece of property."

"It's not that. It's because we were familiar with each other."

"What do you mean? Nothing happened. You told me nothing happened."

He lowered his head. "I told you the truth. We were not close in that way. She kissed me once and I tried to explain. I told her about you. All about you. I told her I wanted to marry you, Colette."

Colette thought about how she'd spent the afternoon with Shelah, trying to find clues, trying to understand. How could she tell him her worries, what she and Jonah suspected, now? "She thinks she will marry you. And now, she's correct."

"Nothing about this is right," he said. "I wish—I wish I'd never gone to Missouri." He stared at his hands. "Saul kept telling me he had to right a wrong and he needed me to understand."

Colette found a chair because her legs wouldn't hold her. Her last hope had been swept away with Mattie's words. "The bishop thinks you should marry her?"

"I have no choice. Your *daed* was with me. The bishop has made his decision." He reached out to her again. "Colette?"

For a moment, Colette thought of taking him by the hand and running far away, of starting over in a new community, of having Mattie with her always. But that would be so wrong. Too wrong. Instead, she said, "I hope you know what you're doing. But more importantly, I hope you know all of what she's doing."

His expression folded into a frown. "What does that mean?"

"I don't think she's being honest with you. That man who came to the frolic—I believe he and Shelah know each other better than Shelah let on."

Matthew lifted his chin, a dark heat in his eyes. "Don't make this worse by accusing her of things she has not done," he said, the flare of anger harsh. "She explained he's just someone she met in town. She didn't want anything to do with him."

"And you believe her?"

"Shelah is a pretty, friendly woman. I've seen her charm people before."

"She has certainly charmed you."

"Colette, you need to understand. I have no choice." His eyes held torment, and his expression was filled with a weary acceptance. "I have no other choice."

He reached for her, but Colette drew back, sat down, and curled into the wing chair, trying to disappear. "Go,

Mattie. Just go and tell her the news. I—I can't be with you. Ever again."

"Colette?"

She heard the tremor in his voice, saw the anguish in his eyes, felt the heat of his heartache and his love, even if he wasn't touching her. "Go."

He looked at her, turned toward the door, and then turned back. "Colette, please."

He stood, waiting, hoping. Colette wanted with every breath in her body to go to him and hold him, but she couldn't move, she couldn't speak. Her heart was shattered into a million jagged pieces. He was going away with Shelah. She might not ever see him again. Was he so blind and weary that he refused to listen to her fears, her worries concerning him? She had no fight left.

"We were supposed to be married," she said, her voice husky and raw. "Now you need to go. You are to marry another. It's over, Matthew. Go to her."

He came back into the room. "Saul is my father. He . . . took advantage of my *mamm* shortly after my parents had married. Shelah knows this and she has threatened to tell it to everyone. The bishop says I should marry her, because Saul is my *daed* and he asked it of me, and because you and I never announced our plans to marry."

Colette sat up and stared at him, speechless, heartbroken, and unable to comprehend what he'd just told her.

Matthew gave her one last look and then he turned and left the room. Colette sat there, watching the fire, shivering, crying, holding herself against the chair.

This explained so much. So very much. And there was nothing she could do to change it. Ever.

She closed her eyes and remembered everything she'd

wanted and knew that dream would never come true now. Then she felt a hand on her shoulder and opened her eyes.

"Daed?"

Her father gathered her up in his arms and hugged her tight. "I'm so sorry," he whispered. "Let's get you home."

Colette clung to her *daed*. He took off his overcoat and wrapped it around her, then guided her out a side door. Together, they walked slowly to the cottage without speaking a word. But her tears ran hot and chilled her feverish skin, wetting his coat. She now had to bear this horrible secret, alone and broken. *How will I ever get through this?*

The lights burning inside welcomed Colette and the scents of supper cooking, candles burning, and freshly washed clothes folded and put away surrounded her, while her father's cloak surrounded her with a warmth that held her broken heart in place.

She'd be okay. She'd find a way, somehow, to get past this. She'd tried all her life to ignore Matthew Mueller and *Gott* had seen that. This had to be His will. She'd wasted time and now time had been taken from her.

She'd waited too long and wasted so many opportunities when she could have been happily loving Matthew. *Gott* had shown her the error of her ways. She'd have to live with the consequences of not seeing what had been in front of her eyes all along.

And Matthew would be far away, living with the woman his dying *onkel—neh*—his dying father had wanted him to marry.

But in her heart, she knew Matthew Mueller would always love her and she'd always love him. In her heart, her world had stopped right here, on this cold December night.

"Here we are," Daed said in his firm, sweet voice. "Home."

Colette nodded and looked up at her father. "I love you, Daed."

Abe's eyes showed the same mist hers held. "I love you, too, Dochder. We will get through this. You will survive."

For the first time in her life, Colette doubted her father's words. And that in itself showed her she needed to turn to the Lord and find her way back to her true home. She had to hold tight to her faith and her family, and her Father in heaven.

CHAPTER EIGHTEEN

"You need to get some fresh air."

"You should finish your quilt."

"Edith is asking for your help in the kitchen."

Colette glanced up from her book. *Anne of Green Gables* was far more interesting than her sisters pestering her. "If Edith is asking for me, the world must be exploding."

"Nothing has exploded yet," Abigail said as she grabbed the book and rudely closed it. "It's time for you to rejoin the world, Colette."

"I am in my own little world," she replied, waving one hand in the air. "I picked out enough books to keep my mind occupied, and I have a whole year to read them. Wait, I have the rest of my life to read, do some quilting, and find about ten cats. Remember Sabra Gleason? She died single at ninety and she had about that many cats in her house. I think they had to condemn it. Poor kitties had to be gathered and taken away."

Eliza looked at the many teacups lining Colette's dresser. "When did you become so messy?"

Colette glanced around, seeing her room through her sisters' eyes. "Messy" was an understatement. "I've been preoccupied."

"Then get unoccupied," Eliza said. "If Mamm sees this, you'll be up scrubbing floors as punishment."

Colette stood. She felt wobbly, dizzy, sick. She sank back down and gave in to the pain. Shaking her head, and wiping at her eyes, she said, "I can't believe this is happening. I can't go out there."

"You will go out there," Abigail said. "You are one of the strongest, most stubborn people I know—next to Eliza, of course."

Eliza frowned. "I'll take that as a compliment because you are correct. We're all three determined, mindful women and we have a *gut* life here. Colette, you can't stay in your room and be pitiful. Get up and get going. You still have time to find out the truth."

"The truth?" She wanted to scream. After Matthew had told her why he had to marry Shelah, Colette had taken to her room. That was two days ago. This truth she couldn't even reveal to her sisters. "The truth doesn't matter now. He is going to marry her and that's that. I have no say, and if I complain, everyone will tell me this is *Gott*'s answer and I must accept it."

"It's hard to accept," Abigail said, shaking her head. "The bishop means well, and he's trying to save our family's integrity, and Matthew's, too. He knows Saul had a big estate, and maybe he's hoping the money can help those in need here and in Missouri."

Colette gritted her teeth. "So Mattie has to marry this woman and give his riches to the poor."

"Well, when you put it like that"—Eliza shrugged—"it's horrible and *gut* all at the same time."

"I wonder what Mamm and Daed said when they found out they'd inherited the inn," Colette replied, her spirit seeming to rise out of the ashes. "Did they think,

'Oh, now we can help the poor'?" She seriously doubted Shelah would encourage such charity.

Fear for Matthew forced her to hold her tongue. He would be in serious danger, and here she lay like a fallen faceless doll.

"That's not a bad thing," Abigail replied. "And we do help the poor with our festivals and our donations, and that is a *gut* thing."

"But they *loved* each other," Colette said. "Shelah has never said she loves Matthew."

She stopped whining, whirled, and started cleaning her room. She might not be able to tell her sisters the many secrets she'd been forced to keep, but she could do something to help Matthew. Somehow. "In fact, she kept saying things like 'Mattie and I are to marry' and 'I must marry him.' She never said she loved him or truly wanted to be married to him."

Colette tossed tea leaves onto a plate and grabbed a linen napkin to cover her mess. "I think she and that man who came to the frolic are up to something, and Jonah—"

She stopped, sat back down, and stared out the window. Why could she not keep a secret?

"Jonah what?" Abigail said, her eyes blazing. "Have you dragged my husband into this? He's been acting secretive about something, so tell me."

"I told him what I saw the day of the frolic." She wished she hadn't blurted that out. She'd promised Jonah she wouldn't tell anyone. But her sisters didn't count as everyone. They were her advisers and mentors and the gatekeepers. They needed to know.

"And what did you see?" Abigail continued, her usually serene face frowning. "You'd best tell me—or tell it to Mamm and Daed."

Abigail had used that threat many times over the years. She'd never had to rat anyone out yet. Colette let out a sigh and touched her finger to a mint-green knitted doily. "He was driving a car. A blue sports car."

"That's news," Eliza said, sinking onto the bed. "You saw this?"

"Saw that and heard Matthew and this man in a heated discussion just before. I glanced out the side kitchen window when I heard a motor running. He'd parked it in a strange place, right there on the far side of the inn where delivery trucks usually park."

"He wanted to hide it," Abigail said. "Okay, so you spoke to Jonah. What did he say and what is he going to do?"

"He said he has friends still—the *locals*—who can check such things. Look for dents in the car. I saw a dent that day. And I remembered Mattie telling me the car that hit the buggy was blue and small. He only got a flash of it before it sped away."

Eliza gasped and grabbed Colette's hand. "Have you said anything to Shelah about this car?"

"I inadvertently told her the man was driving a car when he left the frolic, but I caught myself and didn't say what color or anything else. She denied knowing anything about a car, but she got very nervous all the same. She implied she met the man in town and he crashed the frolic, knowing she'd be there."

"I don't believe a word of that," Eliza said.

"I didn't either," Colette replied. "Jonah told me to stay out of it, but I did try to befriend her to get information. The woman is a fountain of information—about herself."

"That is the truth," Abby said. "She splutters on and on

about her hair, her clothes, the huge house Saul left to her and Matthew—" Abby stopped. "I'm sorry."

Colette swallowed her self-pity. "She did go on about such. She twists her version of everything to suit her needs." Colette was bursting to blurt out the real reason Matthew had to marry Shelah, but she would not reveal that. He was right. It could ruin his family. She didn't want that kind of guilt on her conscience.

Thankfully, her sisters were too caught up in what she had revealed already to see her distress.

Eliza got up and walked around. "You should clean up, get back out there, and try to find out more information. Or better yet, Abby and I can talk to Shelah and Mamm can talk more to Kathleen. She won't tell us whatever Kathleen says to her, but I gather her version of things in Saul's household is different from Shelah's."

"Shelah has not had a proper upbringing," Colette said. "I'd feel sorry for her if she wasn't trying to steal Mattie away. Wait—she has stolen him away, and he will not listen to my concerns."

"Not yet," Abigail said, getting up to find a basket to put empty teacups and dessert dishes in. "I've heard from Aenti that Matthew refuses to leave until after Christmas. He's trying to get Shelah to go back to Missouri and wait there, but she is adamant about staying here. I also heard Matthew is sick with a cold and Shelah has gone to 'help out' at his house."

Eliza shook her head. "I'm loving having Aenti Miriam around more and more."

"I had planned to speak to Agnes," Colette said, feeling better already. "But that might not be possible now." How could she face Matthew's *mamm*, knowing what he'd told her? Impossible. And yet, she needed to see him. Somehow, she had to tell him she understood. But did she really?

"We can find a way to distract Shelah if you happen to want to visit Agnes. Just let us know when," Abby said. "I'm famous for sneaking food to people I'm hiding, so I think I can detain a woman while you're sneaking a talk with Agnes and taking food to Matthew while you're at it."

"You snuck food only to one person," Eliza said with a giggle. "Jonah in that tiny carriage *haus* apartment. And you carried trays of food to him. I still don't know how you managed that and all the work you do. The memory always makes me smile."

"I want us all to smile," Abby said. "Colette, I know Jonah didn't want you to tell anyone about his investigation. He tries to stay out of such doings now, but he does know about the law. I will forgive both of you because this is an urgent matter and we need to save Matthew from whatever Shelah has in mind. Then, once we have proof, Daed can go back to the bishop and tell him what's really going on. You might get your Mattie back sooner than you think."

Colette smiled, causing her face to hurt. It was fake, to keep her sisters off the trail. She hadn't smiled or talked very much since Matthew had told her he was to marry Shelah. After Daed and Eliza had helped her up to bed, she'd stayed out of sight. She'd spent her time wondering how Matthew had presented the news to Shelah. Had he made a big deal out of actually proposing to her? She'd also tormented herself, thinking of how Shelah must be gloating and bragging and carrying on. About a marriage she probably didn't even want, about Matthew having to do as the bishop suggested, about knowing this horrible secret and using it against Matthew. Colette wanted to confront Shelah, but that could cause even more problems. But if they all worked together to prove Shelah was being deceitful, the bishop would surely change his mind.

"There was one other thing Jonah pointed out to me," she said in a low whisper to her sisters. "And you cannot repeat it, not to anyone."

They both bobbed their heads, their eyes wide with curiosity. "Tell," Abby said.

"He thinks if Shelah is involved somehow with this other man, then she might be marrying Matthew for one reason only."

Abby lifted her gaze to Colette. "To get the money?"

Colette nodded. "And then she will get Matthew out of the way as soon as possible."

"We need to make haste in finding out the truth," Eliza said, nodding. "I think we need to meet at Abby's house and explain this to Levi, too. Together, we can figure out a plan to trap Shelah—without violence or ill will, of course."

"Of course," Abby said, nodding.

"Of course," Colette parroted, thinking hard.

Abby gave her a questioning look, then continued. "Tomorrow night. I'll cook supper and tell Mamm and Daed we're trying to cheer you. I'll send them a tray."

"They can't find out," Colette said. "They'd worry."

"They'd also shut this down," Eliza replied.

"Well, *ja*, there is that to consider, too."

Colette hugged both her sisters. "*Denke*. I'm better now. I have hope now. You're right. It's not over yet, and Christmas is a time when wonderful things happen. If I can help Matthew out of this, then it's worth all of the angst. And if I do win him back, I am never letting him go again."

"That's the Colette we love so much," Eliza replied. "Go wash your hair."

Colette laughed and finished cleaning her room. She'd keep her books close just in case. But she had a new reason to leave this room now. And to finish her quilt before Christmas.

Matthew coughed again, and then sneezed. He tried to keep his coughing down. He didn't want Shelah to *kumm* running with more weak chicken soup and that horrible concoction she'd whipped up for his cold.

He should be out helping Daed, but Mamm had insisted he take a day or two to rest.

"You've been through so much over these past months, and your body had become worn down. You've been going, working, and you've had this heavy burden on your back for too long now. Rest." Then she'd leaned close. "And that way, you can avoid Shelah as much as possible, *ja*?" Mamm had promised she'd try to keep Shelah occupied.

Matthew agreed, thinking he wouldn't be able to avoid her after Christmas. She was already planning their February wedding. She'd informed him, right after he'd told her the bishop's news, that she'd need that long at least to gather her maids and have dresses made—probably twelve. She did have some friends, he thought, or she'd force twelve women to show up. She seemed to think she'd be ruling the district, rather than letting the bishop do his job. Although, truth be told, that was pretty much what Saul had done. The bishop back in Missouri had been close to Saul and discussed all matters with him. That bishop probably knew all of Saul's sins. Or maybe not. But he probably already knew about this marriage arrangement.

An arrangement Matthew did not want. He wished he hadn't blurted it all out to Colette. He'd wanted to sit and tell her, make her understand. But his emotions had gotten the best of him. Now she knew everything, all the bitter things he'd had to keep to himself for so long. In a way, it had been better to get it said and then leave. Let her know there was no turning back, no matter how much it hurt.

So here he lay, staring up at the ceiling, wondering how his life could have done such a one-eighty. He would never forget the look in Colette's eyes when he'd told her the truth. Nor the questions in her sisters' eyes, when he'd walked out of that room, unable to explain anything to them. Thankfully, he'd not seen Sarah. She would condemn him, too. *Neh*, that wasn't fair. Abe had not condemned him, because Abe understood, and Abigail and Eliza had frowned, but they'd also shown him compassion later when he told them he couldn't return to work at the inn. It was only when he'd asked about Colette that they'd looked angry.

And Eliza, in her blunt way, had set him straight. "What do you think? That she's all sunshine and moonbeams? She's a mess, and what hurts the most, she's hiding in her room. Colette is no coward, but she is broken now. She's hurting, Matthew. That's how she is right now."

He hated the image of her moping in her room. Colette was full of life, and usually full of mirth and that razor-sharp wit that either stung fiercely or made him laugh out loud. She was like a sunflower blossoming in the midst of ragweed.

Great, now he'd have that comparison in his head. Sunflower—Colette. Ragweed—Shelah.

No wonder he was sick and hiding in his room, too.

His cough returned and sounded loudly in his ears. Hardly a minute later, the door of his room came open and Shelah stepped inside, overdressed and overenthusiastic. "Time for more medicine. I can't have my fiancé sick. I have to keep you healthy for our wedding at least."

An odd way to put it, but this was Shelah, after all.

"I'm fine. I just need some water."

"And medicine."

"*Neh*, I do not want more medicine."

She held her pout and a frown. He'd need to get used to that. She had a spoon and a medicine jar.

When they heard horses trotting up to the house, she ran to the window. "We have visitors." Then she gasped. "I'll get rid of them."

"Wait, who is it?"

But she was gone in a flash. Maybe he'd like to see some visitors. Colette came to mind, but she wouldn't show up here for all the world. Matthew sighed and fell back on his pillow.

At least he'd avoided that oily medicine.

Colette wanted to turn and leave, but Mamm's hand on her arm stopped her. She knew Shelah was here because Kathleen had taken one of the inn's buggies and paid a man to drive them over early this morning. So much for her sisters trying to distract Shelah. Henry had reported to the sisters immediately. Word was out to watch Shelah's every move, and keep it on the down-low, as Jonah had said at their meeting last night. He and Levi had both seemed quiet. How much did they really know?

While she and her sisters were trying to figure out another way for her to see Agnes, Mamm had inadvertently suggested Colette and she could drop off some food to Agnes.

They wouldn't go inside.

Right. What was Mamm up to? Did everyone around here have their own agendas regarding Shelah and Matthew?

Jonah was not happy with her blurting the truth to her sisters, but as usual Abigail talked him down in her serene, calm way. "We are sisters, and we help each other and protect each other. We won't repeat this, especially to Mamm and Daed. We need to shield Colette. She could be in danger, too."

That got Jonah's attention. "If Matthew is in danger, she could be, too. You're right."

After that he told Abigail, Eliza, and Levi what Colette already knew. "I've got people on the car. We don't see that kind around here very often, so it shouldn't be difficult to pin down. If I can get a license number, we'll have title and an owner. I think Shelah's friend might not be Amish. He looked out of place from the glimpse I got of him at the party."

"Same here," Levi said. "I was busy making sure everyone behaved, but I did see him talking to Matthew. And I did see Shelah watching the man, fear in her eyes. Maybe he's threatening her because he knows she's Saul's heiress."

"Well, she thinks she should be," Colette had said. "She wants to be the heiress, and going through Matthew is the only option she has for now." How could Shelah claim love when she was practically extorting Matthew?

"And that right there," Jonah had replied, "is why they are both dangerous."

Now Colette gathered herself and knew she had to face all of them—Shelah, Agnes, and Matthew. She had to maintain a neutral expression and pretend she'd accepted the bishop's decision. Which was the Amish way, after all. A hard way, at times, but a peaceful way. Unless one searched one's heart and found it shattered to pieces. Unless one could prove to the bishop that Shelah had ulterior motives. Sinful motives.

"Are you ready?" Mamm asked after she'd parked the buggy. "No matter what, Colette, keep your grace and dignity. Those two things go a long way in a bad situation."

"I'm trying," she offered. "I'll be fine."

Before they could get out of the buggy and lift the food basket from the back, Shelah came out the door, her eyes full of fire, her smile pasted on. "Good day, ladies."

"*Gut daag,*" Mamm replied. Colette nodded her head.

"Why are you here?" Shelah asked, her tone dismissive.

Mamm spoke. "We wanted to visit with Agnes. We heard Matthew is ill."

"So you *really* came to see him?"

Colette glanced at Mamm. "Of course, Shelah. Even though Matthew and I are only friends now, I still care about him. Of course, we are very thankful to you for taking care of the Mueller family, but it would be remiss of us if we didn't check on him and Agnes, too. Since we've known them for all of our lives."

Proud she hadn't choked on those words, she stared Shelah down.

"That is kind of you, but he's sleeping." Shelah paced

a bit. "It's not like he's dying or anything. He has a little cold, but I'm giving him medicine and tender loving care."

Colette gave her mother a speaking glance that conveyed her concerns. What kind of potion was this woman feeding him?

The door opened and Agnes appeared, her own expression mirroring how Colette felt. It might have held a bit of an eye roll. Colette had to hide her smile.

"Sarah, Colette, *kumm* inside out of the cold. It's so nice of you to visit. Our patient is a bit grumpy, but he is up and bored. So I for one would appreciate a visit, and I'm sure Matthew would, too."

"But he's—"

"Awake," Agnes said. "Let's get you two inside and I'll make tea."

Shelah balked but didn't try to keep them out. Colette might have pushed right past her if she had.

CHAPTER NINETEEN

Matthew walked into the living room and found five women staring at each other. Mamm watched Shelah. Shelah glared at Colette, and Sarah and Kathleen moved their gazes over all of them and back to each other.

"Frolic?" he asked, trying to find the humor in the situation. He'd not seen or talked to Colette since he'd blurted out the horrible truth the other day.

"Hardly," Shelah said, jumping up so fast she almost knocked the teacups off the table. "You shouldn't be up."

Matthew ran a hand over his hair. "I'm feeling better, I think. And it's just a cold."

"So we heard," Colette said, her eyes spitting fire. "Just a little cold. Isn't that what you said, Shelah?"

Shelah pouted. "Matthew, I'm concerned. It isn't proper for your ex-girlfriend to come calling."

The sting of that statement hit him in his core. "Colette will always be my friend. Nothing more." He didn't, couldn't look at Colette when he said that, but it had to be that way now and they both knew it.

Colette lifted her chin, but he saw Sarah put her hand on the table and give Colette a warning glance. "I insisted Colette drive me over since everyone else was busy. I wanted to visit with Agnes and bring you some of my chicken soup."

"We have soup," Shelah replied, proud.

"Not this kind," Matthew said, his gaze finally landing on Colette. "The inn is famous for its chicken noodle soup. Large chunks of chicken, carrots, celery, homemade noodles and a thick, rich, creamy broth with special herbs to make it tasty. It will cure my cold."

Shelah got up to touch a hand to his arm. "But we have soup, and I mixed you a batch of herbs and honey. You just need to rest."

"I'll have some of the soup you brought later," he told Sarah and Colette. "*Denke*."

"You are welcome," Sarah said. "You will always be a part of our family, Matthew."

Shelah dropped her hand away, her eyes going from fretful to shrewd. "I suppose one last visit won't hurt. After all, we'll be going back to Missouri soon. And about time, if you ask me."

Colette only stared up at him, her eyes blue-green like the lake when the sun hit it just right. Her expression was full of confusion and longing. "I hope you feel better soon," she said, her words husky and low.

Shelah glared at Colette. "You did this on purpose. You can't accept that he is going to marry me. You had to go and bring the inn's soup."

"Shelah, we should watch for our driver," Kathleen said. "You've been here all day and he's supposed to return soon."

"I belong here," Shelah said. "She doesn't. All I hear about is the inn. The inn this, the inn that. You are no longer a part of the Shadow Lake Inn, Matthew. You'd do well to remember that."

The room went quiet. Matthew glanced around again, his heart hammering a warning that told him to be very careful here. "*Denke* again, Sarah and Colette, for bringing the soup and visiting with Mamm. And *denke*, Shelah, for also cooking soup and visiting with Mamm. But you all need to understand something about me. I am strong, I am determined, and I will be fine. I've had worse colds and managed to get all the milking and feedings done, so I'm going to go and get cleaned up and help Daed."

He turned to leave and then pivoted back. "Shelah, the Shadow Lake Inn has been a part of my life for all of my life. I will not turn my back on my family or my friends. I will marry you and we will find a way to make this work, but do not ever again suggest these women are not welcome in this home. That would not be wise on your part."

Then he shot Colette one last look and went back to his room to get bundled up. The house was too warm. He needed fresh air and to be with Daed and his brothers. He needed to turn to *Gott* and ask for guidance on how to do this—walk away from one woman and start a life with another.

Dear Father, I love but one only. What am I to do?

What could he do?

He went out the back door so quickly, the women sitting at the table didn't get a chance to see him. He couldn't look at them either. He followed the path to the barn, his head down, his feet shuffling. When he looked up, he saw Daed waiting for him. Matthew studied the quiet earth, the soft snow, the trees glistening white, the sky dark blue with the coming dusk.

He breathed in the cold air, let the beauty of late day

touch his skin, and wished he didn't have to leave Shadow Lake.

What a sweet and beautiful thing, to see his father waiting for him. To know that his heavenly Father waited in just the same way. No matter how Matthew felt in his heart, he had to accept that *Gott* would provide. *Gott* had provided, just in a different way than he'd expected. Should he pray to love Shelah and ask *Gott* to take away his love for Colette? Or should he pray for something to change his fortune from gaining money to being content with what he'd had in front of him all along?

Daed nodded as Matthew approached. "I wondered how long it would take before you bolted out of there."

Matthew studied his father's face. "I needed some air."

"*Kumm*," Daed said. "The cows have missed you."

Matthew followed his *daed*. As they went about their tasks, feeding and checking on the livestock, he heard his brothers fussing in the goat pen. This was normal. This was solid. This was his life. He'd always loved the routine of working all day with his friends, coming home to Mamm and Daed and his brothers, helping Daed, smiling at Mamm, cutting up with Timothy and Aaron. Home, prayers, rest.

Would he ever have that once he left?

Daed didn't ask questions, nor offer advice. He just continued with the chores that had to be done. But every now and then, he'd glanced over at Matthew, his eyes guarded, his expression pinched and strained. What did Daed need to say?

And what should Matthew say to him?

In the end, they finished in the quietness of the gloaming, the sun pouring orange and peach over the pristine white snow. When they heard a buggy leaving, Matthew looked toward the house.

After seeing four black bonnets huddled close, he spoke. "They are all going back to the inn together."

Daed squinted toward the buggy. "I reckon Kathleen and Shelah decided to save money by getting a ride with Sarah."

"I reckon so," Matthew replied, wondering how that ride would go.

Daed echoed his thoughts. "I'd not want to be in the middle of that. *Neh*, not at all."

Matthew nodded. He *was* in the middle of that.

He might not be on that buggy ride, but he had to be in the thoughts of the four women who'd crammed in there together.

A place where no man wanted to be.

He prayed again, silent and steady. *Gott* would see him through. He had to rely on that.

"*Denke* for the ride," Kathleen told Mamm when they pulled up to the inn. One of the workers took the buggy to the stables while Colette and Mamm walked up the side steps by the portico, Kathleen and a very silent Shelah behind them.

After Matthew had left the house, Shelah busied herself with cleaning. If you could call sweeping a hand over the tabletop cleaning. Then she insisted on going to tidy up Matthew's room.

The intimacy of the task had not escaped Colette. Fury burned through her veins. Shelah was a cruel woman to hold his parentage over Matthew's head. Especially if she planned to marry him for the fortune she must surely think was hers and then do something terrible to him so she and that stranger could get together. How could they be happy if they harmed Matthew?

Colette had been surprised when Mamm offered them a ride back to the inn. She had not wanted to be anywhere near Shelah. But Kathleen, who had a cell phone tucked away, called and canceled the other buggy. She wanted to protest, but Mamm didn't know what Colette knew, and maybe Kathleen didn't either. She wanted to scream out her fears and glare at Shelah, maybe even grab her and shake some sense into her.

But Mamm's firm hand on her arm convinced Colette to take the high road yet again.

It had been a quiet ride.

When they were inside the massive lobby, Kathleen hugged Mamm. "I'm exhausted. I'm going up to rest." She glanced at Shelah. "You should *kumm* up, too. We'll get a tray for dinner."

Shelah looked hesitant. "I'd like to talk to Colette, please." When Mamm and Kathleen exchanged glances, she added, "Alone."

"Colette, is this okay?" Mamm asked.

Colette felt weary from her heart to her feet, and she was afraid if she stayed to talk to Shelah, she'd blurt out her anger at the woman. She usually liked winter, but now she shivered like a baby lamb lost in the woods. "I'd like to go home and sit by the fire."

Shelah motioned to the beautiful crackling fire across the way. "I won't keep you long."

Curious in spite of her exhaustion, Colette nodded. She had planned to befriend her enemy—what better time to try again? She prayed Shelah would confess, but that was highly unlikely. "It is time for us to talk a bit more."

She hugged Mamm. "Tell Eliza I'll be home soon. Save me some supper."

Mamm nodded and moved toward the kitchen.

Kathleen went to the front desk and ordered their tray.

Shelah turned to the fire and held out her hands toward the warmth. "I'm sorry I was rude earlier."

Surprised, Colette would ever be amazed at this woman's moods. "This is difficult for all of us." Then she moved beside Shelah, the heat of the flame too inviting to resist. "Do you love Matthew?"

"Well, of course," Shelah said far too quickly. "That's a silly question."

"Not coming from me," Colette replied. "I do love him, with all my heart and soul. I waited too long to tell him that, to even realize it myself. We'd only just—"

"You had a lifetime to figure this out," Shelah said. "I'm sorry for what happened, sorry he had to end things with you, but Saul wanted us to marry. He told me so many times. He said, 'When Matthew gets here, all will be right again. He will take care of you and provide for you. You'll never be alone again, Shelah. I don't want you to be alone.'"

Colette pondered that revelation. Saul had been a bachelor and had no one close to love. He'd found an orphan, a friend's child, and taken her in with a proper companion to help look after her.

But why?

"Saul must have been close to your parents," she finally said, lacking any other explanation.

"He was, even before I was born," Shelah replied. "He and my father were so close, and then they had a disagreement. Right after that, my folks went on a trip. They were considering moving to Ohio, to start fresh, Mamm told me. They left me with some cousins I didn't really know."

"And they never came back," Colette said. With true empathy, she added, "That must have been so horrible for you."

Shelah barely nodded. "It was. By the time Saul found me, I was five and I'd been moved from home to home, unwanted. When Kathleen heard I was living with Saul, she showed up to take me. She and my *mamm* were close. He had a housekeeper who looked after me, but he persuaded Kathleen to stay and help. He put her in charge and kept the housekeeper. It took him two more years to become my legal guardian."

Colette felt a twinge of sympathy for Shelah. "Do you know why he searched for you and wanted to take care of you?"

Shelah rubbed her hands together. "I believe he felt so guilty about the argument with my *daed*—his friend and his employee. He always told me he had to right a wrong, so he found me."

A nagging memory fluttered through Colette's mind. Something Matthew had said to her about Saul.

He told me he had to right a wrong.

And he'd told Shelah the same thing.

She didn't say anything to Shelah about her thoughts, but Saul had obviously wanted to mend all his fences before he met his maker. One of those sins was forcing his brother's wife. Matthew and Shelah both knew that now. That secret could bond them together, but Shelah had made a mistake in using it to manipulate Matthew. How desperate she must be.

"What did you want to talk to me about?" Colette asked. So many questions needed answers.

Shelah turned from the fire and faced her. "I wanted you to understand. I can see the love between you and Matthew, and it makes me jealous. I want him to love me that way, and I want to love him with all my heart."

That admission of what Colette already suspected sent a ray of sharp piercing pain through her heart, followed by a tentative thread of hope. She had to hear the truth from Shelah, so she got blunt. "You don't love him, and he does not love you. Why are you really going into this marriage, Shelah?"

Before Shelah could answer, Kathleen called from the landing just above them, "Shelah, your supper is getting cold. *Kumm* up and let Colette go home."

Shelah shot Colette a gaze full of fear, longing, hope, and regret, all in the flash of a direct stare. "Never mind. I just wanted you to know I understand, and I'm sorry." Then she whirled and ran up the stairs.

Leaving Colette to stare into the fire, hoping to find more answers. But she'd seen one answer there in Shelah's eyes. As she hurried through the inn to the cottage, she whispered, "They do not love each other." *They do not love each other.*

CHAPTER TWENTY

Mamm was with Eliza and Abigail when Colette arrived home.

"There you are," Mamm said. "We were a bit worried about leaving you alone with Shelah."

"Was there blood?" Eliza asked.

"We talked," Colette said as she stripped off her scarf and cape. "It was an odd but telling conversation."

"Well, tell all." Abigail glanced back toward the *grossdaddi haus*. "The men are talking about finishing touches on the new house, so we only have a few moments."

Colette let out a sigh and went to the sink pump to wash her hands. "She apologized for her behavior today and implied she and Matthew don't love each other. I know he doesn't love her, but he's trying. I feared from the start that she might love him and not just for the inheritance he received, but today she showed me the truth. She said they could grow to love each other. She said she believed Saul became her guardian so he could right a wrong. The same thing Matthew told me about Saul giving him the inheritance—so he could right a wrong."

"This is very odd indeed," Mamm said. "Kathleen

opened up to me a bit, too. I mentioned the man who came to the frolic and Kathleen got nervous. She told me she knows of him, and she thinks he's *Englisch*."

"Whatever gave her that clue?" Colette said in a deliberately sarcastic tone. She wanted to blurt out everything she'd seen and heard, but this wasn't the right time.

Mamm gave her a playful pat on the hand. "She also told me he's from Missouri and Shelah met him at an *Englisch* get-together. She had a horrible crush on him, and Saul disapproved. It could be that's why he called Matthew to come and help out. He wanted Shelah to be distracted."

Colette held a hand to her heart. She couldn't speak, but this made sense to her. Now everything she'd discussed with Jonah and her sisters seemed even more ominous. Why hadn't she forced the issue with Matthew? She could have made him listen if she hadn't been so shocked by the bishop's decision, and if she hadn't been so confused by Matthew's confession.

"*Ach, vell*, that sure worked," Eliza said, shaking her head as she buttered biscuits and stirred the chicken and dumplings.

Colette swallowed away her pain so she could focus. But this burden of knowing and not being able to talk about Matthew's crisis was almost too much to bear.

Mamm gave her a curious once-over. "Is this hard for you to hear?"

"Anything regarding the happy couple is hard to hear, but I want to know all of it."

"I suppose this man followed her here," Mamm said. "Kathleen didn't know he was even in town. But she immediately admitted he was trouble." Mamm sighed. "I don't think Kathleen is keen on the marriage. She does feel for Matthew. He has talked to her, but she didn't reveal their conversations."

"Does everyone around here have secrets?" Colette blurted.

"Colette?"

She heard the concern in her mother's tone. "I'm fine."

Abigail poured drinks and checked the table. "So Saul wanted to right some wrongs. Bringing Matthew and Shelah together? The *Englischer* could mess up Saul's schemes."

"It seems so," Colette managed to reply, trying her best to stay calm when she wanted to shout the truth. "I do not like Shelah at all, but I feel sorry for her. She seems desperate."

"Only because she is driven," Eliza replied, glancing at her sisters. "She wants what she wants, and now she's courting trouble."

Mamm's keen gaze pinned all of them. "What does that mean?" She stared down Colette when Eliza didn't explain. "Colette, I can always tell when you're hiding something. You seem ready to burst."

Colette shot Eliza a speaking glance. Abigail stopped pouring water and looked down at the perfectly placed plates.

Mamm put her hands on her hips. "I thought we were to share everything we know. What do you three know that I don't?"

Colette lowered her eyes. Eliza cleared her throat. Abigail stood still, the water pitcher in her hand.

Mamm gave them a stern glare. "Talk, now."

"We aren't supposed to tell you," Colette blurted out. "I mean, I'm not supposed to tell anyone." She'd never been good at keeping secrets, and this one was nagging at her heart. "But it might be wise, so you can be aware." Then she looked at her surprised sisters. "I have something to add, for all of you to hear."

"I do so like being aware," Mamm replied, her serene composure back now. Then she looked at her other two quiet daughters. "I'm waiting. First you two tell what you know. Then we can all hear what Colette is hiding."

"Jonah is checking on the man," Abigail said, giving Colette a questioning stare. "Because Colette saw him leaving in a blue sports car the day of the frolic."

"If that isn't a clue that he's *Englisch*, I don't know what is," Mamm said, sinking down onto a chair. "How did he even drive it in this weather?"

"We cleared the road," Colette pointed out. "And the state cleared most of the highways."

She explained to Mamm what she'd seen that day. "I went to Jonah out of concern. If that car is the same one that hit Matthew's buggy a few weeks ago, maybe it wasn't an accident."

Eliza filled in more. "So we told Jonah, and then Levi offered to help."

"Help Jonah?" Mamm looked worried. "What will they do?"

"Jonah knows people," Abigail replied in a whisper. "He'll do nothing illegal, of course. He can find out about identities and such. License plates, background checks."

"I see," Mamm said. "As long as he's careful and acts in accordance with our beliefs, I suppose it will be all right. But why would all of this make Shelah so driven?"

Colette came and kneeled in front of Mamm. "If she married Matthew, but has this man waiting on the side, we believe something dire could happen to Matthew."

"What?" Mamm's gaze lifted in shock. "You mean, she'd do something to harm Mattie?"

"She and her friend could, *ja*," Abigail replied. "We have no proof, so that's why Jonah told us to keep it quiet." She shrugged. "I tried several times to bring our fears up with Mattie, but he balked and made excuses. She has blinded him to what she's doing, and his honor and duty have taken care of the rest of it. He'll marry her if the bishop tells him to do so, but that could put him in real danger when he's away in Missouri, alone with only her and Kathleen. That man could easily do a lot of harm."

"Did any of you consider that your *daed* and I should know about this sooner?"

"We didn't want to worry you," Colette explained.

"I appreciate that kind consideration, but we are a family. We stick together, and we can't let Matthew fall into this trap. You must talk to him again."

"I asked him over and over—why?" Colette stood and rubbed her hands down her apron. "And the day he came to me to let me know what the bishop said, he finally told me what's going on. I can't contain it anymore, Mamm. Saul had a secret that gave him a hold on both Mattie and Shelah." She held her hands together. "Saul is Matthew's father."

"What?" her two sisters said at the same time.

Mamm's eyes went wide. "What?"

Colette bobbed her head. "He told me. Saul assaulted Agnes, after she and Titus were married. I don't have the details, but Shelah knows the truth and she's using it against Matthew—so he must marry her, or she will tell everyone."

Her listeners gasped.

"Why didn't you tell anyone?" Abigail asked in a loud whisper, her gaze moving toward the back door.

"Matthew asked me not to. He told me all this as he was walking out the door. I've been trying so hard to keep it to myself, but today—"

"I forced you to go with me to their home," Mamm said. "I'm so sorry, Colette. I only wanted you and Mattie to part friends."

"We are friends, but it's a fragile thread holding us together. Shelah does not love him. She knows he does not love her. I think she was about to confess earlier, but Kathleen called her upstairs, and she ran out of the room."

"You are caught in an untenable situation," Mamm said, shaking her head. "Are you sure Matthew is Saul's son?"

"Matthew seemed sure. He's afraid to tell his folks the truth." She shook her head. "That means his mother is keeping a big secret, and now Mattie has to keep that secret, too. But I'm not sure if his mother knows what Saul asked of him. He's trying to protect both of them, I imagine."

"Understandable," Eliza said. "But now we all know, and it's even more urgent to help him."

"If I accuse Shelah," Colette said, "it will only add to his woes. We have to be for certain sure before we confront anyone."

"Even from the grave, Saul is making trouble," Mamm said, worry creasing her face. "I never felt comfortable around that man when we were all youngies." Then she lowered her voice. "We can't tell your *daed*. He might get too excited. He's already exhausted from taking Matthew to the bishop."

"We all agree," Abigail said. The others nodded and

went about their work. Colette fretted about telling Matthew's secret. He had trusted her. *Neh*, he had told her in a moment of intense anger and sadness. Still, he'd told her and now she'd blabbed.

Just then, the back door opened, and the men came inside.

Daed stood staring at all of them; then he shook his head.

Abigail gave Jonah a questioning glance.

"Abe knows everything," he explained as he walked by.

Abigail pulled him back. "So does Mamm."

Daed looked at Mamm. "They told you?" Then he glanced at his daughters. "Does everyone know everything now?"

Mamm nodded and swept her gaze over Jonah and Levi. "And they told you?"

Daed indicated yes.

They'd always had an unspoken understanding of each other, as if they could see into each other's hearts.

Mamm stood. "So we all know that Saul claims to be Matthew's *daed*, and this is why Shelah thinks he will marry her. To keep her quiet for the sake of his family."

Jonah shook his head. "That's the gist of it. None of you would ever last in detective work."

"*Neh*," Colette replied. "But I could not keep it to myself any longer. I needed my family's help, and now we all know."

Daed glanced around the room, his gaze touching on each of his daughters and then going back to Jonah and Levi. "But this will go no further. We stick together to help Matthew. And we pray that *Gott* is leading us, because this could become very dangerous."

Jonah stood still, his hands on his hips. "Well, now

that this investigation is out in the open, let me do the legwork. I'll try to talk to Matthew and explain. He told us about Saul's claim not long after he came home, but we promised, same as Colette probably did, not to say anything until he'd talked to his parents and spoken with the bishop. He has probably told Titus and Agnes by now. But what they do with the information is beyond me."

"He'd want to warn Agnes," Mamm said. "She would be so humiliated if this secret got out."

Jonah nodded. "The rest of you stay alert and report anything that seems odd or dangerous. Abe and I have agreed to talk to Matthew. Alone." He scrubbed his hand down his beard. "We'll do that when I have enough evidence to prove Shelah and this mystery man are up to something. It's obvious she wants the status and money of being Saul's ward, but Saul left her high and dry, essentially forcing her to marry Matthew. If she has this male friend waiting in the wings, things will not end well for Matthew."

"We will not let that happen," Daed replied.

Colette watched as her family formed a shield around her. "*Denke*, for looking after Mattie and me. I love him, but I can't go against the bishop's decision or try to win him back. If we don't prove what Shelah is up to, he'll be walking into a trap."

"He has a right to know what could happen," Levi said. "Matthew is a strong, determined young man who has always done what is right. He thinks he's doing that now."

"Saul wanted to right some wrongs," Colette said. "But in doing so, he's put a lot of people in danger."

"Let's eat," Daed said. "We turn this over to *Gott*."

They all sat down and said their silent prayers.

Colette blinked back tears of frustration coupled with

hope. These last weeks had changed her, rearranged her whole focus on life. She'd been complacent, content, maybe a bit aloof and overly confident that she was safe and loved and happy, and that she had a purpose here at this old inn. Matthew had always been her one and only, and now that she understood that, she didn't know if she could let him go without a fight.

Help me, Lord. Help me to be gracious and to find wisdom. Help Matthew to find the truth. Show us Your will.

She opened her eyes and smiled at her family. Then they all began to eat in a somber quietness until eventually talk turned to the happenings of the day. The normal and *gut* happenings of their simple life that somehow seemed so far away right now.

On the other side of the township, Matthew sat thinking about all that had happened over the last few weeks. He'd had doubts about everything until the bishop had given his decision.

Now, the reality of his situation set in. After Christmas, he'd leave here with Shelah and Kathleen, and his life would change forever. If he went back to Bishop Zook and told him he had concerns, would it matter now? The bishop would probably frown and tell him to man up, a term he'd learned from Jonah. The bishop would explain he had new responsibilities now.

I thought I could handle this. I thought I could walk away from everything and everyone I know and love.

Again he thought of the man who'd come looking for Shelah. She'd waved his appearance away like an annoying fly. But Matthew's instincts told him something wasn't right. The man didn't seem Amish, yet he'd dressed in the proper clothes. Maybe he was on his Rumspringa and had decided to get his haircut in town. Maybe he'd noticed a pretty woman and followed her to the inn, as Shelah had said. She was pretty and she knew it. Had she been so bored she'd decided to flirt with an outsider? The man could be dangerous. Matthew still had that feeling—the man looked familiar, but he couldn't place him.

Could Shelah be lying to him? If she wanted to marry Matthew, why would she risk enticing another man—a stranger at that? Or maybe they already knew each other. That had to be it.

A spark of hope burned through his weary resignation. If Shelah was doing something unethical behind his back, they would need to address the issue. And he might not have to marry her after all.

He needed to find out the truth, and he would do so before he left here and made the worst mistake of his life.

Mamm and Daed came in and sat down at the kitchen table, their expressions somber. The time had come for the full truth between them. Matthew had asked them earlier if they could meet alone.

"I sent your brothers over to visit with Levi's family. They are close friends with Jamie and Laura. Connie and Miriam will watch over them until I go to fetch them home."

Matthew lifted his head to Daed in understanding. "I'm glad we have this time. I only have a few days left here—"

"You do not need to make this marriage," Mamm said, holding up her hand. "I've observed you and Shelah together. You will make each other miserable, and no amount of money can change that. You belong with Colette. She loves you so much."

Matthew wanted to believe that. "So where do we begin?"

Mamm took Daed's hand. "I begin with the truth at last." Her eyes watered and she lowered her head. "I just hope you can both forgive me."

Matthew listened as Mamm explained in detail how Saul had harassed her, followed her around, and flirted with her even before she and Daed had married. She went on to explain to Daed how she'd tried to avoid his brother. Though Matthew had already heard her story, he cringed anyway, the thought of what Saul had done weighing on him like a yoke. He hated the dazed, shocked expression on Daed's face.

Daed teared up, his fist tightening against the table-cloth, his face going pale with shock and anger. Once Mamm had finished with the worst, she turned to Daed.

"I tried so hard to fight him off. I could not. Then, later, I tried to forget. Just forget."

"But you found out you were with child," Daed said, his voice husky and low. Wiping at his eyes, he continued. "I always wondered, but I did not want to see the truth. I knew something had to be wrong when you seemed so sad and distant." He swallowed and looked out the window where a tree branch kept tapping as the wind shifted. "I thought maybe you'd picked the wrong brother. That you really wanted to be with Saul."

"*Neh.*" Mamm grabbed Daed's other hand and held it. "I love you, Titus. I have always loved you. I was so ashamed, so afraid. But the *bobbeli*—I knew it couldn't be yours. I added up the weeks and realized my worst fears had come true." She touched a hand to Daed's cheek. "I love you. Only you." Then she turned to Matthew. "And we both love you, son. You are our child. No matter how you came into the world, *Gott* put you with us and no one else can claim you, because we love you. You are our son, and we all need to agree on that."

"But Saul did claim Matthew," Daed said. Then he looked from her to Matthew. "How did he know?"

Mamm started crying again. "Before he left, he came to me and told me he was sorry. I was terrified." She held her fist to her mouth, tears falling down her face. "I placed a hand on my tummy, in protection of the babe. I had a tiny bump already."

Daed let out a choked sob. "Saul guessed?"

She nodded. "I didn't say anything and neither did he at first, but the way he looked at me and then at my stomach." She stopped, shaking her head. "He asked me. I didn't answer at first, but I finally said I'd tell him the truth, but only if he'd leave and never come back. I made him promise that, and in return I would never tell anyone what he'd done."

"So you told him Matthew was his son?"

Mamm's nod was so slight, Matthew almost missed it. She wiped at her eyes. "*Ja*, I did. I wanted him gone. I was afraid he didn't believe me, would want proof. Instead, he readily agreed. He seemed relieved that I'd taken the burden off him." Her voice strengthened. "He left, because he was a coward who could not face his sin or the brother he'd wronged."

The look of pain on Daed's face would stay with Matthew the rest of his days. How he hated Saul for betraying the trust of his sweet parents. "Daed," he said, pleading. "Daed."

His father stood and paced and stared out the window; then he turned and looked at Matthew. "You are my son. Always."

Matthew wiped at his eyes, the agony of this confession like a knife scarring his soul. His parents' pain was the reason he'd agreed to let Shelah stay on. She would have blurted the truth out in the worst way if he hadn't given in to her demands.

Daed found a dishcloth and touched it to Mamm's face. "And you, Agnes, will always be mine. Mine. If Saul were here, I'd be expected to forgive him. And I would not be able to do so. Never. But he is dead now. It is enough—that he did one *gut* thing by staying away, by letting us raise our firstborn."

Mamm stood so fast, the table shook. "*Neh*, he did one last cruel thing. He gave Matthew his fortune because he thought that would buy him a spot in heaven, and his son's forgiveness, too. My forgiveness, Titus. And yours. He thought we all would just let this go and take his money. But that will let him win. He wanted our son." She shook her head. "The man had everything he could ever need and never once came to us or offered us anything. But we didn't need his money then and we don't need it now. We have the one thing Saul never had—a loving family. And that includes you, Matthew. Always."

Matthew had to turn away. He'd worried about Saul's gift, and now he could see Saul had used all of them, even Shelah, to get his way in the end. Did he think his wealth could cover all his sins? Mamm was right. This was cruel. Saul could have done all of them a favor by willing the estate to someone else.

Except Mamm had needed to confess the truth. She'd held this horrible secret since Matthew's birth. That pained him more than knowing she'd been attacked. Now maybe they could all forgive and forget and never mention it again.

She started sobbing again, but Daed rushed to her and held her tight. "It's over, Agnes. You are safe and he is gone. He's in *Gott*'s hands now. And you and I will be fine. It's almost a relief to finally know what I suspected all along."

Mamm lifted her head. "You thought?"

"I did, but after he left, I let it go. Maybe I was the coward, but I was afraid if I asked, I would not like the answer."

"Oh, Titus, you are the bravest man I know," she replied, relief lifting her shoulders. Then she turned to Matthew. "It will be your decision as to how to handle your inheritance, Matthew. I know you'll make the right choice."

Matthew went to his parents and hugged them both. "I need you both to know that Shelah is aware of what happened, because Saul told both of us. She is using this information to her advantage. I won't let her ruin your lives, too."

Daed looked at Mamm. Then Mamm stood back, straightening her spine as she held her head high. "*Neh*, I will not let you do what I did for so many years. You are not going to live with a lie the way I chose to do. This tragedy will not repeat itself. It ends here with us. We love each other and we will go to the bishop and tell him everything. If I need to stand in front of the church, I will do so. It will be a relief."

Daed took Mamm's hand. "She's right. You don't have to go into a marriage you don't want in order to save us, Matthew. We will stand together. This community is

gracious and forgiving and the brethren know we have
lived a good, simple life. We will be fine."

"I can't let you do that," Matthew said. "What if you
aren't fine? What if Mamm is shunned? You'd have to
move somewhere else."

"You can and you will stop this," Daed replied.
"You've seemed troubled by this marriage from the beginning. You owe Saul nothing more, son."

Mamm nodded in agreement. "Do not let Saul win
again."

They were right. He'd tried so hard to protect them,
and now he could see that keeping this secret would only
damage them more.

He let out a sigh. "I have more to tell."

They all sat down again, and he told them about the
man who'd been sneaking around, asking about Shelah.
"I think those two have something cooked up," he finally
admitted. "But I aim to find out what."

Daed grunted. "It's obvious, isn't it? Shelah wants the
lifestyle she had before, whether she marries you or not."

Mamm lowered her head and then she looked out
toward the fields behind the house. "Why should you
marry a woman who seems to have another man waiting
in the wings? I think this girl has learned some of Saul's
traits. Don't let her fool you."

"I didn't want to see it," he admitted. "But now it's
plain as day."

"You were too caught up in shielding us," Daed said.
"What can we do to help?"

"You don't need to do anything," Matthew said. "I've
told a few trusted friends about this, and I will go to them
for help."

"Abe knows," Mamm said. "I wonder who else?"

He told them about Jonah and Levi. "They are my most trusted friends, and Jonah has a way of finding out the truth about people."

"Are you in danger?" Mamm asked.

"I could be," he admitted. "That's why I need to warn everyone. Now that we've talked, I can be honest with those I trust, and that includes the King family."

"Then go to them," Daed said. "But keep us up-to-date this time, *ja*?"

Matthew stood, feeling better. "I love you both. Never forget that. I will make this right."

"Be careful," Daed cautioned.

"I will."

He'd find out the truth that Shelah seemed to be hiding, because now she had nothing left to use against him. And he had everything, including a loving family, to help him bring her to her senses.

Chapter Twenty-one

Matthew couldn't sleep, so he got up early the next morning. He was still on the volunteer committee for the scholar singing, which was coming up. He'd go to the inn and get the bleachers and benches set up before anyone was around. That way he could avoid most everyone but the night clerk, a young man who only spoke when a guest needed help.

He didn't want to avoid people, but it had become necessary after he'd made the commitment to marry Shelah. She would still be asleep, since she rarely got up before dawn. Or at dawn, for that matter. Now that he'd put together the truth, he didn't trust her at all. But he had to keep pretending until he could find a way to stop her and her dangerous friend.

Proof. He needed proof. After he finished his task, he'd go talk to Jonah.

He rode Sawdust through the fields and valleys. They'd have to buy a new buggy soon, but for now one of his *mamm*'s cousins had loaned them a small one.

He thought about Saul's place and all the money waiting in a bank nearby. He could buy a lot of buggies, or at least send one back for his family. Would they ever be able to accept his help? He didn't know what to do about the estate, but he did know he would never live there, and if he could prove Shelah was out to get his inheritance, the wedding would be called off.

The road was empty at this early hour. The morning light made a timid approach through the snow-covered trees. The world was still and fresh. Soon, the busyness of life would bring everyone out for work or for school. Or for a visit to a loved one.

He thought of Colette, and longing filled his soul. He'd broken her heart over and over in the last few weeks. If he left with Shelah, that would be the end of things. Forever.

Now he might be able to find a way to stop this charade. Saul had asked him to marry Shelah, but she had pushed him to do so. She knew the will stated his wishes, but she also knew hearing the request from a dying man would add more pressure.

Where was the love in that equation?

He led Sawdust up to the stables and found a clean stall. After checking on the roan and giving him some oats, Matthew covered the big horse with a blanket and hurried through the snow to the inn.

It looked dark and sleepy, peaceful and welcoming. He'd have to do his work quietly, so he was careful as he carried the heavy seating into the big lobby. The furniture had already been rearranged so they could get everyone inside out of the cold.

Out of habit, he entered through the back and gently closed the door of the small mudroom, then went through the employee lounge toward the kitchen. Maybe Edith would take pity on him and give him some *kaffe* and a slice of pie.

When he rounded the corner to the swinging kitchen doors, however, he stopped, his breath leaving his body.

Colette stood in the glow of the morning light, her hands kneading the bread dough with a back-and-forth rhythm as old as time. He took in a breath, held it, afraid to move for fear she'd turn and run away. He watched her for a moment, but he clung to that moment like a lifeline.

He must have let out a sigh, because she turned, startled, and stared right into his eyes. "Mattie."

That's all it took for Matthew to march across the kitchen and pull her into his arms. He didn't stop to think of the consequences. He kissed her, the longing in his soul reaching out to her. When she sighed her own sweet sigh, he deepened the kiss and held her there.

She had put her hands behind her because they had dough all over them. Now she grabbed the counter, finding the edge, and held herself steady while she returned the kiss.

Matthew knew in that moment that he would never leave her. If they had to run away together, he'd find a way to be with this woman. *This woman.* No one else.

He finally lifted his lips from hers and saw the gleam of love in her eyes. The surprise of that kiss was on her pink lips, and a sigh of longing slipped through them.

"Mattie," she said again in a soft whisper. "What are you doing here?"

"I honestly don't know," he said, his finger moving down her cheek. "I woke up and decided I'd get here early to set up for the school singing."

"That was kind of you."

"I think I must have felt it—that you'd be here. I didn't know you liked to make bread."

"I learned," she said, still out of breath. "Edith is

teaching me to cook. I need to stay busy. I hope to take over the kitchen after—"

She stopped, her eyes widening as if she'd woken from a dream. "We can't be alone together."

He glanced around. "We can."

"What?" She looked doubtful. Grabbing for a towel, she washed her hands, taking out her frustration with soap and a clean towel. "What are you doing?"

"I had a long talk with Mamm and Daed. He knows everything now. Mamm and I had already talked, and she told me what happened between her and Saul. Now Daed knows, too. He holds nothing against her, or me. We are a family."

"Of course you are," she said, empathy in her eyes. "A strong family. I know that was hard to bear, and I'm glad you've managed to confess all. Your *mamm* has suffered enough. But Matthew, that doesn't change things between us."

"But it can," he said, trying to get the words out before she bolted away. "I also told them about Shelah knowing Saul is my *daed* and how she is using that secret to keep me quiet. When I mentioned my concerns regarding the stranger who came looking for her, we all figured out she's seeing him on the side."

"And they want your inheritance," Colette finished, blurting the words on a fast breath. "You and I need to go talk to Jonah. I saw the man leave in a blue sports car on the day of the frolic, a damaged blue sports car."

Matthew couldn't believe what he was hearing. "Why didn't you tell me?"

"I wanted to, but you'd made it clear you intended to marry Shelah. I was afraid you'd think I was making up things to keep you two apart, but now that I've learned a few things, no one could make this stuff up. Jonah is looking into it—or rather he has friends looking into it. If he learns the identity of the man who owns the car, then we'll know who hit you. And probably on purpose."

Shock coursed through Matthew's veins. If she was correct, they could all be in danger. "So you figured this all out?"

"Well, with the help of Jonah and Abby and Eliza and Levi, and Mamm and Daed."

He stared down at her, confusion rushing through his mind. "Your whole family?"

"*Ja,*" she said, her voice low. "I had to talk to someone, so I mentioned the man and the car to Jonah. He told me to keep it quiet until we had proof."

"Let me guess," he began. "You blurted it out to your sisters, and your *mamm* made you tell her, too?"

"Something like that," she said with a smile. "They were all together, but then Jonah, Levi, and Daed came in to eat supper and they already knew—because *you* told *them*. Imagine that?"

"I only told them about Saul," he said in his defense. "And they told me not to repeat it to anyone except the bishop. I'd planned to tell you in a better way. I just couldn't find the right time. But now that we both know a lot more, and we both think the same thing, I believe we can be seen together."

"I'm glad you told me everything," she said, her hands on his arms. "She has nothing over you now, Mattie. Was that what you meant when you said we can . . . kiss?"

Despite all his problems, Matthew nodded. "*Ja,* that's why I came charging in here and tugged you into my arms."

She bobbed her head and then lifted her chin. "Can you do it again, please?"

He kissed her again, over and over, until they heard a grunt behind them. Colette stepped away, her blush making her even more beautiful.

Edith stood with her hands on her hips. "The bread is rising," she said, motioning to the mound of dough on the aged wooden counter. "It is rather warm in here." Then she grinned. "Matthew, sit down and I'll bring you some *kaffe* and coconut pie. How does that sound?"

Matthew grinned at Colette. "That sounds perfect."

"It was perfect," Colette told her eagerly listening sisters later that day. "A perfect kiss, actually better than anything I've read in a novel."

"That's amazing," Eliza said, smiling. "Go, Matthew."

Abigail giggled, then got serious. "But where does that leave things?"

"Well, Edith caught us, so she might be informing the bishop right now," Colette said. Then she shook her head. "*Neh*, she wouldn't do that. She's weary of teaching me to cook. I'm sure she wants Mattie and me back together."

"Are you back together?" Abby asked, her expression sharp with concern.

"Not publicly," Colette said. "He has to pretend he is going through with the marriage to Shelah. If Jonah learns anything, then we make our move to prove the truth."

Eliza pursed her lips and asked, "What if Edith tells what she saw?"

"I don't think she will. She is definitely Team Colette."

Abby shrugged. "I don't know many that are Team Shelah."

Colette let out a sigh. "I think the kiss was Matthew's

way of apologizing to me and letting me know he still cares. But when . . . we stopped to compare notes, he told me his parents know everything, and there is no horrible secret between them now. So Shelah has nothing over him."

"That's *gut*," Abby replied. "But we still need to get the facts straight."

"*Ja*, we do." Colette rubbed a hand across the quilt she was working on. It really was pretty—reds, greens, browns, and ycllows shone brightly against the lush green background. She'd put a tree in the middle with a star on top. Simple, but it showed her faith. She had to have faith. "So for now, he pretends—about the marriage, about the inheritance—and he will not mention that he knows about the blue car."

"*Neh*, he can't, or Shelah might alert the other man."

"When will we know more?" Eliza asked. "It's been days since that man showed up at the frolic."

Abby stood and paced. "Jonah doesn't tell me much, for my own protection. He did say it's an 'active case,' which means someone is working on it. I hope he'll tell us more at family supper tonight."

"Speaking of that," Eliza said, "I'd better get downstairs and heat up the ham-and-cheese chowder that Colette helped Edith make earlier. We'll have corn bread with it, and I grabbed a few tea cakes for our dessert."

"I'll be there soon," Colette said. "I need to freshen up."

After her sisters left her room, she got up and stared out the window toward the inn. She knew Shelah was still visiting Matthew's family, but he'd told her his parents would not divulge anything to Shelah. "Daed leaves the house when she is there, and Mamm keeps her busy, hoping she'll give up. I think they've burned more biscuits than I've burned trash."

Colette grinned at that. Today for just a few hours, it had been like old times. If Shelah knew where Mattie had been all day, she'd be furious.

When Colette was leaving the inn earlier, she'd stopped in the gloaming to admire the sunset hugging the lake and to relive the kiss she and Matthew had shared. Matthew had come up and pulled her into his arms. "The best day," he'd whispered, his warm breath on her neck.

"Ever," she'd replied. "Mattie, I'm so sorry you had to bear this alone for so long. This explains why we argued on the phone. You couldn't tell me anything."

He'd given her a brief kiss. "I hated hurting you, but at that time I thought I had no other choice, so I picked a fight. I believed I had to carry out my duty to Saul. But Shelah is only going to betray me. Just a few days more and then we'll finally be able to plan out our lives."

Now as she stared at the big upper suite of the inn, she prayed for this situation to end and soon. Shelah and her friend needed to be held accountable for what they were trying to do—*allegedly*, as Jonah always told them.

She turned to stare at her quilt. Its panels would show the world that she and Matthew belonged together. But a new question popped into her head. What would Matthew do with such a big inheritance? She didn't care about the money, but he could help his family and a lot of people with such a vast fortune.

Please keep him safe, Lord. She could deal with everything else.

* * *

Everyone gathered at the table that night for supper. The soup and corn bread brought comfort from the cold and from their concerns. They all quietly prayed and then started eating.

Until Colette put her soup spoon down and asked, "Well, does anyone have anything new to say?"

Then they all started talking at once.

Mamm held up a hand. "I only have two ears and they are not very sharp. One at a time. Jonah, you start."

Jonah put down the spoonful of chowder headed for his lips. "I had thought to wait until we'd eaten."

"I can't stand it," Colette said. "Have you learned anything?"

"I have a name," Jonah said. "Gabriel Moser. He used to be Amish but left when he was young. He and Shelah knew each other for years. Now he's come back and is willing to return to the brethren all of a sudden."

"Umph," Daed said. "He's returning to take over Saul's place, and Matthew is in the way."

"It would seem so," Jonah replied. "My friends are looking for the car, but if Gabriel is smart, he'll get rid of it quickly. I plan to check the local car dealerships."

Colette told them she'd talked to Matthew, leaving out the kissing parts even though her sisters kept smiling sweetly at her. "His parents are fine now. They were going to see the bishop today. Imagine carrying such a secret all your life."

"A horrible way to live," Mamm replied. Then she smiled at Daed. "I don't think we've ever had a secret between us."

Daed laughed. "Other than the secrets you and the girls pass back and forth."

"Whatever do you mean?" Mamm asked, looking completely innocent.

They all laughed at that.

Colette smiled, so glad her family had stood by her this whole time. Daed would explain things to the bishop once they had enough information, and she'd pray for the truth to be exposed.

"I want what you and Daed have," she said to Mamm.

"That's the best gift," Jonah added. "To have a long, happy marriage, even in times of trouble."

"Especially in times of trouble," Levi said, smiling at Eliza. "Soon, Colette, your Mattie will be sitting at this table with us."

Colette hoped her brother-in-law was correct. "I shall pray that is so," she said. "Now pass those tea cakes."

CHAPTER TWENTY-TWO

Colette kept up the ruse she and Matthew had agreed on. Whenever she saw Shelah, she tried to be contrite and somber, without being rude. But today, Shelah seemed flighty and nervous. Something was up.

The scholars' Christmas was the big event for this week; perhaps Shelah was concerned about that. She'd already complained about all the noise of benches and chairs being shoved here and there too early in the morning. She could have come down to help, but she was busy making plans for her wedding and pestering Matthew about every little thing.

Colette had to grin in secret about her complaints. If Shelah had come down, she might have heard some sighs and kissing going on, too. She and Matthew had met in the kitchen at dawn. Then they'd shared lunch in the employee lounge, and another kiss in the quilting room. They didn't talk much, but they sure made up for lost time. Kisses, sighs, quiet whispers. She refused to feel guilty because of Shelah now. But she wished she could get solid proof of what was going on.

She found her opportunity when Shelah came through the inn wearing her wool coat and dark bonnet, her head down and her feet swift. Dusk colored the sky with a rich burnish wrapped up in delicate pink. A winter sky, so beautiful but so chilly and mysterious. Why would Shelah decide to go for a walk now?

Finished with her work, Colette grabbed her own cloak and bonnet and decided she'd follow Shelah. She needed some fresh air and exercise. Patches of frozen snow crunched underneath her sturdy boots, so she tried to move through the fallen leaves to cushion any sounds.

She watched as the other woman hurried down the path to the lake. Shelah probably needed some air, but why go down that slippery walking trail to the blustery wind that howled over the beach?

Remembering how Abigail had found Jonah there with a gunshot wound and unconscious, Colette thought the lakeside must be a place for a clandestine meeting.

Then she let out a gasp.

Of course. Her heart beating as fast and furious as the waves hitting the beach, Colette stayed up on the main path, hidden behind shrubs and trees. She had a view of the beach below and the curve that jutted back into the cove.

Shelah had to be meeting someone. And Colette thought she knew who that someone might be.

When she heard voices, she moved as close to the curve as she could get. Then she found a tree and peeped through the dry, bare branches.

Shelah stood by a big rock on the shore, talking with a tall man in a dark jacket.

Gabriel!

Trying to get closer, Colette strained to hear their words.

"I can't do this anymore," Shelah said, her arms clutched

over her cloak. "We can just leave, Gabriel. We don't need the money. We'll make do."

"I don't want to make do," the man replied. "Saul owes me. I kept his secrets and did his dirty work for years. You should be the one who inherited, not Matthew. He just shows up for a few weeks and now he gets the pot of gold. It's not right and you know it. You're used to the life Saul gave you. If we do this the way we planned, we can share that life together."

"I just don't think I can go through with it," Shelah said. "Matthew's a nice person, but he doesn't love me."

Colette watched as Shelah placed her hand on Gabriel's shoulder. "And you know I don't love him. I'll get the money somehow. At this point, I think he's ready to give me anything I want just so he won't have to marry me."

Colette held a hand to her mouth to keep from screaming. These two were quite a pair. Gabriel seemed to have forgotten the parable in the Book of Matthew about the workers in the vineyard, who learned the last shall come first. Not surprising then, that her Matthew had come first with Saul even though he'd only worked for Saul a few weeks.

Gabriel pushed Shelah's hand away. "We agreed to do this together, Shelah. If you can't follow through, I'll find another way. And I can guarantee you'll be a widow before you even marry that poor misguided man."

"*Neh*, you will not hurt him," Shelah retorted, her words angry. "He's a *gut* person and he's willing to marry me even though he loves another."

"So you do have feelings for him." Gabriel shoved her and she tumbled to the ground and started sobbing. "I knew you were up to something when you wouldn't talk to me at that stupid frolic."

"I still love you," she whimpered as she tried to stand, her hands brushing sand off her soiled cloak. Grabbing the rock since he didn't offer to help her, she added, "I won't help you commit a crime."

Colette stood still and prayed. She wanted to do something to help Shelah get away from this horrible man. But if she showed herself now, it would only make things worse.

Gabriel let out a snarl. "That's always been the plan. You were agreeable until you came here with him."

"I made him bring me," Shelah replied, a bit of grit in her words. "And I regret that—I regret all of this—now."

"You can't back out at this point," Gabriel warned. "I've got big plans for us, and I can only make those plans work if you marry him and then inherit the estate."

"I'm well aware of that. I'll try, really I will. But I don't know how much longer I can pretend. I didn't think we'd be here all month."

She continued to worry at the damp dirt on her cloak, her fingers frantically brushing away dirt. "I have to go back before Kathleen misses me and sends out a search party. You take the path the way you got here so no one will see you."

Gabriel swiped a hand across his wind-blown hair. "Get it together, Shelah. Or else."

Colette didn't move until she knew the man was gone. Then she found a spot farther up the path to the inn and waited for Shelah.

When the woman came around the curve, her head down, Colette stepped out in front of her. "We need to talk."

Startled, Shelah gasped and glanced back. "About what? I was just out for a walk."

"*Neh*, you were not just out for a walk. I heard voices and then I heard you sobbing." She didn't tell the other woman she'd heard their whole horrible plot and seen Gabriel push Shelah. "What's going on? Who were you talking to? Are you in danger?"

Glancing back, Shelah shook her head, looking nervous. "What are you talking about? I only needed some air. I wanted to see the big lake up close."

"So you were alone?" Colette asked as she guided Shelah back up the path. "I thought I heard you talking to someone, but maybe it was the birds or an echo from the road."

"That had to be it," Shelah said, her brown eyes looming like two dark orbs.

Colette had never seen the woman so jittery. Shelah held on to Colette like a lifeline, her hands clammy and shaking. She was scared of Gabriel Moser. Colette could see Shelah's relief once they were safely on the inn's front lawn, where the patches of crisp snow crackled into mush as their boots pushed through.

"Wait," Colette said before they went inside. "Let's talk in the small parlor—the library. I'll have some hot tea brought in."

"I should go upstairs."

Colette held the other woman's cloak, her gaze fixing on the soiled spot. "Shelah, we need to talk. Go into the parlor and wait. I mean it."

Shelah inclined her head in a nod, tears in her eyes. "I'd like a cup of tea."

Colette didn't go to the kitchen. She went to Henry, who'd been watching them. If Shelah tried to bolt, they'd both see her. After she ordered the tea, she found Shelah in the small parlor. Colette entered and shut the door.

Then she sat down on the high-backed settee and grabbed Shelah's hand. Shelah gasped in pain. Colette looked at her hand. Her palms and fingers were raw from where she'd scraped them when Gabriel had pushed her. Thankful Shelah hadn't fallen over the slippery bluff, Colette glanced up. Shelah was crying.

"Shelah, tell me the truth. I heard all of it on the path out there. I saw him push you, so don't lie to protect him. It's over. All over. You can't go through with your plan."

Matthew had looked for Colette everywhere. Jonah had told him Gabriel Moser had been spotted in the area, driving a beat-up tan pickup. The locals were searching for the blue car, and they'd finally located it in a used lot near Shipshewana, the bent fender still visible.

"The salesman said Gabriel didn't even care that the car was worth a lot more than the truck he traded it for," Jonah had told him and Levi earlier. "Moser wanted a nondescript vehicle, and now he has one. But we found the pickup. Now we just need to find him in it. The locals, I mean. We don't condone such things."

Levi and Matthew had grinned at that. Jonah still had a lot of the detective in him, even though he'd been baptized into their faith.

Matthew wanted to tell Colette this news, to warn her. When he didn't find her in the kitchen, he went to the lobby to talk to Henry. The man had eyes on everyone around here.

"Hello, Henry," he said as he came up to the old mahogany counter that stretched across the entryway. "Have you seen Colette?"

Henry, robust and career military, nodded toward the

closed pocket doors just off the lobby. "In there, but I must warn you, she's with Shelah."

"Shelah?" Matthew shook his head. "This can't be *gut*. But I need to speak to Colette."

Henry eyed the closed doors. "You are a braver man than I," he said with a grin.

Matthew couldn't tell Colette his news with Shelah standing by. Before he could think what to do next, the pocket doors flew open, and Colette stood there, glancing around.

"Matthew, I was about to go looking for you."

"I need to talk to you, too," he said, rushing to her. Checking behind her, he spotted Shelah sitting on the settee. "Somewhere private."

Colette whispered, "I believe you need to hear what Shelah has to say."

Matthew's heart rate accelerated, but he was ready to get this confrontation over with, and this might be the time. "Okay."

He went into the room and sat down, his eyes on Shelah. The tension in the air sizzled like the wood in the small fireplace. "What's going on?" he asked the two women he'd been caught between for so long.

"Tell him," Colette said in a demanding tone he'd heard before when she was angry.

Shelah started crying.

Colette kept talking. "Shelah, if you tell the truth now, you might have an opportunity for redemption. If not, you will create your worst nightmare—being shunned and alone for a very long time."

Matthew glanced from Colette to Shelah. "She's right, Shelah. We've pieced things together and we think we know the truth. But I'd like to hear your side of the story."

Shelah's sobs grew louder. Colette sat down beside her and put a hand on her arm. Matthew thought he must be imagining things, but he didn't dare break the mood.

"I've been lying," Shelah announced as if they hadn't figured out that already. "I'm so sorry, Matthew. It's a long story."

"I want to hear it," he said, immeasurably relieved. "And now, before we ruin our lives altogether."

"Mattie," Colette said, "Shelah wouldn't have just ruined your life. If she had gone along with what Gabriel wants her to do, you'd lose your life."

He had hoped and prayed they were wrong, but now Shelah's sobs showed him the truth. "I'm so sorry," she kept whispering. "I've made a terrible mistake, and I don't know how to stop it now."

"The truth," Colette said. "*Now*, Shelah. Gabriel is back and he wants what he wants, regardless of your sudden change of heart. You should have known from the beginning this was a bad idea."

Shelah wiped at her eyes and nodded. "A bad idea, but love has a way of blinding a person. You and Matthew belong together. That was obvious from the time I got here. Even before that, really." She paused and found a handkerchief in her cloak pocket. "I have loved Gabriel since the day I met him in the stables. He taught me how to ride, and we were so close. He was Amish then. Saul didn't like us being so friendly, but I convinced him we were just friends. He didn't want me hanging out with the hired hands, but Gabriel was different. He wanted to leave the Amish and make a name for himself."

Colette gazed at Matthew. "Did he want you to go with him?"

Shelah took in a breath. "Not at first. He left for two years and then came back. Saul listened to his pleas and hired him again, but only if he'd leave me alone. Saul always told me he had someone in mind for me to marry." Her gaze held Matthew's.

"Me?" he said, knowing the answer.

"You." Shelah shrugged. "I didn't know that until he got so ill. I was sneaking out with Gabriel, planning our future. Gabe said we'd need money, and he knew how to get it. He wanted me to steal from Saul, but I refused."

"She was about to explain when I thought I heard you talking to Henry," Colette told Mattie. Then she turned back to Shelah. "Why are you messing with this man now?"

"Go ahead, Shelah," he said. "I really need to hear this."

Shelah took a sip of her tea, her worried expression changing as her eyes softened and a trace of resolve and relief flittered across her gaze. "I'm actually ready to confess. This whole time here has been so trying." She smiled at Matthew. "You are one of the nicest men I've ever met. But I already loved Gabriel when you came into my life. Saul wanted us together, and as usual, he did not allow for discussion. His was always the final word."

Matthew gave her a frown. "But you could have told me the truth, Shelah. All you had to say was that you loved Gabriel."

"I couldn't. Gabe had jumped the fence to go out into the *Englisch* world. I was fascinated by that, but he had no money and no job. He tried to come back into the fold, and Saul paid him a nice salary, but Saul forbade me to see him." She wiped at her eyes. "Saul also convinced me that if I left with Gabriel, I'd lose any inheritance coming my way. I believed him."

"And yet, he lied to you and left everything to me to force us together." Matthew would never claim such a conniving man as his earthly father. Daed was his father.

"He did," Shelah said. "When I realized that, I found Gabe and told him I'd go along with the plan to get some money for us, but Saul became ill. Gabe and I had thought that once Saul died, we'd take as much money as possible and get reestablished elsewhere or sell the whole place. He was angry when he heard what Saul had really done."

"Did you two harm Saul?" Matthew asked, his heart filled with doubt and guilt.

"*Neh.* We truly planned to wait until he died, so I'd inherit. We bided our time and met up once or twice a week to solidify our plans."

Colette stood and placed her hands on a chair, her knuckles going white as she gripped it. "But you two defied his rules and he caught you together?"

"*Ja.*" Shelah lowered her head in shame. "He fired Gabriel, and then you showed up. He called you to come because he knew you'd distract me, and he also knew he was dying. And it worked. When he told me he wanted me to marry you, I had only two thoughts. One, I'd be secure the rest of my life; two, but without Gabriel. I found a way to meet with Gabe, and that's when he suggested this plan."

"That you'd force me to marry you and then, later, something foul would happen to me. You'd be a wealthy Amish widow."

"Not Amish," she said. "I'd leave with Gabriel but keep

the property. Have a land manager and hire local Amish as Saul had always done, but from far away with Gabe."

She stood and looked out the window. "Now he still wants me to marry you, just so we can get the estate. What was I thinking to agree to this—to agree to harming you, Matthew? I'm so sorry."

CHAPTER TWENTY-THREE

Matthew didn't know what to say. He met Colette's gaze, saw the hope in her eyes, and wondered how he'd ever sort out this mess so he could stand beside her as his bride.

"Tell him the rest," she said, watching Shelah.

Shelah nodded, took a breath. "Gabriel is back, and I talked to him today down on the beach. He's impatient to see us married and I'm afraid he's getting desperate."

"I followed them and watched them arguing," Colette explained. "He pushed her, Mattie." She reached for Shelah's hand. "She grazed her hands on a large rock when she caught herself."

When he saw the raw welts across Shelah's hand, Matthew's anger knew no bounds. "This man is dangerous, Shelah. To you and me, and to my family and my friends. There is now a witness to his threat." He gave Colette a thankful nod. "And what were you thinking, following her? If he'd seen you, you'd be floating in the lake."

"I had to find out," Colette replied, her eyes bright with the defiance he knew so well. "And now we know the whole truth. What are we to do about this?"

Matthew studied the floor. "We could offer him some money and tell him to go away."

Shelah shook her head. "I told him I'd try to get some money early—for the wedding—and I'd give it to him. He wants it all, Matthew. I can now see he only pretended to love me when he returned. But he loves power and money more. He thought I was the heiress and he could just sweep me off my feet and take what was mine. But to force me to marry another man so he can do harm, that doesn't feel like love to me."

"*Neh*, that is *lecherich*," Colette replied.

Matthew stood and paced. "It is ridiculous. We need to trap him. Shelah, do you still love this man?"

Shelah started crying again. "I will always love Gabe, but I can't go through with this. He does not love me—he loves money and power. I'm afraid I'd be next on his list."

"You mean after he'd done in Matthew?" Colette said, her tone harsh.

"I can't let him harm Matthew or anyone," Shelah replied. "What can I do to help . . . bring him to justice?"

"You keep doing what you're already doing," Matthew said. "You pretend. We pretend. Find a way to meet with him and tell him we've moved the wedding up to the week after Christmas and we're having it here. To save time and to halt rumors."

Shelah nodded. "Okay."

"You and I will walk about and pretend we're close," he replied, sending Colette an apologetic glance. "You mustn't tell Gabe that we're onto him, Shelah."

"I won't," she said. "I'm ready for this to end. I want to go home, and . . . I'll understand if you want me off Saul's property."

"We'll discuss that after we have Gabriel Moser in custody," he said. "Tonight, we'll meet here at the inn to discuss our strategy further. That way, he won't be able to see you coming or going and it will look natural, as we all are always moving through here."

He glanced from Shelah to Colette. "Can you two work together without animosity and without showing him we know?"

"I'm ready," Shelah said. "I feel as if a tremendous burden has fallen off my shoulders."

"Murder is a tremendous burden," Colette replied. "*Denke*, Shelah, for telling us the truth. You've not only saved Mattie from harm, but yourself also. If a man would push you against a rock face near a cold, deep lake, he'll do much more to hurt you when he's sure no one is around. Especially if he is a greedy, self-serving man who has threatened to kill another."

"I know," Shelah replied. "He's been angry at me before." Then she glanced at Matthew. "I wish he could be more like you."

"You will find the right person," Matthew told her. "And that person will not treat you so callously, I promise."

Colette nodded in agreement. "We will take care of you until you're safe, Shelah."

"I don't know how to thank you," Shelah replied, her tone and demeanor full of regret. Holding her hands together, she glanced from Matthew to Colette, her eyes full of humility. "After all I've done, you're still kind to me."

"You told us the truth," Colette said. "That counts."

They opened the parlor doors to find Abigail, Jonah, Levi, and Eliza waiting for them by the roaring flames of the main fireplace.

"What's up?" Jonah asked. "We followed Matthew here in case we were needed."

"We must gather the whole family," Colette said. "Shelah is willing to cooperate with us. She has confirmed that Gabriel Moser is a dangerous man."

As planned, they met in the inn's employee room so no one would see them all together. Shelah had told Henry to please ask Kathleen to come, too. The poor woman had been asleep, but she got herself together and hurried to the big room.

Mamm and Daed came in and found seats, their expressions caught between curiosity and frustration. It was close to their bedtime, too.

"What has happened?" Kathleen asked in the weary voice of a woman who'd dealt with this kind of discussion before.

Shelah took her by her arm. "You'll find out. Please, just listen. This will all be over soon."

"That sounds ominous," Kathleen replied. But she sat down and placed her hands in her lap, ever the lady. "And everyone is here, I see."

After the others were seated, Jonah remained standing. He glanced from Abigail to Mamm and Daed, and then his intense gaze moved to Matthew and Colette, then Eliza and Levi, and finally settled on Kathleen and Shelah.

"Gabriel Moser used to be Amish, and he worked for Saul Mueller. He is the man who showed up at the frolic, asking for Shelah. And we have reason to believe he was driving the car that hit Matthew's buggy."

Shelah gasped and shook her head. "I never thought of that and I wasn't a part of that. I didn't see the car."

Kathleen's shrewd gaze zoomed in Shelah. "Oh, no."

"Oh, yes," Colette blurted, but Mamm gave her a warning stare.

Jonah continued, explaining how his contacts in the police department had tracked down the vehicle that had rammed into Matthew's buggy. "I don't believe it was an intended hit, however. I think he was following the buggy and skidded on the ice."

Shelah turned to Kathleen. "He could have killed us all."

Kathleen huffed a breath. "Go on, Jonah."

"That was just the beginning," Jonah explained. "He's got an impressive criminal record. It seems that after he left the Amish community in Missouri, he fell in with a ruthless group and learned how to con innocents out of money and valuables."

"But he returned," Kathleen said, her voice rising with surprise. "Saul let him come back."

Jonah nodded. "There was a reason for that, just as there was a reason for everything Saul did."

Colette sat up straight and Matthew gave Jonah a quizzical look. "What else have you learned?" Matthew asked Jonah.

"Gabriel Moser and Saul went way back. One of my friends asked around in Missouri. It seems Saul and Gabriel's *mamm* knew each other." He stopped, shrugged. "In the biblical way."

Kathleen gasped. "What?"

Jonah held up a hand. "Gabriel is not Saul's child. His mother and Saul had an affair after he was born, but no children were conceived."

Colette and every other woman in the room blushed. Daed grunted and lowered his head.

Matthew shot a glance at Shelah. "I'm sorry. I know

how hearing that must feel." Then he punched a fist against the table. "And I'm guessing it wasn't a consensual encounter."

"I thought the same," Daed said. "It wonders me how many *affairs* my brother might have had, how many lives he's ruined."

Kathleen gave Shelah an empathetic stare. "I've held this secret for a long time. I'm afraid that's why my cousin and her husband left." When Shelah's eyes widened, she added, "It happened after you were born."

Shelah's eyes misted over. "Are you telling me Saul abused my *mamm*, too? And that Gabriel wanted revenge on Saul so he used me to get it?" She held her hand to her throat. "Gabriel was always dropping hints, but I was too infatuated to understand what was really happening." She crumpled into Kathleen's arms. "How could I have been so naive and stupid?"

Kathleen patted Shelah's back. "I tried to warn you about so many things, but I'm sorry for what he's put you through. I should have told you what I knew about your folks leaving. They wanted to get away, but they had to find a place first."

"They left me," Shelah said, anger filling her words. "They left me all alone."

"They had much to discuss that they didn't want you to hear," Kathleen replied. "They loved you so much."

Colette's heart went out to Matthew and Shelah. "This explains why Saul wanted you two married. He took you in, Shelah, out of guilt. Your parents left to find another place to live, but they never made it home to get you. Saul knew this and he had to have known it was his fault. In the same way, guilt caused him to ask for Matthew to come to him. He thought if you two married and shared his wealth, it would wipe away all his sins."

Shelah put her head on the table. "This is a nightmare."

Jonah gave her a moment and then continued. "So now we've put it all together. Gabriel found out the truth about his mother and Saul, and he came back for revenge after his *mamm* told him why she didn't want him around Saul. He must have forced Saul to hire him back, and he probably demanded money from Saul. How else could he have afforded that sports car?"

Matthew stood and started pacing. "Gabriel believes Shelah should be the rightful heir, but he probably doesn't know about Shelah's *mamm* and Saul. He might have put two and two together, but Saul picked me to inherit. So then came the desperate plan for Shelah and me to get married. Saul wanted it and now I know why. He couldn't tell us the truth—that Gabriel was extorting him. Besides, he did want us to get married, because he is my biological father. It was his way to protect both of us and to ease his conscience, I believe."

"What happens next?" Kathleen asked, her frown full of rage. "I for one want this man to be put away for a long time. He's done enough to all of us, and so has Saul, God rest his soul. But it's high time we get this over with."

"I think we can all agree on that," Jonah replied. Abigail and Eliza sent Colette quiet glances of reassurance.

She'd like nothing more.

Daed nodded. "I shall talk to the bishop at once." He looked at Shelah. "He will want to hear from you, too."

Shelah nodded. "I don't know how I'll keep up this charade with Gabriel. He's got a bad temper."

Kathleen puffed up like a protective hen. "You will not keep up a charade. We are going home."

"That's too dangerous right now," Jonah told her. "Gabriel is getting desperate. If he hears you've left, he'll be waiting for you in Missouri, and . . . things won't go well for either of you."

Mamm nodded. "He's right, Kathleen. You're both safer here, and you can stay as long as needed."

Kathleen wiped at her eyes. "You've all been so kind. I had no idea what was really going on. I've failed you, Shelah. I should have told you my suspicions and kept you in Missouri."

Shelah grabbed both Kathleen's hands. "You've been the only relative who has been honest with me. And I've lied about everything. This is my fault, for loving the wrong man."

Colette stood, wishing she could be anywhere but here. "Saul started this a long time ago, and his sins caught up with him. I hope he made his peace with the Lord. Because he ruined a lot of lives here on earth."

"We will let the authorities find Gabriel, but I'll alert my friends at the station about what we've discussed here." Jonah stood and shifted his gaze to Shelah. "Meantime, Shelah, if you hear from him, try to set up a meeting. We can call for help, and at the least, he'll be taken in for questioning regarding the accident. We know he was driving the car from the license plate, and the township police can gather DNA samples, too. They'll need to send them to the state lab for verification, but if they find a match, the information can be used as evidence."

"This is all too much," Kathleen said. "Shelah, you let me know if you hear from him. I mean it. I won't mess things up by confronting him, but I can at least make someone aware to watch over you."

"If you stay on the property, you should be safe," Levi

offered. "We're all aware of what's going on. And I'm glad. In this case, the more of us here who know, the better. To protect all of us."

Kathleen nudged Shelah toward the hallway leading to the lobby. "*Kumm*, you need to rest."

Shelah turned and faced Colette, contrite now. "*Denke*. If you hadn't followed me today, I don't know what I'd have done after seeing Gabriel. I'm so relieved this farce is over."

Colette lifted her chin, not ready to forgive but very ready to help. "It's not over yet, but it soon will be. You were brave today, Shelah. The kind of brave that takes a lot of guts and a strong faith."

Shelah looked sheepish, her gaze hitting the floor. "Not as brave as you've always been, but I'm going to do better from now on."

Matthew stood nearby. "I'm proud of you, Shelah."

Shelah nodded at him, her gaze dancing with hope. "I wish I could love you, Matthew." Then she turned and headed upstairs with Kathleen.

Colette stayed behind when the others had left. Matthew waited for her. "I'll walk you to the cottage."

"I'd like that," she said, the discomfort she'd felt around him all these weeks now disappearing. "This is so hard to believe. Your uncle—"

"—was what the *Englisch* would call a womanizer and a predator."

"*Ja*." She didn't say anything more, mindful that Saul was his biological father. "I'm sorry, Mattie. Sorry for doubting you, for being so bitter and angry. I should have trusted you no matter what."

He pulled her into his arms and held her close. Colette fell against him, the strength of his arms and the warmth of his heart filling her with something she'd missed these many months while he was gone.

"I should have told you the truth from the beginning," he replied, his breath warm against her neck. "I wanted to, so many times. But I didn't want to hurt you."

"Just come back to me," she said. "No matter what happens from here on out, don't leave me again."

"I won't," he said. "I promise. And that means I'll be keeping an eye out for you until this is finished." He drew back and held a hand to her cheek. "Because you could be in real danger now, too. You're the one reason I have refused to marry Shelah, and that makes you a target."

CHAPTER TWENTY-FOUR

Everyone was on alert now.

The staff had been warned, and the family stuck close to each other. Matthew had informed his parents of the latest discoveries so they could be wary of any strangers prowling around their home. His brothers, as mischievous as they could be, knew how to take care of such things.

Matthew came to the inn as usual, falling into the old habits of helping out, working on the kitchen equipment, and lending a hand wherever needed.

He arrived early so he and Colette could have some quiet time. Now, they were putting the final touches on the lobby so the singing could take place. Fresh snow covered the grounds and the trees, making the whole place look like a winter wonderland.

He found Colette in her usual spot at the work counter. She was making Christmas cookies and cupcakes for the big event. The scents of vanilla and almond wafted through the long kitchen. They planned to serve the treats with warm apple cider and hot chocolate.

He stopped to watch her work, as had become his habit. Thankful that she'd never given up on him, he took this time to pray for her, to ask *Gott* to provide, to show them the way. She was so beautiful there in the soft light of day, tendrils of loose hair curling at her neck and temples, the kitchen warm and smelling of Christmas.

She lifted her head as if she knew he'd be there, glancing over her shoulder. "Mattie."

He moved toward her, wanting her, loving her, needing her.

He pulled her back against him and held his hands across her stomach. "I thought I might be able to bribe a cookie from you."

"You might," she said, giggling as she fell against his chest. "It feels nice to snuggle with you. It's fearsome cold out there."

He kissed her neck and was rewarded with a sigh. "That it is, but we'll make sure the roads are clear to get everyone here. Though I think the parents would walk if necessary to see their scholars singing Christmas songs."

"That they would."

She pivoted and handed him two fresh cookies on a napkin. "I made *kaffe*, and we have the best breakfast tea. A new brand for the holidays."

"I know. My *mamm* brags on that tea. I'm going to wrap her up a whole box for Christmas." He kissed Colette's neck again. "She says it's spicy and sweet all at the same time. Kind of like my girl."

Colette sighed and giggled. "Am I like that?"

"You are like that and more," he said. "But we won't tell my *mamm* about this conversation."

"How is she?" Colette asked as they managed to pull away from each other to sit at the big counter. "I've thought of nothing else but this horrible predicament."

"She's holding up," he said. "She's stronger than I

gave her credit for. Daed loves her so much, and now, they seem to be rekindling that love in an even deeper way."

"Oh, I like hearing that." She looked into his eyes. "And we seem to be doing the same."

"At last," he said, biting into a cookie. "This will be over soon and then—"

"—and then, we will decide our future," she finished. "Shelah and Kathleen met with the bishop yesterday. She will confess in front of their brethren when they return to Missouri."

"And I met with the bishop not long after they had seen him," he replied. "I'm free and clear. On the market again."

She smiled, then lifted her gaze to him. "I'll keep that in mind. For future reference."

He understood. They didn't dare plan their future until Gabriel Moser was out of their lives. Shelah was working on becoming a more pious, quiet, considerate person. It was clear she only wanted to end this disaster and go home. She'd put on a bold front, but her charade had come crashing down. Matthew felt for her, but he could never love her. All he could offer her now was shelter and some kind of financial support. Being her guardian might be the one kind thing Saul had done, even if he'd done it for his own dubious reasons.

As if sensing his thoughts, Colette asked, "Have you decided what you'll do with the property, Mattie?"

Matthew finished his *kaffe*. "I don't want it. I know that. Shelah and Kathleen will live in the guest cottage, which is finer than most homes and has plenty of room. I've talked to a man I got to know when I was there about running the place, and he will be paid to do so. He can live in another house on the property. I've told him he can renovate it and I'll cover the cost."

"Do you want the money, to help your parents?"

"They say *neh*, but I feel I should give them something to tide them over. Saul's money won't change how they feel, but it can serve as restitution at least."

"Maybe you can talk to them again and explain how the money could help them. They can set a limit. We know they don't need much; it's not our way. And yet, knowing they can rest easy might be worth accepting some of the money."

"You mean, they could be blessed and that makes the money okay?"

"Something like that. But only if they agree. They won't take it easily, and I suppose they might resent you for giving it."

"You're a smart woman."

"Hardly. I almost let you get away. During these last few weeks, I thought of how I ignored you all those years, how I tormented you with grunge work and teased you with my flirting."

"I loved every minute of that," he admitted. "Because at least you were noticing me."

She put her hand on his cheek. "I have always noticed you, Matthew Mueller. I think in my own confused way, I wanted your attention right back. I was just too afraid to let my feelings show."

He got up and tugged her close. "You've got me now."

Someone cleared their throat. Loudly.

Edith stood at the door. "Honestly, do I need to send you two to the bishop for a talk?"

"I have had enough talks with the bishop," Matthew replied with a soft smile.

She grinned at both of them. "Don't mind me. I love seeing you together. But I think I smell cookies burning."

"Did someone burn cookies?" Aenti Miriam asked as she swept into the kitchen later. "That won't do."

"I did," Colette admitted, her smile creeping out even when she tried to look contrite. "It's okay. I fed those to the goats and started a new batch. We'll have plenty for tomorrow."

Aenti gave her a long appraisal. "You're back with Matthew, ain't so?"

"It is so," Colette admitted. "But we are being very cautious. The bishop has heard the truth of everything, and Matthew is a free man."

"He and Shelah will not marry?"

Colette figured her *aenti* had heard this already, but she had to step lightly here. Mamm had not shared the details with anyone, especially her nosy sister. "Shelah called the wedding off. Seems they are not compatible after all."

Miriam surveyed the kitchen, trying hard to find something to criticize. "*Ach vell*, a fly could have seen that. But you mind your decorum, you hear? You don't want to go and mess things up after all this turmoil."

"I won't, I promise," Colette said while she sealed up cookies in sturdy containers and cleaned the kitchen. The café had been busy today as tourists came through on their way to somewhere else and returning guests showed up for a home-cooked feast. They'd served turkey and stuffing, baked ham, a variety of vegetable casseroles, red velvet cake, and several choices of pie. "What a busy day. I'm so glad we have everything ready for the singing tomorrow."

"I hear it will be crowded since the committee moved it here instead of the schoolroom. That place is stifling when it gets crowded."

Colette agreed with her *aenti*. "I think we'll have a large crowd, because the *Englisch* townsfolk seem to enjoy it, too."

"I plan to stand in the back so I can get fresh air if I need it," Miriam replied. "I don't want to have a fainting spell from getting too hot."

"We wouldn't want that," Colette replied, laughing at Miriam's drama. She could not recall her *aenti* ever having a fainting spell. "How is Connie, by the way?"

"She's doing remarkably well. She hopes to be here to see Jamie and Laura singing. Her Parkinson's is under control for the most part, but we know that can't last."

Colette was so glad her *aenti* had found a purpose by being Connie Lapp's helpmate and nurse. Aenti Miriam was a smart woman, and she had the energy to help Connie on bad days. Levi and Eliza had sung her praises for helping his mother. Helping Connie kept her out of the inn kitchen, where she and Edith had been known to go a round or two in one-upping each other.

"I hope she'll be able to attend and enjoy herself," Colette said. "I plan on having a *gut* time."

Aenti Miriam huffed and went in search of something to fuss about, but when Colette heard Henry laughing, she had to grin. Aenti had a crush on Henry, but it was an innocent thing. They were just friends. She was learning how important friendship could be.

Her sisters came into the kitchen. "We've hung the quilts, sister," Eliza said. "Aenti is admiring them."

"Oh, or checking for mistakes," Abby said on a snicker. "Your quilt is beautiful, Colette."

She'd worked on it late into the night over the last few days, her heart going from heavy and burdened to free and happy. "Can you see a difference?"

"*Ja,*" Eliza said as she helped put away clean dishes and pots and pans. "The man and woman standing by a Christmas tree is lovely. The snowy background and the glistening of the trees with silvery thread is perfect. Even Aenti was in awe."

"Then I have succeeded," Colette said. "And *denke* for the help."

"We have all three of them up now," Abby said. "I think they are beautiful, and we've had tourists wanting to buy them."

"They are not for sale," Eliza added.

"Of course not," Colette replied with a nod. "I want Mattie to see mine. I hope his whole family will be here tomorrow."

"It's going to be a great day," Abby said. "Then we have Christmas Eve, Christmas, and Second Christmas. What a *wunderbar* weekend."

Eliza smiled, tears in her eyes, as she put away silverware. "It's a special time. My first Christmas as a married woman."

Mamm walked in and searched her daughters' faces. "What is going on?"

She glanced from Abigail to Eliza and then to Colette. "I hope soon all of you will be married. Then I can plan on more *kinder* running through these hallways."

They all ran to Mamm and hugged her tight.

Colette pulled away. "Let's just hope nothing goes wrong and that will soon be our reality."

"We will continue to pray on it," Mamm said. "Now let's finish up here and go home to the white bean chili I've had simmering all day long."

Colette moved through the kitchen to make sure she'd cleaned it properly. Everything was in order for the big event tomorrow.

Even though she felt better knowing Matthew and she could be together again, that nagging worry still hovered over her like a thundercloud ready to burst.

Where was Gabriel Moser? And when would he show up to talk to Shelah again?

Matthew got home late and took Sawdust to the barn. The big horse was still skittish from the accident, but Sawdust was also loyal and a fine quarter horse. "You did *gut* today," Matthew said. "All this getting up early to see my girl has worn both of us out, but she's worth it, ain't so."

Sawdust neighed a reply, ready for his rations and his stall. Aaron and Timothy came running in. Those two never slowed.

"The back fence has been cut," Aaron said, huffing breaths of air. "We fixed it."

Timothy had a workbag slung over his shoulder. "We crimped it back together, but someone sure cut it and stretched it."

Matthew grabbed an ax. "I'll go check."

"We can come," Aaron said. "We'll show you the footprints."

"And why are you taking an ax?" Timothy asked. "We fixed the fence."

"I might need to chop down some of the dead shrubs

near the fence," Matthew said. He couldn't tell them he needed a weapon. He had an idea who might be snooping around, but he couldn't tell his brothers that either.

"Where's Daed?" he asked, trying to sound casual, as they hurried across the fallow fields.

"He finished up some work in the barn and went to the house. He was cold," Aaron said. "We saw you first, so he doesn't even know about this."

"Okay, well, we won't upset him until I see what's what. We've never had an intruder back there before."

"Just possums and snakes," Timothy reminded him.

Possums, raccoons, snakes—anything but a human, Matthew thought. He knew exactly who had done this. And he'd need to alert Jonah and the rest of the family soon.

Dusk settled like a golden blanket over the field and forest, creating long shadows. He saw the footprints immediately. *Didn't even try to cover them up*.

"Did either of you see anyone coming onto our property?"

"*Neh*," Aaron said. "But we did hear a vehicle cranking deep in the woods."

"A vehicle? So *Englisch* maybe?"

"For certain sure," Timothy said while he pointed to the patched fence and the soggy footprints in the dirt and snow. "They stepped through, and look." He pointed to the path of footprints. "They stopped here and turned around. Left the same way they came."

"Probably because we were out here looking for kindling wood," Aaron said. "We found some twigs and broken limbs. Whoever it was had to have seen us and heard us. But we didn't see them."

He imagined his brothers had been busy trying to outdo each other and tossing the occasional snowball. "It's okay. You both did *gut* coming to find me."

He studied the fence. It had obviously been breached with a wire cutter. "Why don't you two run on home and take in the kindling wood. I'll check around, and first thing tomorrow, I'll check the whole fence line."

They ran off, chasing each other. Matthew stood and stared out into the forest, the sounds of snow melt and nocturnal animals breaking the eerie silence that held him there.

Was someone out there waiting to attack his family?

None of them would be safe until they stopped Gabriel Moser. He'd get word to Jonah as soon as possible.

And he prayed nothing bad would happen to those he loved.

CHAPTER TWENTY-FIVE

Early-morning sunshine glinted through the kitchen windows while Colette started the cinnamon rolls. She'd learned a lot at this old counter, working alone. Edith had listened to her worst fears and her long rants, taking the conversation back to food each time Colette would veer off on her personal problems.

Today, she'd already gotten the hefty turkey, which she'd rubbed down with oil and sprinkled with sage and rosemary, into the big oven. They'd have sliced turkey with gravy and stuffing again today. It was a tradition the week of Christmas, before they shut down the inn to the public and held their own family meal there. They'd have three days off at the end of the week, and then back to work.

She moved the dough between her hands as Edith had taught her, back and forth, back and forth. Today, she was making dinner rolls.

"It's the love you put in it that brings out the sweetness, the goodness of food," Edith had said. "The touch of someone's hands is always a comfort, and it brings out the best in the food. Whether you are kneading dough or stirring with a spoon, your touch of love is the secret, Colette."

Colette believed that with all her heart. Matthew had come back to her, and he wanted to spend the rest of his life with her. Shelah had seen the error of her ways and now only wanted to be done with Gabriel so she could return home. Hoping that wasn't too little, too late, Colette prayed everything would fall into place soon, because she'd learned to cook and make a quilt with her *touch of love*, and now she wanted to give Matthew the same.

Matthew hurried in and came up to her, his expression sharp with worry and anger, his frown worse than the ones Jonah made when he was mad.

"What's wrong?" she said, dropping the round bread dough onto the floured counter and wiping her hands on her apron.

"Someone cut our fence line late yesterday," he said, the grit in his words showing his frustration. "I had to get here early to let Jonah know. He's in contact with the township authorities right now. My brothers heard a vehicle cranking, and that's when they saw the tear in the fence."

"Is everyone all right?" she asked after wiping her hands again and hurriedly putting the dough in a bowl with a towel over it so it could rise on the warm cook top.

"*Ja*, but he might come back at any time. My whole family is coming to the singing today. It's a relief they'll be here most of the day."

"They should be careful when they return home. Gabriel could be waiting there for them. Maybe they should stay here with us."

"I told Daed and Mamm what's happening. I cautioned my brothers that a stranger has been prowling around."

"Then they should plan to spend the night here. That will be fine—they are family, too."

"We don't want to impose, but that could be a solution. Maybe the township patrols can check on the property."

"Or Jonah can ride over. He has this certain look that scares people. Especially bad people."

"I'll talk to them when they arrive," Matthew said, his hand touching hers. "You must be watchful. Don't go off after anyone alone, promise?"

Colette glanced around as early staffers started pouring in. "We have extra people to help today. I need to be mindful. Did Jonah warn everyone?"

"He was headed toward the cottage while I came here. He said he'd call the police and get someone out here to patrol the inn."

"I'll feel better knowing that."

Matthew tugged her close. "Don't leave my side."

"I have to go and change, and I need to help serve everyone," she said. "But I will be careful coming and going. I'll bring my clean clothes and get dressed here. I won't leave this area all day, I promise."

"And I'll be here all day." He gave her a quick kiss. "I'm going up to find Shelah and alert her and Kathleen."

Wishing he could stay, Colette nodded. "You be careful, too. He's getting desperate and that means he could do anything to any one of us."

"My point exactly," Matthew replied. "Has Shelah been downstairs yet today?"

"Not yet. She tends to sleep in."

He nodded at that statement. "That's true, but I'm sure glad you are an early riser."

"I'm thinking I like being the first one here every day when I know you're waiting for me."

"I'll always be waiting for you, Colette."

After he left, Colette told the kitchen staff there was a stranger lurking about. "We believe he is the *Englisch* who hit Matthew Mueller's buggy a few weeks ago. He's probably trying to make sure no one here knows that— so he could threaten any one of us. Or all of us. He's toying with us right now."

Everyone nodded and assured her they'd be on the watch.

Edith came up to her after the others had moved on to their tasks. "Shelah has something to do with this man, ain't so?"

"She did," Colette admitted, "but she finally told us the truth. Now she is trying to make amends, but her friend has other ideas. He's a criminal. That's all I can say right now."

Edith went to the open shelf where they kept the cast-iron pots and pans. "I've found a *gut* frying pan can knock a person out cold."

Shocked and impressed, Colette asked, "And how did you find this out?"

"That's all I can say right now," Edith mimicked Colette's own words with a smug smile. "But trust me, it works in a pinch."

"I'll remember," Colette said. Then she added, "*Denke*, Edith. You've been a true friend through this whole ordeal."

Edith's eyes misted over. "I'm just the cook."

"*Neh*, you are more than that," Colette replied. "You've helped Mamm raise all of us and you've been a constant presence in this inn and in our lives. You show up, you work hard, and these past few weeks, you've listened to me lamenting about everything. But you taught me to cook, really cook, to create food that nourishes the soul and makes people happy. You were just what I needed during this horrible time. So *denke*, Edith."

"Your dough is ready," Edith said, reaching for her apron to wipe her eyes. "And I have work to do." Then she rushed toward Colette and took her in her arms. "You King girls always amaze me."

With that, she pulled away, winked at Colette, and went on with her work, her composure intact.

But Colette had seen beyond the bossy cook attitude. Edith was a dear friend who needed to be needed. If Colette had learned anything during this time of torment, it was to cherish those she'd taken for granted, from Matthew to her sisters and her parents to Edith and the entire staff.

She'd be better about that now, because now she understood what it meant to rejoice even in your struggles, to love the Lord through the good and the bad, to praise Him even when she had doubts and distractions.

Denke, Lord.

She said her prayer, opened her eyes, and picked one big, long-handled frying pan to use as a weapon if she needed it.

An hour before the singing started, Jonah gathered everyone and explained who Gabriel Moser was and why he might try to crash the party.

"He's dangerous and he's desperate," Jonah explained. "The township authorities are aware, and they've put out alerts regarding him. If you see the man I've described, or if you see anyone who looks out of place or suspicious, let one of the family know immediately. Do not speak to or approach the man yourself."

"Well, that put a pall on the whole day," Eliza said after the staff members went about their business. "The parents will be arriving soon. I want the *kinder* to be safe."

"The *kinder* and everyone else will be safe inside the inn and out near the pavilion as planned," Jonah said. "We've got the entries covered. Henry brought in a few friends to help with parking and crowd control. They will watch out for us."

Matthew found Colette and tugged her close. "Stay near your family and I'll keep an eye on mine. I went home and told them to come prepared to spend the night."

"We'll find them rooms in our homes, so they'll be comfortable," Colette said, relieved that Matthew's family would be nearby. "I think we have the best plan possible, and we've covered everything. I hope we can enjoy the singing without any disruptions. The *kinder* and the volunteers have all worked so hard."

He gave her an intense gaze. "I talked briefly to Kathleen and Shelah. Shelah is so afraid, she said she might just stay in her room. She can watch from the landing up there if she wants."

"I can understand her being scared. She's turned on Gabriel and he won't like that. It means he won't get what he really wants—Saul's money."

"Let's get through this day and then you and I will take some time for a real adventure," he replied. "After all, it's Christmas. I think a nice buggy ride in the snow with you is the only gift I need."

Colette sighed. "That sounds *wunderbar gut*, Mattie." She saw Maggie motioning to her and hurried off, giving

Matthew one last glance. They might not have time later
to speak much.

The lobby was completely full now. Fifteen minutes
until the scholars came in and took their places. They
were in the employee lounge with their teacher and
Maggie, going over the last-minute details.

Colette knew they would sing beautifully. She'd heard
them practice enough to see they took pride in their task.
And the parents held anticipation in their gazes and in the
way they waited patiently for the singing to begin.

The big room had been decorated with holly berries
and magnolia leaves, along with cedar branches and
pine cones. The *kinder* had made cards for their parents
to view and take home once the event was over. Those
hung on a string over the fireplace. And several of the
quilts the women of the community had made were lined
up in the small sitting room that Colette loved so much,
her quilt amongst those displayed there.

She wondered if Matthew had had a chance to go in
and view them yet. She wanted him to see her quilt, to
see how she'd displayed their times together and her love
for him.

Despite her worry, she loved this time of year, and this
year especially. She'd almost lost hope, but Christmas
always brought hope. A few more days and maybe she
and Matthew could start all over again. A second chance
she wouldn't squander.

As the audience settled down, Maggie and Linda
walked in and nodded. The scholars followed, filing in
quietly, one after another by age, leaving the youngest

ones on the bottom of the bleachers, giggling and waving to their folks.

The whole room laughed and waved. Colette's heart purred like a contented kitten. Would she and Mattie be sitting here one day, waiting for their children to sing? She hoped so.

Linda Gaber said a few words, thanking the parents for all of their help and praising the scholars for working so hard. "Now let's listen and rejoice in the birth of our Lord," Linda said.

After that, the room went quiet while the children went from High German hymns to more traditional *Englisch* songs. The backdrop of green trees with snow tipping their branches was so beautiful. It looked perfect here in this vast old room that had survived centuries. Some of the guests had come down to listen, too, and they smiled and clapped even when they didn't understand the language. Christmas brought everyone together.

A chill went over Colette, a kind of premonition of how things could change in the blink of an eye. She held still, taking in the moment, glancing toward the spot where Matthew sat with his family and Eliza sat with Levi and his family. Mamm and Daed sat with Abigail and Jonah and little Jon, who tried to sing along.

Colette caught Matthew's gaze and they smiled at each other. She stood in the back off to the side, so she had a perfect view of him. He gazed at her more than he paid attention to the scholars.

The program was over in forty minutes, just as Linda had planned it. Applause filled the inn. When Linda invited everyone to get refreshments, more applause sounded, echoing happily along the hallways and stairs.

The parents and their children made their way to the

huge center table that had been set up in the café. The King sisters helped serve the treats and handed each scholar a warm drink. Some braved the outdoors even though a light snowfall and a crisp breeze kept the temperatures low.

After they'd served everyone and the guests had complimented Linda and her crew, people began to disperse. Colette glanced up once again to see if Shelah had come out of her room, but there was no sign of her. Kathleen sat near the stairs, watching, always trying to protect her ward, but Aenti Miriam was talking to her about something. Those two loved to gossip.

Deciding she'd be kind and take some food up to Shelah, Colette mingled a bit more, then grabbed a plate to fill with cookies, pinwheel ham-and-cheese roll-ups, and other nibbles. She'd check on Shelah, and then she'd spend some time with Matthew and his family. Mamm had invited them to stay for an early supper.

That would cap off a perfect day.

Chapter Twenty-six

Colette knocked on the door of the suite, thinking surely Shelah would be hungry after hiding all morning while the singing went on. When she got no answer, she almost turned to leave. But she noticed the door wasn't closed all the way.

Would it be rude to just walk in?

She took her chances and decided she'd leave the food on a table. Why she was being so considerate she didn't know. But Shelah had come clean with them about everything, and Colette did feel grateful for that.

She went in and placed the food on a side table, but the room was a mess. Then she noticed a half-eaten breakfast and the door to the bedroom ajar. "Shelah, are you in there?"

No answer. Colette took a deep breath, telling herself not to panic, not to let her overimaginative brain go right to the most frightening scenario. But when she turned to see the balcony doors open, she knew something had gone wrong. The wind lifted snow drifts against the old French doors and the room was chilly. Shelah must have been gone for a while.

And Colette could guess she'd sneaked down the balcony stairs to the front of the inn for only one reason.

Could she had left to meet with Gabriel Moser?

Colette's stomach roiled. Had Shelah lied to them, only pretended to disagree with Gabriel?

Colette went out on the small balcony, remembering how she used to dream of seeing her hero riding up on a big horse to rescue her. Now that dream had turned into a nightmare.

When she heard a scream echoing through the trees, she rushed back inside and hurried down the stairs to find someone to help her.

"Kathleen," she called, "have you seen Shelah?"

"*Neh*, she wanted to stay in today. She wasn't feeling well."

"I was just in the suite," Colette said as she hurried down the stairs. "She's not in there and the balcony doors are open."

Kathleen stood so quickly, her napkin fell to the floor. Aenti stood, too, both of them calling out to anyone who'd listen.

Henry shot out from behind the check-in counter. "Is everything all right?"

Abigail came running. "What on earth is wrong?"

"Shelah is missing," Colette said. She told Abigail what she'd found. "She must have gone down the balcony stairs."

Kathleen shook her head. "I never dreamed she'd sneak out that way. I thought those doors were sealed shut."

"They are hard to open," Abigail said. "No one ever opens them because the balcony is so narrow, and the stairs are steep. It would take strong hands to pry those little doors open."

"You mean a man's hands?" Aenti Miriam asked.

"Exactly," Kathleen replied. "He's taken her. He's taken our Shelah. We have to find them."

Everyone sprang into action.

"Where is Matthew?" Colette asked, searching for him.

"I think he went to the stables to get the family buggy put away," Mamm said from the hallway. "His folks are staying here for the night."

"I heard a scream down on the path, close to the stables. I have to let him know," Colette replied, grabbing her cloak as she ran out the back door.

The snow had stopped, but the chill of winter hit her with a fierce blast. She had to find Matthew and warn him. She didn't know if Shelah had left with Gabriel of her own accord or if she'd been taken against her will. And right under their noses at that.

Colette's heart hammered against her ribs. What if they'd all been fooled? Had they played right into Shelah and Gabriel's hands?

She rushed into the stables, the bright light of the snow and sun causing her to blink. She heard the horses neighing in agitation. "Matthew, are you here? Jonah, we need to talk."

She hurried up the alley, trying to find someone who could help. Where was everyone?

When she heard footsteps coming from Levi's farrier shop, she headed that way. "Matthew?"

"He's not here," a voice said.

Then she saw them—Gabriel Moser held Shelah in front of him like a shield.

And he had a gun aimed at Colette.

* * *

Matthew had been at the cottage getting his parents and brothers settled in. The boys would sleep upstairs, and Mamm and Daed would stay with Abe and Sarah, since they had a small spare bedroom in the *grossdaddi haus*. He'd sleep in the carriage *haus*.

He was on his way to find Colette so they could finally be alone when he heard voices in the stables. Maybe Jonah and Levi needed some help in there.

But when he entered, he saw his worst nightmare. Gabriel Moser had one hand wrapped around Shelah and he held a gun on Colette with the other one.

"Stop," Matthew said, causing all of them to look toward him. "Let her go. Let them both go."

Gabriel laughed at him. "Why should I? You couldn't decide which one you wanted, so I think I'll just take both of them."

"*Neh,*" Matthew replied as he eased forward, his hands out in front of him. "You don't deserve either of these two women. You won't get away this time."

Another chuckle, and the gun remained pointed at Colette. She glanced back. "Don't listen to him, Matthew. He won't hurt Shelah. He loves her."

"She has a point," Gabriel said. "Shelah is a beauty, but she let me down." He tossed Shelah to the side, causing her to hit the edge of Samson's stall. The big horse neighed his displeasure as Shelah screamed in pain.

Before Matthew could get to them, Gabriel grabbed Colette.

"You'd best get out of here," the other man said, his eyes wild, his tone gravelly. "This woman is standing in the way of what should be mine. If I take her, I'm sure you'll be quick to give me all the money I want to get her back."

Shelah moaned and sat up. She glanced from Matthew to Colette. "I . . . I didn't invite him. He startled me and made me stay quiet. Did it while everyone else was focused on the singing. I'm sorry."

"Stop your whining," Gabriel said to Shelah. "Soon you'll have everything you've always wanted. We just have to finish our plan."

"There is no plan," Shelah said. "Let her go. I'll go with you, Gabe. But you need to end this, and now. Don't hurt anyone else."

"What's going on here?"

Matthew pivoted to see Abe coming up the alley. "Go back," he shouted.

Abe kept walking, squinting as he realized what was happening. "Matthew? Colette?"

"Stay back, Abe," Matthew pleaded, moving toward Colette's *daed*. "Stay away."

Abe took in the scene, his words breathless and angry. "He has my daughter. I will not stay away."

He moved toward Gabriel and Colette.

"Stop," Colette said. "Daed, stop. I'll be okay. I'll go with him if he'll let all of you live."

Matthew couldn't let that happen. There was a chance Gabriel would kill Colette. "Let her go and I'll give you whatever you want."

"Sorry," Gabriel said, his gun waving each time Matthew tried to move forward. "I have to take her now. She's with me until you get me the money."

"*Neh*," Abe said, stepping forward. Suddenly he went

still, his hand on his chest. Grabbing for support, Abe slid
to the floor, still holding his chest.

"Daed, Daed," Colette screamed as Gabriel started
dragging her away. "Daed?"

Abe lay gasping. Matthew had to help him. "Please
don't do this. Let her go. Her *daed* needs her."

Gabriel smirked and grunted. "Can't do that. Daed
should have stayed away. And you should have done the
right thing and married Shelah. We had a plan."

Gabriel raised the gun, but Matthew watched in horror
as Colette kicked his shin to distract him. The gun fired
and Shelah screamed. Matthew glanced at her. She had a
wound in her arm. Blood spilled out over her cloak and
her hand.

Abe moaned. "Colette . . ."

Gabriel backed out of the stables. "Don't come after
us. I'll kill her right in front of you."

"Taking her won't help you," Matthew said, his heart
beating so fast he thought his chest might explode. "Take
me. Let them go. Shelah is wounded and Abe needs
medical help."

"Daed," Colette cried out, trying desperately to get
away.

Matthew rushed forward to charge at Gabriel, but
Gabriel lifted the gun and shot again, causing Matthew to
drop to his knees, thinking Colette would be dead.

But she was still there, crying, her eyes on Matthew
and Abe.

"I have no choice," Gabriel said. "Someone has to pay.
Now I have the woman you really love, so you decide
how much Saul's land and wealth mean to you. Do you
want them still, or do you want this woman?" He backed
away and then shouted, "Think on it and I'll get back to

you. And you'd be wise to remember, I will kill her if you decide the wrong way."

Matthew screamed. "I want Colette. Don't take her."

But Gabriel Moser wasn't listening. He shot again, hitting Matthew in his leg. Shelah screamed and tried to get to her *daed*. And while Matthew was down, Gabriel got away.

And he took Colette with him.

Colette went back over the day. They'd taken every precaution, had people stationed at every driveway and throughout the property. But no one had considered that old forgotten door hidden behind the curtains in the big suite.

The suite Shelah had insisted on taking. Had she been sneaking out that way before when she'd wanted to meet secretly with Gabriel?

Colette shivered, from the cold, from the pain, from what she'd witnessed there in the stables. Her *daed* dropping, sliding down the stable wall. Was he still alive? Shelah, bleeding and begging Gabriel to stop. Did she really mean that? And Matthew taking one last chance as he'd charged toward Gabriel.

Had Gabriel killed him? She remembered the gun going off, but had he shot Matthew?

If I hadn't tried to be kind, she thought.

If I'd listened and not gone up there alone.

If I'd just left Shelah to her own devices.

Shelah might be held captive or, worse, dead right now if Colette had not decided to check on her.

But I'd be safe, and so would Matthew and my daed—

She refused to think about that. Daed had to be okay.

Matthew had to be alive and Daed had to be okay. Even Shelah needed to be all right. She prayed over and over as Gabriel dragged her through the woods. She remembered how Abby had been overtaken on the beach and had almost died at the hands of a criminal.

But Jonah had saved his Abigail. Matthew would be a wreck, thinking he'd failed Colette. But love never fails, she reminded herself.

Matthew would save Daed. That was all she asked. She had to turn to *Gott*, and she had to believe there was a reason for this, for her being cold and afraid. She was determined to get away from this evil man. Somehow.

"Taking me won't solve your problems," she said as he pushed her through the snow. "You've messed things up— even with Shelah. We know your plan now. It's over."

Gabriel shoved her so hard, she fell to her knees, her hands hitting the cold, wet dirt and weeds. "It's not over. I have you and I have a weapon. They won't dare try to follow us. But I can get what I want after all. Your dear Mattie will sign things over to me, make it legal. Then I won't need anyone to help me get what I deserve."

Colette sat back in the snow and stared up at him. "You'll be a wanted man, and all the money and status in the world can't save you from your sins. Matthew would have gladly handed over the whole estate if you'd left me with him. He is in no need of all that complication and angst. He is true to his faith and his family. And he's true to me. You'll never have that kind of love."

For a moment, she believed he would shoot her and get it over with. His dark expression showed the evil in his heart; his eyes gleamed with the need to act on his immediate anger.

"I will get what I want, and if you want to live, you'll stop taunting me or trying to change my mind."

"Very well." She got up and shook the snow off her clothes. She wanted to tell him that he didn't know her family, her brothers-in-law, her sisters, her *mamm*, her *aenti*.

Cold and near shock, she started giggling. "You don't know my Aenti Miriam. She will find me." The image of her *aenti* traipsing through the woods with a frying pan, just as Edith had suggested, brought her some comfort. She'd have to remember to give Aenti a big hug.

"I don't care. They won't find you."

"They know these woods a lot better than you."

That made him mad. He shoved her again and then stood over her with the gun inches from her face. "You talk too much."

"Oh, I'm only getting started," she said, defiance and her faith taking over. "I talk when I'm nervous, and you make me extremely nervous."

Yanking her up, he laughed. "You should be nervous. And you should keep your comments to yourself. I won't be swayed."

"Where are we going?" she asked, her mind on the many ways she could try to run. Which way to go? Where to hide? She'd freeze to death before she'd let this man kill her.

"Shut up."

He kept pushing her deeper into the woods. Colette watched as the sun moved toward the west. They were headed east.

Cold. She was so cold, and now they were climbing up a steep embankment. She wouldn't cry. She wouldn't let this man get to her. But when she thought about the buggy ride Matthew had promised her, she wanted to curl up in a ball and cry like a baby.

"We're here," Gabriel finally said, his eyes wild, his expression dark. "Now they'll never find you."

She saw the tan pickup truck and knew if she got in that vehicle with him, she'd never make it home again. She had to find a way to escape.

Somehow.

CHAPTER TWENTY-SEVEN

Somehow.

He had to find Colette somehow.

Matthew turned back to where Jonah stood near the window of the cottage. "I couldn't save her. I tried, but Abe . . . Abe was having a heart attack. Shelah was shot, I got shot running after them. Jonah"—his voice broke—"I tried to save her."

Jonah put a strong hand on Matthew's shoulder. "You did the best you could. You did save Abe and Shelah."

"If Abe lives," Matthew said, running a hand over his hair. "He looked so pale when the paramedics took him away. He has to live, Jonah."

Matthew relived those last few moments, when he went down with a shot to his calf and watched in horror as Gabriel lifted Colette up and ran out the open barn doors and into the woods. Then he heard Abe moaning and Shelah screaming for help.

Jonah had come running, Levi behind him. They'd taken over.

He'd failed. Why hadn't Gabriel let Colette go? Matthew would have offered him everything, including his own life, just to save the woman he loved. He'd told him so, but Gabriel had taken the one thing that could hurt Matthew the most. Colette.

He'd failed. He'd never forgive himself for letting her come to harm. Or worse.

Levi came into the living room, his expression grim. "Sarah made it to the hospital. Eliza and Abigail are with her. Henry will bring them home later if—"

"—if Abe is okay," Matthew finished. "He has to be okay. I can't face Colette if anything happens to her *daed*."

Levi and Jonah exchanged glances. "You did the best you could," Levi said. "We'll find her. People are looking everywhere. The township police are aware and on the lookout."

"But he got through all our precautions today," Matthew said, standing to pace the floor. "He could have killed Shelah and Abe, and he . . . he might harm Colette." He whirled. "I'm taking Sawdust and I'm going to find her."

"*Neh*," Jonah said. "Not a *gut* idea. You'll freeze out there, and you're wounded. You don't need to be riding a horse with that bandaged leg."

"*Colette* could freeze out there. I must go."

"Stop," Levi said, grabbing Matthew's arm to hold him back. "Think about this. If he's using her to get what he wants, he won't kill her. He's desperate and he has run out of plans. Shelah has condemned him, so he's lashing out to hurt all of us."

"How is Shelah?" Matthew asked, remembering her wound. Remembering how she'd cried over Abe and begged Matthew to forgive her.

"She's okay," Levi said. "The first responders said the bullet only grazed her, same as your wound. This man wounded you to slow you down. And Shelah got in the way of his bullet, but she's alive." He glanced out the window. "We can be thankful for that at least."

"I'll be thankful when I have Colette back," he said. Then he pushed away. "I won't go anywhere. Mamm and Daed are too upset. But I need to do something. I want to go back to the inn and look at the quilt Colette made. Mamm said I should do that."

"I'll walk with you," Jonah replied. "Aenti Miriam is staying here tonight. She'll listen for your parents and the boys."

Matthew nodded. "I won't be long."

"I'll wait here," Levi said. "In case anyone comes by."

Jonah and Matthew walked toward the inn. It was dark out now, and still no word from the authorities. Matthew didn't want to think of Colette out there in the cold and dark with such evil.

"I can't lose her," he said to Jonah. "I can't. We've been through so much. So much."

"We will pray," Jonah replied. "For all of us."

They entered the inn through the kitchen, just as they always had. Matthew went straight to the lobby, where Maggie was watching the counter and hoping to hear some news.

She came around the counter when she saw him. "Matthew, I'm so sorry. I'm praying."

He nodded and headed for the small parlor, remembering the day he'd told Colette they couldn't be together. Now that moment stood out starkly in his mind, but tonight he could only keep Colette's image in his heart while he studied the beautiful quilt she'd made.

He turned up the light and gazed at the panels, his heart burning with torment and love. His eyes watered; his throat grew tight. It was all there. From the time they'd been born right up to the present. School, work, smiles, laughs, Matthew and Colette, walking on the beach by the lake, working in the kitchen, a loaf of bread on the counter, and finally standing by a Christmas tree, hand in hand. They'd fallen in love by a Christmas tree. At first, they'd been shy, thinking they were only caught up in watching both of her sisters marry.

But it was more than catching wedding fever. He loved her, and she had finally admitted she loved him.

They'd had it all, and she'd threaded the tapestry of their lives together during the worst time they'd ever been through.

"We almost made it."

Matthew touched the quilt, feeling its warmth shoot through him. He gasped and then he felt a hand on his arm.

"Mamm."

Agnes took her son into her arms and held him tight. "She loves you so much, Mattie. Hold on to that. She'll be back. She'll be home for Christmas. This quilt shows her love, and it shows her strength. She never gave up on you, so don't you give up on her."

Matthew held his mother close. "I won't, I promise. I'm going to find her."

He turned and headed out the back way. He'd made it to the stables when Jonah ran up behind him. "You're not going out there," he said. "At least not without me."

Matthew stopped. "You don't need to do this, Jonah."

"I'm going with you. I can't stand waiting either, and I know these hills and woods now. Let me saddle Samson. That horse has a nose for finding people."

Matthew breathed a sigh of relief. "*Denke*, Jonah."

"Let's go before anyone misses us."

They hurriedly saddled up and headed out the way they'd seen Gabriel going. Jonah had brought two old-fashioned lanterns to guide them. No guns, no weapons, just two men and their horses, following the messy trail that a kidnapper had left.

Matthew would find Colette, and when he did, he'd never let her go again.

She wanted to sleep for a very long time, but Gabriel wouldn't let her.

He nudged her again. "You have to stay alive."

"I'd like to stay alive," she retorted, hoping someone would find them in this old, abandoned shack.

They hadn't gotten in the truck after all. Gabriel must have driven it here on a dirt road that led up to the other side of the shack. How would anyone ever think to look here? She'd checked all the exits. Only one way in and out. A few broken windows and some loose boards.

If she could find a gap in the boards nearby . . .

Gabriel held the gun in one hand while he peeped through the broken glass of one of the windows. "Dark soon, then we'll head out. Have you ever been to Missouri? It's beautiful there."

"I'm not going to Missouri," she said, her teeth chattering. "I have a home here and I want to go back to it. Gabriel, sit down and talk to me. You had good in you once, I'm sure. What changed?"

He whirled in a frenzy, and she braced herself for either a gunshot or a hard slap across her face. Instead, he started laughing, the echo of his chuckles coming back to her with an eerie clarity.

"You want to know about me?" he asked. "Are you stalling or trying to trick me?"

"I figure since we're here together and we've both lost the people we love—Shelah and Matthew—we might as well rant to each other. I'll go first. I didn't like Shelah at all when she first showed up. She took my man away and I didn't understand why. I was hurt and frustrated, but I got to know her over time. The truth has a way of coming out, ain't so? She began to confide in me. And then of course, I saw you push her against a rock by the lake. Then I felt pity for her. You're a cruel man, but I know you couldn't have been born that way."

He bent down to where she sat against a cobweb-covered wall. Colette swallowed her fear of spiders and her fear of this man. *Gott* would see her through.

Your will, Lord. Your will.

"You want to know about me, right?" Gabriel's dark eyes flamed with anger. "You think just because I was born Amish, I wanted to stay that way? *Neh*, as soon as my Rumspringa came, I wanted nothing but to leave and never come back."

"But you did come back," she said. "Were you pretending, wearing the proper clothes, acting in a proper way? Why would you do that if you wanted to jump the fence?"

He pulled at his thick black hair. He wasn't a bad-looking man, but his soul was rotten.

"I wanted her," he finally said. "I wanted to work for Saul so I could be with her. She talked me into going back to being Amish, but it didn't work for me anymore. I've always wanted Shelah, but she thought she was better than me. I had to prove to her I could live up to her standards."

"By asking her to marry another man, just so you could kill him and take that tainted inheritance?"

"When I came back, Shelah was ready to go along with me, to become *Englisch*. Only, we needed money. I couldn't make her live in poverty, like I did for most of my life." He gave her a pleading glance, then turned mean again. "Saul Mueller owed me something for what he did to my *mamm*! Then he gave it all to a man none of us even knew existed."

Colette felt a trace of pity and understanding, but it didn't stop her. "It's horrible what Saul did to many women, so many that it makes me sick to think about it. But he has paid for his sins now. He could never be a real husband or father, so he took Shelah in to ease his guilt. You weren't the man he wanted for her, and that is a shame. You two make such a *gut* match."

He stood and paced again, sweat pouring from him despite the chill surrounding them. "We did, but Saul wouldn't have it. He fired me and sent me away, but I never left. I was always nearby, and Shelah and I had a plan."

"And you don't like having that plan disrupted, poof, up in smoke."

"*Neh*, I do not like that. So you will be with me until Matthew pays me off."

"He's willing to give you the money. Think about it. You have me as a hostage, and you can keep me alive and name your price. He'll get you the money, and you and Shelah can run away as planned. You might not have the entire estate, but you'll have cash to start over wherever you want."

He hit his hand against his forehead. "Stop. I need to think."

He was obviously getting weary and hungry. Well, so was Colette. She let him stew for a few minutes while she searched for a weapon. He had the gun, but he hadn't thought this kidnapping through. He had not tied her up. Only told her to sit in the corner with the dead bugs and dry crumbling leaves. At least most of the spiders were dead now. She shuddered again and slipped away from the grimy wall. When she spotted a broken board a foot away from her, she scooted inch by inch toward the board, waiting for each time he turned away to pace and stopping when he turned back toward her.

Could she do this? Hit a man over the head and run out into the snow, lost and cold, and growing weaker by the minute?

She couldn't sit here and wait. That was not her style. She thought again of Mattie and the buggy ride he'd promised her.

Tears threatened to spill over, but Colette refused to cry. She had to stay alert and strong. Gabriel was a mixed-up person who'd lost the love of his life and the plan he'd worked so hard on. A misguided, ugly plan that involved killing another human being. The human being she loved.

Ja, she could do this. And she would once she had the opportunity. Meanwhile, she prayed over and over that somehow, someone would find her. She needed a hero, and she needed him now. She'd keep praying and she'd keep inching toward that old piece of wood.

CHAPTER TWENTY-EIGHT

Matthew kept praying with each mile he and Jonah made. They'd found footsteps here and there in the forest, because no one came this way a lot. But Jonah knew where this path led, because he'd brought Abigail this way the day he remembered his past.

"Are you remembering?" Matthew asked him now, knowing how his friend must have felt that day.

"I am," Jonah admitted. "It makes my stomach roil, but we survived that turmoil, and we will survive this. Gabriel's so far gone, he didn't bother to hide their footprints. The falls are to the east, so that means he's headed up above the falls. That's wild country, but the snow is helping us. We only have to keep climbing. Fortunately, the snow has stopped falling, so the footprints are intact. We'll find them soon, Matthew."

Sawdust snorted his disapproval of being out in the cold, but he kept moving, following Samson's lead. Samson seemed to sense where he needed to go. Did he find scents he knew belonged to someone familiar?

They huddled against their horses, not needing to talk. Jonah had always been a big, quiet man. He spoke when it was necessary and not much more. All business and always super-focused. Matthew used focus himself to stay on the lookout. The full moon glimmered above them like a guiding beacon.

Samson stopped at the top of a bluff, neighed, and shook out his mane, one hoof lifting and kicking the dirt.

"I think Samson likes it here," Jonah said in a whisper.

Just then, they heard a gunshot, followed by a motor roaring to life. Leaving the horses behind, they both took off running toward an old lean-to cabin.

Matthew watched, his anger growing by the minute, as the truck spun out on the icy roads down the bluff, its taillights shining like two red eyes as it slipped away.

"He has her," he said, falling to his knees. "We're too late. He's taken her again."

Colette had heard a horse neighing. Gabriel had rushed to the door, and that's when she used all of her strength to roll over and get the board she'd been eyeing. She'd somehow grabbed it and rolled to her feet in one quick movement, adrenaline flowing like water through her veins.

She'd whacked Gabriel *gut* and hard across the back of his head. He'd turned, letting out a groan, his hands flailing. The gun had slipped away and fallen to the old dirt floor.

Ready for him, Colette kicked the weapon into the corner with the dead spiders and roaches, then hit him again, this time across his face and chest.

Gabriel fell through the door, and before he could get up, she grabbed the gun. "Get out of here. Leave!"

"You're nuts. I'm not going without you. I'll kill you first."

She moved toward him, cocked the pistol, and aimed it at his heart. "My *daed* taught me to forgive people who wrong me, Gabriel. But he also taught me how to shoot a gun. For protection against varmints, and you are one of the worst varmints I've ever encountered. I'm giving you one more chance to get out of here. Go or I'll end this here and now, and I'll ask forgiveness later. But you'll be the one who'll suffer."

To prove she meant business, Colette had shot at him, missing on purpose. He'd run out the door and cranked the truck, the sounds of the wheels spinning giving her some comfort. She'd rather die right here than go anywhere with him.

Now she sat huddled in the corner again, wondering what had become of the horse she'd heard. Afraid to move, afraid to breathe. She'd stay here until morning, until she could find her way back down the trail toward the falls and the lake. She prayed in silence, listening to the sounds of snow clumps falling from the trees. Thumping as if someone was running over the soft forest floor, their footfalls breaking the snow and ice.

She had to be imagining things. She was in shock, and cold, so cold. She was wishing she could tell Matthew how much she loved him when the door burst open. She sat up, startled and afraid, searching for her weapon.

"Colette?"

Was she dreaming? That couldn't be Matthew's voice.

"Colette, it's me. Mattie."

He held the lantern up and she saw his face. His beautiful, brave, loving face. The nicest dream.

When he rushed forward and bent down in front of her, she cried out, "Matthew?"

Someone took the lantern from him, and he pulled her up and into his arms. "I'm here. I'm here. You're safe now. I'm taking you home."

"Okay." She nodded, still disoriented, and held him as he gathered her in his arms and walked toward the moonlight. Then she balked. "Daed. I have to get to Daed."

"*Neh,*" Matthew told her. "He's in *gut* hands. He's with doctors."

She sank against him. "I was so worried."

Someone spoke. "I'll get the horses. We should be able to find our way to the road from here."

"Jonah?"

"I'm here," Jonah said, touching her cloak. "With Matthew. Samson and Sawdust brought us right to you." Then he asked, "Are you all right?"

"Did he hurt you?" Matthew demanded.

"No, but he sure aggravated me. I'm better now. Much better."

They both chuckled at that.

"What happened?" Matthew asked, his chuckle sounding more like a sob now.

"I took his gun," she whispered, her voice raw from the dirt and too much emotion. "I hit him with an old board when he heard a horse neighing—Samson or Sawdust— one of them saved my life by distracting him. I fought him and he dropped the gun." Pointing to her little corner, she said, "Find it, in case he comes back."

Jonah moved toward the darkness. "Got it. I'll be right back with the horses."

She started crying then. Soft, hot tears that silently fell

down her dirty cheeks. Touching Matthew's face, she whispered, "I fought him."

"You scared him away all right," Matthew said, kissing her tears as he sat down on the rickety porch stoop and held her against him. "I'm so proud of you. I love you so much."

"I love you, too," she said, clinging to him so he wouldn't disappear. "So much."

Then she fell sound asleep. Safe and warm, she lost herself in dreams. No more nightmares, no more snow and cold and fear and danger. She was with her Mattie, and if she died this very moment, she'd die happy. So happy.

Two hours later, Matthew and Jonah reached the steps of the cottage. Abigail ran out, shouting to anyone who happened to be with her, "They're home!"

Matthew held Colette tight in front of him as she clung to Samson's mane. She'd been in and out of sleep for most of the trip, sometimes waking with a scream or twisting to grab him around his neck so she wouldn't fall off Samson. The bigger horse fit them better than Sawdust. Jonah rode behind, watching for anyone who might be lurking about.

"Maggie told us what you two were doing," Abigail said, running to Jonah to hug him close. "I was angry at first, but now I love you both so very much. We were terribly worried."

"I thought you were at the hospital," Jonah replied after they'd hugged. "How is Abe?"

"He's alive and stable," she replied on a whisper. Matthew knew they were trying to protect Colette.

"Mamm stayed, but she is so frightened and worried. She wanted me here in case—"

Jonah nodded, kissed his wife, and came to gather Colette in his arms so Matthew could hop down. Matthew took her right back. He didn't want to be apart from her. Levi came running from the house. Eliza took his hand as they stood nearby.

"Am I home?" Colette asked, her voice weak.

"You are," Abigail said. "You're home, little sister."

"And Matthew is here," Colette replied. "He's never going to leave me again."

"That is correct," he whispered in her ear. "I'll explain everything later," he said to the others.

But once they were inside, the idea of waiting went up in a cloud of dust as the women gathered around Colette.

"Let's get her to the couch," Miriam said, her hands waving in every direction. "I wish Sarah was here. She knows how to handle these things. But we'll make do."

"I'll find some blankets," Eliza said, hurrying into the mudroom. "And I'll stoke the fire."

Matthew laid Colette down on the couch and took the first blanket handed to him. "Rest now. You'll need food when you wake."

"You'll be here?"

"Always," he said. "Nearby."

"I'll heat water for tea," his *mamm* said as she grabbed him and hugged him close. "I'm so glad you found her. So glad I can't even be mad that you did such a dangerous thing."

He held his mother tight, thankful for these people and this place. He would never leave again.

"*Kumm,*" Mamm said. "We have food and coffee."

Glancing over at Colette's pale face, he said, "Will she be all right, Mamm?"

Agnes took his hand. "We have prayed since we heard she'd been taken and even more after we got news that you and Jonah had gone after her. *Gott* will see us through, Matthew."

He nodded. "You are right there. He guided Jonah and me right to her, and Mamm, she fought Gabriel Moser off, took his weapon, and made him leave. She's so brave."

"So are you, my son," his *mamm* said. "So are you."

He brushed that away and asked, "Where are Daed and the boys?"

"He's got them in the *grossdaddi haus*, distracting them. You know they are the curious type."

"Smart move," he replied, so exhausted he was unable even to chuckle.

Abigail and Eliza had heard what he'd said about Colette. "Matthew, you are *brave*. She could have been killed," Abigail said.

"Jonah helped a lot. Samson seemed to sense where she was. I couldn't have done it alone."

"No matter, we will never forget this," Eliza replied.

Levi and Jonah came in from taking care of the animals.

"Jonah told me what happened," Levi said. "I'm glad Colette got away, but Gabriel Moser is still out there. We need to be mindful."

"I'm not going anywhere," Matthew said, worry for everyone on his mind. "Shelah and Kathleen need to know this."

"We left word with Henry," Jonah said. "He volunteered to guard them, so he's staying at the inn. It's closed for the next three days, at least. It is locked up tight. The door to the balcony has been locked, and we put a big board across it for now."

Relieved, Matthew wanted to go and sit by Colette, but her sisters and *aenti* were cleaning her up and wrapping her in blankets. So he asked more about Shelah and Kathleen.

"They are both fine," Mamm said as she heated soup and made sandwiches, even though it was well past suppertime. "Shelah's wound is sore, but healing. She's still a bit shocked and so frightened she won't leave her room. Jonah's officer friends have checked on all of us, including them."

"Did you tell them we'd gone out?"

"*Neh,*" she replied. "But I think they guessed when Jonah was nowhere to be found."

"I'll let Jonah deal with that," Matthew said. He took a plate and went to the living room, then pulled up a stool near Colette. She was sleeping so peacefully, one would never imagine the ordeal she'd been through.

"Will she be all right?" he asked Miriam. "Mamm says so, but should we call a doctor?"

Miriam shook her head. "Not at this hour and with the snow starting up again. *Neh.* We've checked her for frostbite. Her feet are fine. She had on high sturdy boots, her warm leggings, and her wool socks. Her hands were cold, but we've made sure they are clean and pink. Maybe a little frostbite, but she probably kept her hands inside her cloak for warmth. She's a smart one, Matthew."

"She sure is," he said. "But she'll need food and something warm to drink when she wakes."

"I'll take care of that," Miriam assured him. Then she shook her head again. "These three sisters will be the life of me. Too bold and brave, these three. My sister Sarah is the same way. I could learn from all of them, ain't so?"

"I think you've not only learned from them, but they have benefited from your bluntness, even if they won't admit it," Matthew told her. "And you were brave to move here to be near the family. They are thankful for that, and I know Levi's *mamm* is thankful, too."

Miriam's smile beamed. "I am happier than I've ever been, I have to admit. Connie is the sweetest woman, and Levi is a testament to her parenting skills." She glanced at Colette. "Now to get that evil man out of our lives."

"Amen to that," Matthew said, his eyes on Colette, too.

She stirred and opened her eyes. "I'm starving."

They all laughed. Miriam and Abigail helped her sit up. Matthew handed her his uneaten soup and sandwich. "Here. We have plenty."

And right now, they did. Colette was safe and warm and alive. Shelah was alive and Kathleen would look after her.

But the burning question remained: Where was Gabriel Moser now?

CHAPTER TWENTY-NINE

Christmas Eve

Colette walked through the inn, taking in the pretty decorations provided by nature. Christmas was her favorite time of the year, even though the Amish didn't go all out on decorating or exchanging gifts. It was more about reflecting on the birth of Christ and the year that had passed. She was even more thankful this year than usual.

I'll never take any of this for granted again, Lord. All good things come from You, and I know that now better than most. I will follow You and I will trust You. Denke for bringing my Mattie home. I love him now more than ever.

The family planned to have a big Christmas dinner at the inn this year. They'd enjoyed the Thanksgiving one so much, they planned to do that again on Second Christmas, and they'd feed the local underprivileged people as they'd done in the past. But this Christmas would be a quiet one with just family—to rest and get past the horror of her kidnapping.

And the trauma of almost losing Daed. She was most

thankful that he was getting better and should be home later today. She was also amazed that he'd only been in the hospital one day. It seemed like a lifetime to her.

Jonah had eased their worries when he'd reported that Gabriel Moser seemed to have disappeared. They'd found the old pickup near the bus station, and according to one of the attendants, he'd bought a ticket to Minnesota. He was long gone before the police could reach him, however.

Colette wanted to believe that. She hoped it was so, and that someday he'd be held accountable.

"There you are." She pivoted from her window overlooking the lake and saw Matthew standing there. "I figured you'd be in here."

She smiled and looked at the King sisters' quilts on display across from the fireplace. "This room has a new meaning to me now," she said. "It's where I lost you, but it's also where you found me. And the quilts do tell interesting stories, ain't so?"

He crossed the room and pulled her into his arms. He smelled fresh like evergreen and clean like the winter air. "Your quilt is my favorite. Our story."

"Did you see that?"

"Of course, after Mamm insisted I needed to see the finished quilt. To see the love we've shared through the years."

She giggled at that. "Men can be daft at times."

"I have to agree," he said. "I can't believe what we've been through lately, but this—this I believe, and I know. And to think, I almost lost you."

"I'm fine, Mattie," she said as she noticed the worry in his dark eyes. "I'm content."

He stood back and looked her over. "You look so pretty. The rosiness is back in your cheeks."

"That's a blush. I get all warm and tend to blush when you look at me that way."

"Get used to it," he said, giving her a kiss.

They held each other for a while, and then Colette asked, "Have you heard? Shelah and Kathleen are leaving after Christmas."

"I know," he said. "That's why I came to find you."

"Do not tell me anything that will change my happiness."

"Nothing like that. I've hired a man to drive them to Missouri, and they have agreed to take the guesthouse there. I've also alerted the man I hired as foreman. Not easy this far away, but we've sent letters back and forth, and then I used the inn's computer and phone. He's fully vetted and he's a *gut* man."

"But—"

"But I'll need to go there after Christmas to decide what to do with the estate. The house is huge, and the land is well over one hundred acres. It takes a lot of people to run the place. I thought you might be willing to go with me?"

"Really?" she asked. "That's so nice of you. I have to admit I'd like to see the place. But what are your plans once you're there?"

He sat her down on the high-back sofa. The fire crackled and the wind hissed. But they were warm and cozy here. She waited, wondering if they had yet another hurdle to jump. Would he expect her to move to Missouri with him?

"I've discussed this with Mamm and Daed," he said. "Yesterday we had a long talk. I'm going to keep the place for now, but I will not live there. A lot of the Amish in the area depend on Saul's estate for work. So there's that to consider. I have a foreman I can trust, and he's in no hurry to go anywhere else, since he has family there. His mother lost her job at the bed-and-breakfast one county over, so I'm going to talk to her about turning the estate into a bed-and-breakfast, which would give even more people jobs and purpose."

"That is a fine idea, Mattie," she said with a bit too much glee. "Shelah and Kathleen could help."

"I did mention that to Kathleen, and she was interested. She knows the man I hired, and she remembers his mother. I think I saw a matchmaking light come on in her brain. She will bring it up with Shelah.

"I also explained my idea to the foreman yesterday in our long phone call," he said. "He and his *mamm* are excited about possibly working together. I just need to work out the details. And the best part is that once I take over and have everything in my name, my parents have agreed to take a portion of the profits going forward. The rest will remain in the bank for use to keep the place going for a long, long time. But I want them to feel secure, and I think in his own way, that is what Saul wanted, too. He couldn't leave the place to Daed. That would be an insult. So he left it to me, his only other blood relative. This will be money earned under my watch. I can make sure my parents are cared for the rest of their lives. And you, too, Colette."

Colette pulled him close. "I have all I need right here, but if we're to start our own life—"

"We'll need our own home," he finished. "The other reason I came here today. Your father has suggested we build a home on the other side of the cottage, near the big lake. Near the place where we used to play on the beach as *kinder*."

Relief washed over her. "So we won't be moving to Missouri?"

"Not ever, but I will make the occasional trip there to see how things are going. And I'll want you with me. It can be our turn to stay in the big suite at the top of the house."

"I'm blushing again," she said. "This is the best solution, Mattie."

"I think so. I want that place to be filled with happy workers and happy guests, the way this inn has always been."

They hugged and then he said, "It's time for that buggy ride I promised you, but Jonah told me to take Samson and use the covered buggy. It's cold out there."

"I'll bundle up," she said. "Gloves, and my big bonnet and my warmest cape."

"I brought our thickest blanket," he said. "Finally, we can be alone together, free and clear."

"I'd like nothing more."

A few moments later, they were bundled and had a cover over their heads to block some of the wind. Matthew took the trail through the apple orchard that would bring them around back toward the inn's property line, where they hoped to build a home just beyond the cottage.

They rode in silence for a while, smiling at each other as she clung to his arm. Samson kept shaking his mane, his eyes rolling toward them as if to say, "Finally."

Colette giggled at that. "You know, I've learned a lot about cooking. Edith became my confidante and mentor."

"So I hear," he said with a laugh, his gaze on the snowy landscape. "I think she might retire soon, and I know she wants you to take over."

"I think I'd like that, and I know Abby and Maggie will help me. We've all learned from Mamm and Edith."

"That's *gut* then," he said as he watched a covey of quails lifting out of the trees ahead of them. Had something startled the pretty birds?

"I've been offered a new job," he replied, ignoring his worries. "Your sister Abigail has named me kitchen manager."

"Really now?" Colette grinned at him. "We've never had one of those before."

"I know. Edith was the boss, but no one dared call her a kitchen manager. I guess I'm the first one, but I don't have to cook. Mostly I'll be a maintenance man. It's perfect because I'll get to see you every day. The pay will be great and the money will help us build our home. I know I have money now, but I want to earn my own way, too."

Colette laid her head on his shoulder as they approached the big curve back toward home. Then everything happened at once.

Colette screamed as a figure darted out onto the muddy lane. Samson whinnied and lifted his front legs, his hoofs reaching up and out, kicking high.

Gabriel Moser!

Matthew tried to pull the big horse back, but the Percheron knew danger when he saw it. And so did Matthew. In the end, he wouldn't have been able to stop what happened next.

Dirty and unkempt, Gabriel lunged toward the buggy, but Samson's big hooves hit him and knocked him down, then the enraged animal stomped on the man as they passed in a whirlwind.

His heart racing, Matthew finally brought the runaway horse to a stop. "Stay here," he told Colette.

"*Neh*, we are together now," she said, her voice breathless. "I'm not letting you go to him alone."

Matthew helped her down and held her close as they hurried to where Gabriel lay still, blood seeping out near his left temple. Colette gasped as Matthew bent to feel his pulse.

"He's dead," Matthew said, shaking his head. Then he stood and pulled her into his arms. "Samson always did have a *gut* memory. And Samson has a sense of justice, too, I believe."

Colette nodded, shocked yet relieved. She could forgive, but she would never forget. "Take me home," she said.

And so he did.

The next October

"You two have a great time."

Colette smiled at Mamm and Daed as the bus pulled into the station. "We will. We get to spend our honeymoon in our very own bed-and-breakfast."

Matthew's parents waved at them. "Be safe and take care of each other," Agnes called out. Titus nodded to Matthew.

Their parents had insisted on bringing them to the bus station after the wedding day came to an end. They were now married, and their home was ready and waiting. It had taken almost a year, but they were husband and wife at last.

Jonah and Abby, Eliza, who was expecting, Levi, and little Jon had hugged them at the inn, where they'd had a wonderful fall-themed wedding out under the pavilion. Everyone they loved had been there.

"I can't wait to see what Kathleen and Shelah have done with the bed-and-breakfast," Colette said once they were on the bus to Missouri. "And we get to attend *her* wedding. Can you believe that?"

"I wouldn't have a year ago," Matthew said. "But she seems so happy now, and Jason loves her so much."

"He is a *gut* foreman and he'll make a fine husband," Colette said, relief mixed with her own happiness. "And his *mamm* is such a hardworking person. Priscilla has done so much to make the bed-and-breakfast a success."

"It's a happy place now, and I can't wait to have you there as my wife," Matthew replied. "I have loved you all of my life, and I will love you the rest of my life and beyond."

Colette smiled and thought of the quilts. "Every quilt tells a story," she said. "I believe that's because they are made with a three-cord-strand of faith, hope, and love."

Matthew kissed his bride. "And the greatest of these is love."

Colette believed that with all her heart. She'd witnessed the truth of it in the last few years. Memories, forgiveness, and love truly did conquer all. Such was the thread of life, woven like a beautiful quilt.

You can visit the King sisters
and the Shadow Lake Inn again in

AMISH CHRISTMAS KINNER,

available now!

This trio of heartwarming, inspirational
Amish holiday stories captures the gift of family
and the childlike joy of Christmas . . .

CHRISTMAS EVE BABY
* Lenora Worth
It's a Christmas Eve to remember when a laboring
mother-to-be shows up at the King sisters' Shadow Lake
Inn amid a snowstorm. Midwife Sarah King and her
three daughters go into action, while the men of the
family search for the woman's husband.
And with faithful hearts and helping hands,
this magical night may unite a brand-new family
just in time to share a Christmas blessing.

BEST CHRISTMAS PROGRAM EVER
* Rachel J. Good
On Emily Flaud's second day of work at the Green
Valley Farmer's Market, two hungry children in tattered
clothes snitch some cheese samples—and Emily's heart.
Her coworker, Hosea King, is less beguiled. He is still
grieving the loss of his wife and daughter two years
before, especially as Christmas approaches. But when
the children are in need of adoption, Emily longs to
become their mother—in a prayer that includes Hosea . . .

LOVING LUKE
* Kelly Long
*Wanted: Amish Mail Order Groom. Must be excellent
with kinner.* Recently widowed, Grace Fisher must be
practical. She has a general store to run and needs a
gentle man to help raise her *kinner*. But when Luke King
appears, Grace sees a scruffy man who looks far from
husband material, while Luke sees a woman who
deserves better than he. Yet with faith, each may gain the
courage to see beneath the surface—and create a family
for many Christmases to come . . .

Visit our website at
KensingtonBooks.com
to sign up for our newsletters, read
more from your favorite authors, see
books by series, view reading group
guides, and more!

BOOK **CLUB**

BETWEEN THE CHAPTERS

Become a Part of Our
Between the Chapters Book Club
Community and Join the Conversation

Betweenthechapters.net